I0665049

The Prodigal Sons

Michael Jasper

UNWRECKED PRESS

The Prodigal Sons
Copyright © 2011 by Michael Jasper
michaeljasper.net

Cover art by Lauren Rinder

ISBN: 978-0692627983

Published by UnWrecked Press

Also by Michael Jasper

The Family Pack series: The Finder Team series:
Family, Pack   *Finders, Inc.*
Hunter's Moon   *Lost & Finders*
The Finder Pack
(a Family Pack/Finder Team crossover)
Augie and Ozzy Take Back the Mountain (a Finder Team prequel)

The Contagious Magic series:
A Sudden Outbreak of Magic
A Wild Epidemic of Magic
A Lasting Cure for Magic
The Last Sorcerer (a novella)

Standalone novels:
The All Nations Team
A Gathering of Doorways
Heart's Revenge
The Prodigal Sons
Unassisted Living
The Wannoshay Cycle

Story collections:
What Was Left Standing
UnWrecked Tales
Gunning for the Buddha

Graphic novel:
In Maps & Legends (with art by Niki Smith)

Chapter One

On a gray March afternoon, three months to the day after William Koopman's wife left him, his worthless younger brother John returned home.

Back in December, on the morning Marcy left, William had been yanked out of sleep by the furtive sound of drawers opening. It was still dark, a half-hour before chores, a winter morning when all the world felt dead and frozen. He opened his eyes, and in the weak light saw his wife of four years stuffing as many of her belongings as she could into black garbage bags. William tried to convince himself that he was still dreaming, even as Marcy slipped out of the bedroom door with two bulging plastic bags in each hand.

When she began creaking down the steps, he realized he was awake. He forced himself up and out of the bed, his heart suddenly pounding and his breath catching in his throat. On his way down the cold wooden steps, he avoided the squeaky ones without conscious thought, not wanting to wake his parents or his grandmother.

By the time William had caught up with her, Marcy was bundled up in her coat and gloves and heading for the back door. Blinking fast to clear his vision, he followed her out of the house where he'd lived all his life, even after his marriage to Marcy. Dad needed his help on the farm, he'd told her then, and it had been easier to simply stay right here rather than move out and have to commute.

No way, he thought, numb to the bitter winter cold, even though he wore only a black T-shirt and long underwear bottoms outside the old Iowa farmhouse. A tall young man with the chunky build of a farm worker—all knotted muscles with the hint of a beer belly—William watched his breath cloud in front of him as his bare feet crunched in the day-old snow.

Still he hadn't said a word. He simply followed Marcy, his mouth stuck shut, as if his vocal cords were frozen by the chilly air. After Marcy threw the garbage bags into the trunk of her rusted white Chevelle and slammed it shut, she turned to look at him for the first and last time that morning.

"I have to go," she said. Her words popped in the cold morning air, making him flinch with each syllable.

Her stubborn chin poked out from under the hood of her red sweatshirt—*my* sweatshirt, William thought dully—while she waited for him to say something. As if to protect it from the bitter air, Marcy had shoved her long blonde hair under the hood. In the dim gray light, her eyes remained hidden.

William could only stand there, his bare feet melting size eleven outlines into the snow under him, and gape at his wife. I'm dreaming, he told himself.

With a wordless sound of frustration, Marcy finally moved, turning away from him. Her boots slipped in the packed snow, and William fought the urge to try to catch her, to keep her from falling.

If you have to go, he thought, watching her arms go flying into the air for balance, I guess you're on your own now. But you'll be back, he wanted to say.

Regaining her balance, Marcy closed the car door behind her with a hollow slam, and William jumped. The cranking of the car's big engine cut through the silence of the early morning like the hacking cough of an old man.

Wait! he thought suddenly as the headlights washed over him, snapping him out of his numb lethargy. You can't *leave!*

He took a step forward and opened his mouth to call his wife's name, to tell her not to go, but the winter air rushed into his lungs, silencing him. Marcy was already backing her car around in a half-circle. Her brake lights covered William in a blood-red glow.

2

"I have to go," she'd said, as if everything were that simple.

The last thing that William allowed himself to remember about that cold December morning was what had happened when Marcy drove off in her big white two-door. A chunk of icy gravel shot out at him from under her back tires, as they spun trying to get traction in the snow, and even though he was still mostly asleep and in a growing state of shock, he had somehow caught the rock in his hand.

Then her car's taillights were fading to pink in front of him, the car was shrinking down the lane, and all he was left with was the mutter of the Chevelle's muffler and the sickly-sweet stink of exhaust.

William looked down at the rock in his calloused hand.

How the *hell* had that gotten there? he wondered, staring until the sound of his wife's car faded and the night was silent again. One second his hand had been empty and cold, and then the next second it was stinging hot and bleeding, a piece of random gravel clenched inside it.

And now, three months later, William was again feeling that same sense of numb surprise, as he stood outside the hog barn and watched John drive up the gravel lane in a new red Ford. The wind flared up as if in response to his memories, peppering him with hard pebbles of rain. He fought the urge to turn his left hand palm-up to see if the chunk of gravel was still there.

Instead, he turned back to his work, to the hogs and their food, the constant intake of sustenance accompanied with the constant exhaust of shit. The rain was coming down harder now. His constant companion for the past few weeks, the rain had sometimes slipped into wet snow as the temperatures dropped, the constant precipitation keeping the ground soft and muddy.

With his back to both the house and the red Ford parked in front of it, William emptied four pails of feed into the trough on the other side of the fence. The William of March was about twenty pounds lighter than the William of three months earlier. His jacket and work clothes hung on him as if he were the younger brother, forced to wear hand-me-downs from an older brother.

"Eat up, stinkballs," he muttered, watching the pigs push against each other for their meal, forming one hairy, grayish-pink mass of flesh. William pressed his boots deeper into the mud and manure below him, breathing through his mouth to keep out the ever-present stink of manure. The pigs, he knew, had been keeping the Koopman farm afloat in the past few years.

Smells like money, his father would always say, breathing deeply of the pig stench. Then he would laugh and—in the last few months—try to get William to crack a smile. His efforts rarely worked.

Shaking his head at the thought of Dad joking around in the face of the farm's problems, William wondered how long would it take before the little shit would leave this time, running from the family and the stink and the unending labor of their Iowa farm. He felt generous that gray March afternoon, with rain dampening the back of his neck and his exposed hands; he gave his brother John three days, tops, before John left them again.

I'm *not* avoiding him, William had repeated to himself all afternoon and all evening. I just have work to do. And out here or in town, there was always work to do.

As the rain continued that day, William had kept himself busy grinding feed out in the barn until darkness fell. At that point, faced with the prospect of going inside the house to deal with John and the rest of his family over supper, he'd escaped into town for a couple of hours instead, shooting the breeze with his buddies and helping them with repairs at their automotive shop.

"Chicago blow up or something?" he said to John that night, finally dragging his tired body into the house at half past eight.

John shrugged at him from the couch, where he'd been staring at the TV with his legs thrown onto the cushions as if he'd never been away. His blue eyes were watchful as he grinned up at William, and then he winked.

Using his salesman's charm to win everyone over, William thought, without returning John's smile, and ignoring the wink altogether.

"William," John said, his voice steady as if he'd practiced his response. "There's this thing called vacation. It's when you take a couple days off, you know, maybe even a week. That's why I'm here. Vacation."

"Brought a lot of extra shit with you for just a week off," William said, hitching up the jeans that had become too big for him in the past three months.

John sat up straight, his blonde hair wild at the back of his head from lounging inside all afternoon. He'd lost his salesman's smile. "As far as *they* know," he said, nodding toward the kitchen where their parents sat, finishing a late supper with their grandmother, "I'm on vacation."

William felt himself being pulled into an argument, John's overly-patient voice baiting him. John grinned again, and William felt the words "pretty boy" jump to his lips. All his life John had been the golden child, with his wavy blonde hair and straight teeth, while William had suffered through braces for three years as a teen, and he still could never get the cowlicks from his own thick brown hair. And, as if adding insult to injury, John had always been able to burn up the heavy dishes of meat and potatoes served up at nearly every family meal, but William had fought his baby fat all his life. It was only recently, in the months since Marcy left, that he'd been able to shed some weight, without even trying. At least Grandma had stopped pinching his thirty-year-old cheeks.

When he noticed John's gaze still on him, waiting, William turned away. For the first time in months he looked around the living room, *really* looking at it: the sagging couch with the green and yellow afghan covering it, the dented TV, the two windows covered in plastic wrap to keep out the cold, the dusty yellow light fixture dangling above them, and the old framed pictures hanging crookedly on the wall. William focused his gaze on his round face from his senior picture, almost a decade old now. He was wearing the dark blue suit he still wore to funerals and weddings.

His picture sat to the left of John's graduation picture, above a portrait of the family when William was probably ten, John about eight. Dad's hands rested on John's small shoulders from where he stood stiffly posed behind the two brothers. Mom's shoulder was touching Dad's, and the fingers of her left hand brushed against William's upper arm, as if attempting to hold him in place with her delicate touch. Both parents carried half as much gray in their dark in the old photo than they now had. John's smile, even back then, had been all white teeth and innocence. But William could recognize the mischief—or at least the potential for it—in his brother's bright blue eyes.

William jumped when he heard John getting to his feet on the other side of the room. John stretched and groaned dramatically, arms raised to the ceiling, and then he walked into the kitchen, where Mom and Dad's voices brightly welcomed him. Tearing his gaze away from the history on the wall in front of him, William trudged upstairs to his room, his appetite for supper gone.

The afternoon of the sixth day of John's so-called vacation, William looked up from the fence and the string of barbed wire he'd been tightening and saw his father hiking across the muddy pasture toward him. Dad walked with a hurried gait that William immediately recognized as trouble, even though he couldn't see his father's face under the hood of the long black rain slicker he was wearing to protect him from the steady drizzle. Wearing a slicker of his own, William hadn't even noticed the rain until that moment.

"You need to come to supper tonight," Dad said in his usual abrupt manner, scratching his gray-brown beard with a wet glove, his eyes bright with enthusiasm under his hood. "John has something he wants to tell us all."

Of course, William thought. John. He wasn't even back for a week, and it was already all about John, just like it had been before the little shit moved away and went to college.

"I told the guys that I'd meet them at the Lounge tonight. It *is* Friday, you know," William added, turning back to his work. He usually grabbed something to eat in town or ate at home after everyone else had eaten, though lately he'd been skipping supper altogether.

"William. I don't think you should miss this. Here, let me hold that and you can nail in that staple." With a sharp movement of his big arms, Dad jerked the wire tight next to William and held it, quivering. After a moment's hesitation, William pulled the hammer from his work belt. He hated when Dad told him what to do, even when he was helping him. *Especially* when he was helping him.

"I know I wouldn't want to miss it," Dad said. He was impossible to deal with when he got all excited like this. "When's the last time we saw him? A year ago? A year and a half? I just couldn't believe it when he said he wanted to spend his vacation with us."

Me neither, William wanted to say, but gritted his teeth and pulled hard on the wire instead.

"I'm thinking he's got a new job, something that makes even more money than before. He does have that new car." Dad let go of the wire, and it remained tight, though some of the tension had escaped from it. He gave William a long look that betrayed the enthusiasm in his voice. "Either that or he really screwed up and needs us to help him out. What do you think?"

William blew out the air he'd been holding in his lungs and pounded in the staple. *You don't want to know what I think, Dad.*

"Doubt he has very good news," he said out loud. "When's the last time he came home because he wanted to?"

Dad shrugged. "I can't make him do what he doesn't want to do. He's a grown man, and he'll do whatever he wants, no matter what I say to him."

"*That's* the truth," William said under his breath, moving to the next fence post. He had a pretty good idea what John was going to say at this important meal. There was no vacation, and never had been, and John was either leaving again or planning to stay a while. With John it was best to prepare for the worst, which for William would be if John remained on the farm.

"Just be there tonight for supper tonight," Dad said. He turned and walked off without waiting for a response.

William let the heel of his hammer rest on the tightened row of barbed wire in front of him as he watched his father leave, surprised Dad hadn't tried to argue more with him about John's motives. Staring at his back, William felt something give inside his chest. Dad was moving slower on his way back to the house than he'd moved on his way out to the edge of the field, as if the thought of one of his sons in trouble weighed him down a little bit more with each step.

William rubbed his sore hands. Stretching away from him on either side, the fence formed a barrier for the one hundred dairy cattle the Koopmans had maintained since his father took over the farm from William's grandfather, back when William was twelve and already working hard every day with his chores. Ever since that morning's milking at half past four, William had been steadily working his way down the fence, stretching the top string of barbed wire at each metal post. He took pride in the taut line behind him, traveling back in a straight horizontal a half mile to the wooden end post sunk into cement.

Dad had maintained that William was wasting his time with the fence, but William could see the slack in the mile and a half of fence ahead of him, and it had bothered him for weeks until he'd found time to repair the fence today in the rain. This was a problem he could tackle and force into submission, one fencepost at a time. He picked up the hammer and moved to the next post.

By the end of the day William's back was throbbing and his hands were raw from pulling wire all day in the cold, wet weather. After helping Dad with the evening milking, he walked slowly back to the house under a blue-black sky already littered with clouds and the occasional burst of stars. William found his brother inside, sitting on the couch again, in the dark. John wasn't lounging this time but watching TV with intense concentration, his face caught in the glow of the screen, working his hands together as if they were cold.

William doubted that his brother's nervousness came from the forecast on the six o'clock news for yet more rain—in the back of his mind, William blamed his brother for bringing the rain that had continued since his return—and he stopped himself before saying something encourage to John. He wasn't ready to make peace and play nice yet.

"How's that vacation?" he said instead. He clicked on a lamp and flooded the room with light.

"How's Marcy?" John shot back, squinting.

Fighting the urge to grab him and knock him to the floor, William shook his head at John as if he were a misbehaving child and walked into the kitchen.

I asked for that, he thought, still surprised at the sudden ache the mention of her name evoked. It figured—even after all these years, they still knew how to hit each other where it hurt the most.

In the kitchen, his grandmother was slowly setting five plates around the table, sighing after each one. She squinted at him with ancient, crooked bifocals that she was too stubborn to replace. Her white hair, cut and styled a day ago by William's mother, her daughter-in-law, was standing up in the front like a tiny crown. Queen Grannie, William thought with a smile.

Still sighing heavily, she walked to the silverware drawer and counted out knives, forks, and spoons. Mom had stayed late at work for a teacher's meeting, and Grandma was not pleased to be preparing supper in her absence.

"Here," William said, taking the loose silver from her hands. "I'll finish setting the table. Way you're carrying on, you'd think you were having an asthma attack or something. Sit down."

Grandma drew in a breath for another sigh, but after a warning look from William, she let it out in silence and sat down. He passed her a knife, fork, and spoon, and she squared the silver on the place setting in front of her, watching him over the tops of her glasses.

"What's put you in such a foul mood?" he said.

"Oh, the usual. Your mother working late, your dad getting all excited about this big important meal we're supposed to be having, the damn rain, and, you know." She pointed toward John in the living room with one hand, running the other through her hair, which was sticking up in more places, in more odd angles. "He's been around the house all week, driving me nuts, getting in my way, and making all sorts of phone calls."

"Really?" William lifted the lid to the big Crock-Pot to make sure the pot roast wasn't getting dried out to the consistency of jerky. He knew John wasn't making local calls while everyone but Grandma was out of the house. He also knew John hadn't done a lick of work since coming back, and everyone else in the family had to know it as well. John hadn't been fooling anyone. "Who's he calling?"

Grandma motioned for William to move close. "How the hell should I know?" she whispered, grabbing his ear with her cold fingers. "Do you think I'd eavesdrop on my own grandson? Shame on you, William."

William freed his ear from her grasp and laughed, knowing full well she would indeed eavesdrop on John, or anyone else in the house. He sat down at the table across from her to wait for his parents to come in.

Might as well enjoy this Friday night at home with the family, he thought, with a glance at the living room. But I am *not* avoiding John, he added.

As if sensing William's lowered guard, Grandma turned to him with a knowing look in her eyes. "Lots of people coming and going on this old farm, wouldn't you say?"

He shrugged and didn't answer.

Grandma sighed again. "All this craziness. Makes it hard on a lady of my age. Gets my nerves all bent out of shape. Makes me grumpy." She gave him another look. "How do *you* feel about it, William?"

Oh no you don't, William thought, leaning back in his chair. She could try, but she wasn't going to get him started down that road. That road led to Marcy, wherever she was now. Nobody in the family asked about her anymore. Except for good old John, five minutes ago.

"Did you hear about the Deutmeyer's cows getting out this morning?" he said instead. "It took everyone in their family, and about ten other people, including me, to get them all rounded up. Some of us had to get in our trucks to find all of them. I found two down by the highway, right at the edge of the shoulder, eating grass and shitting in the ditch like they were at home." He rubbed his sore arms. "That's what *I* call craziness."

Grandma made a pushing gesture with both hands, as if to dismiss William's story in order to get at what she *really* wanted to know. "Cows? I've seen more cows in my lifetime than you and your brother will ever see." After glancing into the living room, she lowered her voice. "'Course it's hard to see cows when you live in the city. Right?"

"True," William said, checking the clock. Dad ought to be coming in any minute, he thought, and Mom was already ten minutes late. John hadn't made a sound in the living room. Was he in there, William wondered, listening to us? Gathering ammunition for sneak attacks later, just like when we were

11

kids? He caught himself holding his breath and forced air out of his mouth.

"Once people leave here, must be hard for them to ever come back," Grandma said in the same soft voice, without looking directly at William. She touched her hair tentatively, messing it up. The kitchen was silent as she waited for his reaction, the TV in the living room a dull buzzing.

William told himself to let her comment go. But his stomach was trying to tighten up on him, the same feeling he felt most days around mealtimes. He'd dealt with that ache by throwing himself into his work instead of eating. In his mind he heard the hollow slam of a Chevelle's door followed by the spitting of gravel from the tires. It was going to be another long meal, he decided: pushing food from one side of his plate to another as the others ate with abandon, not a worry in the world. He didn't say anything further to his grandmother.

Finally, with an excited glow in his eyes, William's father stomped into the house, kicking off his work boots and peeling off his wet jacket in the mud room. His face was flushed, either from the late winter cold or excitement. Not two minutes later, William's mother walked in, her dress clothes slightly rumpled from a day of teaching second graders, the bright colors of her pink blouse and dark red skirt looking out of place around the faded, no-nonsense work clothes of William and his father. The tension left his shoulders and lower back after seeing his parents again. Grandma had been close to breaking him down.

John wandered in from the living room, and all five adults sat down to the table for a muttered prayer over their food. As William crossed himself at the end of the prayer, completing the familiar motions without even thinking about them, he realized with a jolt that John was sitting to his right, in Marcy's old place.

During the meal, William ate slowly, barely listening to his mother across the table from him, next to John, complaining about the students getting cabin fever as winter lingered or his father's gossip about the farming problems of their neighbors. To improve his mood, William kept himself occupied by watching his grandmother watch John. She would nod along with whomever was talking, then look to John next to her, as if to make sure he was following along. Then she would look back to the speaker. Back and forth like a cat.

Grandma had lived with the Koopmans for as long as William could remember. Grandpa Koopman had lived there too, before his death fifteen years ago, in the downstairs bedroom that Grandma now had all to herself. She had been the referee in many of William and John's fights while their father had been outside working, their mother taking classes and teaching. Grandma couldn't stand William picking on his smaller brother, even though William was convinced that as the oldest he was her favorite.

Caught up in his memories, a goofy smile on his face, William lifted his head to find everyone else looking at him, waiting for him to finish eating. They were all done, and his father tapped his thumbnail on the edge of his empty plate, anxious to get to John's announcement.

"I'm finished," William said. He pushed away the half-full plate of beef, carrots, potatoes, cabbage, and bread. It all tasted the same anyway, and his stomach was full. Full enough.

"All right," Dad said. "John wanted to talk to all of us about some important news, and he only wanted to say it once, so, well, go ahead, son."

John pulled his chair up closer to the table, glanced at William for the first time in the whole meal, and took a deep breath. "Things have been rough for me the past year or so in Chicago. The brokerage was making me work these long hours to bring in more and more clients, and the money just wasn't there in a lot of cases. People get nervous about the market, I guess..."

John looked down at his plate, his mouth quivering the slightest bit, and in that instant, William knew his brother was lying.

"Go on," Dad said.

William glanced around the table, looking for some hint of doubt in the older faces around him, but he could detect nothing. The little shit had them suckered.

"To make a long story short, some people had to be let go. Even though I'd been there almost two years, they cut the least productive people first." John winced, as if that had hurt him physically just to say it. "So. I looked for work at a bunch of different places the last few months, but nobody was hiring. Or my old bosses had blackballed me."

"They did what to you?" Grandma blurted out, holding a hand next to her ear, a look of confused shock on her face.

"Blackballed," John said. "You know, made me look bad to all my potential employers. I'd used up most of my savings on rent and a new suit for interviewing, so the cash flow just wasn't there for me."

"What about that new car?" William said. He regretted it immediately when he saw the look on his mother's face.

"William," she scolded, shaking her head. She touched her gray-black hair, straightening a wild strand, then rested the same hand on John's forearm. "Why didn't you tell us about this sooner?" Mom said. "We could've helped you, you know."

John shook his head, then glanced at William. The same thought must have entered John's mind at the identical instant that William had thought it: there had been no money to give, and there hadn't been any for quite some time. William was glad that John had at least had the decency, at the time, not to ask.

"I know," John said. His voice took on the rehearsed tone William had heard earlier that week. "You must think it's funny, a stockbroker who can't keep track of his own finances, but it happened. So I wanted to tell all of you that I'm not really on vacation. I'm moving back, with Mom and

Dad's permission, of course, to stay a while until I'm back on my feet."

His parents looked at each other and nodded. "It's a great idea, John," Mom said. "You know you're always welcome here."

"I don't think it'll be for long," John added, as if trying to convince himself. "I can just stay in my old bedroom. Plus, I want to help on the farm."

William barked out a laugh before he could clap a hand over his mouth.

"Sorry," he mumbled into his plate, afraid to meet his mother's withering gaze. Grandma stared at William a few seconds longer, and he tell she was coming around to his way of thinking.

The thought of John, who had bitched and moaned his way through every early morning of chores before school and every night of chores after school, now wanting to be a farmer tickled William. After graduation from high school, John couldn't have gotten out of Holy Cross fast enough. William remembered watching his mother's face drop while she was on the phone with John, asking him to come home, nearly begging, and his anger had grown. And when John *did* come back to visit, he never once offered to help with the chores. Just like this past week.

"I can start tomorrow," John said, helping Grandma pick up the dirty supper plates. "I can be ready by six-thirty, to help with the milking, if you want?"

William looked at his father, whose face had held a bemused expression ever since John's announcement to be the new hired hand. His eyes were unreadable under his upraised eyebrows.

"Shoot," Dad laughed. "Six-thirty's when we come in for *breakfast*, son. Have you been away that long? We're up at four, before the roosters even wake up." Dad stopped laughing and looked across the kitchen at John. "Still want to help us?"

"Sure," John said, his face red. "No problem. I just forgot. How early we used to get up, I mean."

William caught the trapped look in his brother's eyes and smiled. John hadn't given much thought to what he was getting into, coming back here, and he doubted John knew anything about the problems they'd been having on the farm lately. The weather, the finances, the broken-down equipment. None of it was smelling like money, lately.

When William turned around, he saw that his grandmother was once again looking at him. Her eyes were narrow behind her bent glasses, but she had a tiny smile on her face.

Damn, William thought, embarrassed that he'd been caught. Everyone was watching everyone else. But nobody would admit it, and nobody would want to act like anything was out of line. They were just a regular family, finishing up a meal together.

After supper, William had hoped to go into town to salvage some of his Friday night, but his parents had insisted they all sit together in the living room and "get reacquainted," as his mother called it. He shuffled into the suddenly-cramped room and sat on the floor across from his brother, feeling like a kid about to be punished. Grandma continued glancing at William as if her actions were dependent on how he acted.

The five of them ended up watching a bad edited-for-tv movie for an hour in awkward silence, and then his parents had gone to bed. William suspected that they'd set it up that way so he'd be forced to talk to John alone.

Nice try, he'd wanted to shout at them as they retreated into their bedroom. But it's not going to work.

At least Grandma hadn't deserted him. As John turned the channel to catch the sports section of the local news, grumbling about the lack of cable and the bad reception, William moved over to the couch to peer at his grandmother's book. "What're you working on, Grannie?"

On her lap she held an overstuffed scrapbook open to a page filled with yellowed newspaper cuttings. The book contained, among various clippings and letters, a complete genealogy of her side of the family and most of the Koopman side, going back in time to recount ancestors William never knew he had. He usually didn't ask about her book of history—he knew once he got her started she'd never stop, and he didn't want to be reminded of his own, more recent history—but the alternative was to try and talk to his brother. John sat sprawled out on the floor, watching the news, but he had turned slightly towards them, listening.

"I was just thinking about my uncles, for some reason." Her thin hand, dotted with liver spots, touched the faded rectangle of newsprint in front of her, smoothing it. "Local Farmhouse Burns During Night," the headline read in small capital letters.

William relaxed into the faded cushions of the couch and tried to read the tiny news story. "What were their names?"

"Hubert and Albert."

"Hubert? Now *that's* a name," William said, nudging her with his forearm. "You just made that up."

"Show some respect. This is a sad story." She closed the book, placed it carefully on the end table next to her, and rested her hands in her empty lap. It was a posture William remembered well from childhood. "Hubert and Albert were barely a year apart in age, and while they were growing up, most people around here—and back then, right after the 1900s had started, there weren't that many people around here—most of them thought they were twins. They both had dark blonde hair and the bluest eyes. I remember their eyes more than anything else.

"But they were cold eyes. Uncle Hubert hardly ever smiled the few times I saw him as a child. And Uncle Albert was even less friendly. According to Daddy, Albert and Hubert had had a big fight when they came to America from Germany, and they carried their anger around with them like a weight on their backs wherever they went. And the funny thing was, they lived in the same house together, paid for it together even though they never spoke to each other.

"After a year of living there, my mother forbade me to visit them, because she said they'd split their little house on their acreage right down the middle, and it was something no child should see. Put a wall in the kitchen that ran halfway through the living room, back to the two bedrooms. One of them had cut a new doorway into the side of the house so he could get in and get out without ever having to see his brother."

John had turned down the TV, and William squirmed, trying not to look at him. But his eyes betrayed him, and he saw the half-smile on John's face before looking down at his own hands. Grandma and her damn stories, he thought.

"They lived like that until they were in their thirties. This was about 1915. By that time I had grown older and wanted to see this house, but I still wasn't allowed. 'Worse than children,' my father said about them. Then, one hot summer night, when it hadn't rained in weeks, their place caught fire. Everything burned to the ground, the extra walls and all, but they made it out without a singed hair. The next day, Hubert took his money out of the bank and moved west, and Albert took his money and headed east. People asked about them for a while, but after Daddy bought up their land, people pretty much forgot about them. They were just too bitter and sour for anyone to want to visit them or even learn their whereabouts. They just left, my Uncle Hubert and my Uncle Albert, and nobody missed them."

John whistled lowly from the floor. "That is one freakin' depressing story, Grandma." He looked at William and laughed, and William shook his head and glanced away.

The three of them sat without speaking for a minute, the story rerunning itself through William's mind, the TV playing softly in the background. The news had ended during her story, turning into a rerun of "Cheers," the Boston bar a million miles from their Holy Cross farm. William stared at the TV instead of looking at his grandmother or brother. Then the phone rang.

"Damn it," John whispered. His face was suddenly pale as he started to get up from the floor.

"I got it," William said, easing around his grandmother and catching the phone in the middle of its second ring. Every time he heard the phone, the thoughts entered his head: she wanted to see him again, she was so sorry, she'd just needed some time away.

But as soon as he said hello, he heard a click and the line went dead. He glared at John, whose face held the same nervous intensity that it had held before supper that night.

"No one's there," William said before hanging up. The sound of the phone hitting the cradle too hard bounced around the room.

Grandma jumped and closed her genealogy book. John turned off the TV, and everything went still. William imagined that somewhere in the world a house was burning, lighting up the night. He shivered and walked to the window, the plastic that covered it rustling slightly from the late-winter wind. The darkness outside reminded William at last of how late it was, and how soon the morning of another day of hard work would arrive.

Chapter Two

John Koopman knew that, if simply given one more chance, he could make his life work.

He'd needed a clean break from the life he'd been living in Chicago—from Jamie and the drugs to Andrea and the drinking—even if that clean break had brought him back to his childhood bedroom, where he lay staring at the bare rectangles of wall where his old posters used to hang. At five minutes past midnight, the rest of the Koopman family was asleep in preparation for the chores the next morning, but it was still early to him. Back in Chicago, they'd be just getting started on their Friday night.

After tossing and turning for an hour, John got up from the bed, threw on his clothes, and crept back downstairs in the dark. Another phone call wouldn't hurt, he thought, wincing at the traitorous squeaking of the steps. When he picked up the phone, he remembered the look on his older brother's face from earlier that night. How William's flicker of hope had hardened into a mask of desperation and rage when the person on the other end hung up on him. Aside from the hint of anger William had shown before supper, when John had mentioned Marcy, the shifting emotions William had shown on the phone had been the first signs of life John had seen on his big brother's face since John's return to Holy Cross. The rest of the time, William had simply looked dead. Or at the very least, wishing something would come and put him out of his misery.

In the unlit living room, John dialed a number from memory, using the moonlight coming in through the window.

He knew who had been calling and hanging up—or, rather, he'd had the list of suspects narrowed down to about half a dozen people. With static buzzing in his ear, John thought about how the past was proving harder to elude than he'd ever imagined. He closed his eyes in the dark and held his breath until his arms stopped shaking. This was the first call he'd made in the past week to this particular long-distance number.

"Been sleeping well lately?" he murmured into the mouthpiece before she said hello.

"What do you think?" she said. John imagined hearing someone else with her. A rustle of her sheets that could have been someone shifting position so he could hear better. He bit down on his lower lip to keep the venom from his voice.

"So what've you been doing this past week?" he said, eyes still closed. "How are you?"

She whispered again, "What do you think?"

John smiled. "I think you went out with some people from work, and you probably drank too much, talking about the loser guys you're friends with. And now I'm guessing you've been in bed less than an hour. Alone, maybe." He kept his eyes shut, hating the way it made him feel better to talk to her this way.

"At least I'm still here," Andrea said after a short pause, during which John could see her pretty face scrunching up in frustration. "I didn't quit my job and run away. I visited him today on my lunch break, by the way. Today was the first day he could have visitors."

"Great," John said, his mouth clenching. She didn't waste any time, he thought, cutting right to Jamie. She still could get to him, all these miles away. "Just wanted to see how you're doing. Sounds like everything's just fucking peachy there. I guess I'll talk to you later then—"

"He didn't ask to see you, by the way. He has the shakes now and then, and he says he doesn't sleep well." Her voice raised a notch, becoming slightly hoarse. "How have *you* been sleeping, John?"

"Look, I'm going to visit soon," he said. The walls of the old house felt like they were leaning in on him, sucking up the scarce light and air around him. The inside of his right arm itched at the elbow, where he'd slid the needle that night in Jamie's apartment, pushing the junk into his blood. He'd thought he'd left all that behind him when he left the city, but the scar was still there, permanent as a tattoo.

He took a deep breath. "Dad needs my help here on the farm. Things are bad here, financially, from what I've seen. You know, he can't *pay* someone to help him out—he doesn't have the money. He can barely pay my brother anything other than room and board. And, speaking of money," he added, almost out of breath, "I couldn't afford to stay in Chicago anymore, anyway."

"We can wait for you to come back, if that's your plan," Andrea said. But I don't know for how long. Mark and Christine are ready to write you off already for running out of here after that night. I'd like to see you again, if that means anything. But like you used to tell your clients, your window of opportunity is starting to close."

"Damn it," John whispered, rubbing his inner arm, the phone wedged between ear and shoulder. "You just don't get it, do you? How coming here was something I had to do?"

I *had* to come back, he repeated silently to himself. I had no choice.

"John," Andrea said. "I think that's just great. But while you're finding yourself out on the farm, I'm trying to keep everyone else's lives together here."

"Don't do me any favors," John whispered, and he pushed the disconnect button.

He fought the urge to slam the receiver down the same way William had done earlier, but he set the phone down in the cradle without a sound. The darkened house was oppressive in its answering silence, as if waiting for John to return to bed so it could carry on its nightly vigil of the moonlit prairie.

I should have waited another week to call her, he scolded himself. He'd been convinced Andrea had been miserable in his week away, without him. As if I could make everything better with a phone call, John thought, shaking his head in the darkness, all alone. If not better, maybe just a little less hostile. Wrong again.

Walking though the kitchen, wide awake at this late hour, John could still smell the roast from supper hours ago. He was beginning to understand why he was having trouble sleeping. It was as if the same air from the past century had been reused again and again in this house, nothing fresh getting in. Like he was being suffocated on a daily basis. In the mud room off the kitchen, he pulled on his father's heavy coat and a pair of boots before slipping out the back door into the cold darkness outside. Sleep was not an option anymore tonight. The hell with getting up tomorrow at four fucking thirty.

Outside, the world of the farm was quiet, something John remembered from childhood but had since forgotten in the bustle of city living. The silence was different from the strained silence at supper time, with everyone waiting for him to start talking. This was true quiet. Yet in the middle of this flat expanse of cropland, John felt exposed. He fought the crazy sensation that he would just drop off the world and go sailing out into the night sky.

Looking up, though, he had to give his family and his ancestors credit—their farmland had a view that could never be duplicated in the city. The stars burst from the sky above him in brilliant white flashes. He remembered some of the constellations from an astronomy class he'd taken back in college, a class he knew his brother would have found useless. The clump of stars straight above him was the Pleiades, or the Seven Sisters. Further north, the heroic stance of Orion the Hunter. The Little Dipper. And the millions of tiny stars he could see with his naked eye, the stars he could only see out here, with no city lights to obstruct his view. Andrea would've loved it.

John began walking. The main buildings of the farm fanned out in a rough half-circle, with the house at the center. To his right, hidden in the darkness down the sloping lawn, stood the hog pens and three small, leaning barns. To his left was the three-story barn that stored hay, cows, and the milking equipment. The metal walls of the machine shed stood next to the cow barn, the closed double doors dented and slightly off-kilter. John remembered backing the tractor into those doors more than once during his rush to get through his chores.

The sides of the cow barn looked like they had been rubbed raw in places, and it was only when John squinted at the barn that he realized they had been sanded as if in preparation to be painted. The job had been left unfinished. A checklist started in the back of his head, tentatively titled "Projects to Do to Make John More Useful." As he looked around, the list grew. The lumpy front lawn covered in weeds and dead grass. The equipment spilling out from the machine shed, rusting and exposed like the skeletons of metal animals. The broken shingles at his feet, ripped from the house by some sudden wind. Everywhere he looked, another task beckoned.

"Damn," he whispered to himself. "I need to stop looking."

Turning away from the buildings in front of him, John buttoned the bulky jacket to his chin and walked up the gravel lane, just to keep moving. From the house the gravel road curved gently to the south, then made a mile-long straightaway to the west, connecting to the country road. Out here, all the roads except the highway were gravel. The dust his old car used to raise on his trips to town or school or any other place but home would tickle in his nose for hours afterwards. He swore the smell of dust had covered him for the first eighteen years of his life, until he left for college. *Escaped* this place for college, he thought. Holy Cross had held nothing for him then.

At this late hour, the lane and the country road and even the highway four miles distant were dark and deserted. With each footstep crunching into the gravel, John felt himself stepping closer to the edge of the known world. Or maybe, he thought to himself, looking down from the night sky at the unplanted fields on either side of him, he just needed a strong drink.

Drinking was what had gotten everything started with Andrea. The night they first met had been clear like tonight, though much warmer. John slowed in his determined stroll down the lane. Had it been a year, already? He shook his head and walked faster.

They had gone on a blind date with his best friend Mark and her best friend Christine. Mark and Christine had been dating for half a year, and they'd wanted John and Andrea to meet from the start. This was back when John still cared about his job, and didn't want any distractions to get in the way of his career, before any of them even knew Jamie. They'd agreed to meet a year ago last April.

"I like to be on the cutting edge of something new," Andrea had said on their first date, after a few drinks. She grinned at him, a sudden burst of light that cut through the smoky air of the bar. "Or at least feel like I am."

She wore a black jacket and skirt, and her pale skin was flushed pink by the time the two of them had eaten and moved to a smaller table to listen to the jazz quartet onstage, leaving Mark and Christine behind. The long bangs of her bobbed black hair slipped into her face as she talked about her work, covering her eye in a teasingly annoying way that John couldn't help but find attractive. She would touch his hand as she spoke, leaving his forearm with a tingling that remained after she had moved back to her glass of wine.

Tapping his foot in time to the bass and sax's dueling harmonies, John savored the looseness in his muscles that always accompanied a good buzz. He talked about spending his college years in a rundown house in an old section of Iowa City. She talked about one day publishing her own magazine, and how she was "starting at the bottom" as an editor at some small journal whose name he couldn't remember now. They kept it up for two hours, a drink always next to each of them, long after their friends had left them. For every story he had, she had one just as outrageous, and he enjoyed the challenge he found in simply talking with her. He always welcomed a good competition.

"Let's go for a walk," she said at last, her hand falling on his forearm and resting there. The band had played their last song, and the crowd at the bar was beginning to thin out. It had to be close to midnight.

They ended up walking through the too-bright lights of Navy Pier in the unseasonably warm air of early spring, staggering slightly, still talking. Something about the intensity of her gaze when he spoke to her made John say more about himself than he had with anyone else he knew. But she had paused too long when he said he didn't really have any lofty goal outside of working hard, making good money, and enjoying Chicago with his friends.

"Yeah," Andrea said. They stopped to sit on a bench that faced the glittering lake. "I guess that's pretty cool."

She swung her legs, almost invisible in her dark tights next to the bluish-black water of Lake Michigan. Her black skirt crept up her leg to mid-thigh. Trying to distract himself from those legs, John counted back in his foggy mind the number of beers he'd downed, along with the glasses of wine Andrea had sipped. She'd kept pace pretty well.

She turned to him, not ready to let the topic slide. "But isn't there something *bigger* out there, waiting for you?"

"I don't know. I just think people have to enjoy what's going on now in their lives, you know, and not get caught up in worrying about what the future may bring. Because tomorrow could show up before we know it, and then before we know it we're old and wishing we'd done something different with our lives." John paused for breath, his face suddenly flushed and warm. "Or something like that," he added, hoping this girl he'd known for less than four hours didn't think he was a complete idiot spouting drunken wisdom.

She nodded, and a few strands of dark hair fell into her face. With her eyes not quite focused on him, but on something just beyond him, Andrea looked like she was turning his words over and over in her mind until she saw his perspective. In the past year, he had grown to love the way she could focus herself in this way, even if she was drunk. Especially if she was drunk.

John, on the other hand, was too easily distracted by things like the slap of water against the ledge where they were sitting, or the headlights slashing through the city streets and bouncing off the lake, or the clanging of the moored sailboats in the distance.

"So what happens tomorrow?" Andrea said. "Or more importantly, what happens tonight? Do you think that far ahead? I want to know."

John shrugged, and a thrill ran though him that he tried to pass off as a shiver from the chill in the air. "Me too. But I don't want to worry about all that. I just like to see what happens." A breeze blew in off the water, slightly rancid from the exhaust of boats and the stink of fish, and it threatened to steal away his confidence along with his buzz. "You know, don't plan every second of your life, just take it as it comes."

"Have you always been like this? Or did someone come in one day and take all your ambition away?"

"Nah. It's not about ambition. Take right now for instance. There's a lot going on right here, but you and I aren't noticing it because we're too busy talking and analyzing everything. Look out at the lake, at the way the lights bounce off the water, or the way sound carries for miles across it." He moved closer to her, flashing her a smile. "Or think about us, here, sitting almost perfectly still while the city just hums with action and people. Sometimes it's nice to get away from all that, you know, if only for a few seconds."

Still looking thoughtful, Andrea slid closer to him as he talked. He kissed her. She smelled like lilacs and something almost hidden, a smoky scent that offset the flowery aroma perfectly. She pulled back gently, stopping inches from his face.

"Maybe you're onto something," she said. "So. Will you escort me home, Mr. Present-tense?"

"Why not?" he said, his head feeling light as they rose from the bench. The huge Ferris wheel on the pier was turned off for the night, and the evening became perceptibly darker. The sounds of traffic seemed to grow louder as the night deepened. "I don't have anything better planned."

John was close to running by the time he reached the end of the lane. His breath steamed out in front of him as he looked back at the dot of light from the farm over a mile away. Not quite the same as Chicago's Grand Avenue. After the crush of people, buildings, and cars in the city, he'd completely forgotten about the sheer amount of *space* that was available on the farm. He half expected a taxi to pull up beside him at any minute.

Pulling the bottom of the coat down over his rear to protect him from the wetness from the rain of the past week, John sat at the end of the lane and waited for his breath to return. Inside the heavy jacket, his upper body was warm and he was almost sweating, while his legs were freezing in his worn-out jeans. He wasn't ready to turn back yet.

Digging his hands deeper into the pockets of his father's coat, John decided he'd call Andrea again tomorrow, if he had time. In the left pocket he felt something hard inside the lining of the coat, and he reached inside the coat front to pull the object from an inner pocket.

"What the hell?" he whispered. His voice in the silence of the night gave him a chill as he tried to make out what was in his hand. It felt like a flat, smooth rock, though the shape reminded him of an arrowhead. Dad must've found it while he was out working in the fields, and then forgotten about it. Or kept it there as a good luck charm.

Squinting at the rock in the dark, John felt suddenly sad for his father. Dad had lived his whole life on the farm, probably working since the day he learned to walk and hook up a hose to a cow's tits. He didn't know any other way of life, though John could tell that some days his father's heart wasn't in farming. He would catch Dad looking off into the distance, oblivious to the rest of the world, thinking he was alone while they baled hay or rounded up the cows before milking.

During each visit home after he moved to Chicago, once he started learning more about finances and running a business, John often wondered if his father wasn't subconsciously running the farm into the ground. The clutter of broken equipment and the creep of weeds in the fields increased with each of his visits, to the point where John hated returning home. The guilt he felt from leaving home would nearly choke him, cut off his air like the claustrophobic feel inside the old farmhouse. So he'd stopped coming back.

Cold air seeped into his lungs, making him want to cough, but he felt too tired to even do that. He was painfully aware of the long walk home. Still holding the arrowhead, its sharp sides pressing into his fingers, he stood up in the darkness in the middle of nowhere. He squeezed the triangular rock, memorizing each ridge and scar. It seemed like such an innocent, boyish thing for his father to do: saving something that could be an ancient artifact, or just a worthless rock.

John slid the rock into his pocket. A month ago, if anyone had told him where his life would take him in the coming weeks, he would have laughed long and hard to dispel the possibility of ever returning to Holy Cross. Yet here he was, back on the Koopman farm. He stretched, feeling his back pop, and hoped like hell he wasn't going to have to get up at the crack of dawn as he had promised at supper.

An insistent beeping pulled John too soon from his hard-fought sleep. After coming in from outside last night, chilled and bone-weary, he'd tossed and turned for another hour until his body had given in at last. He couldn't have slept more than three hours before the alarm went off on his old digital watch. He wanted to go back to sleep for the rest of the day. But on this, the first day of his new job, he'd decided not to give William the pleasure of getting up before him.

With his head swimming, like a hangover without the pain, John sat up and placed his feet on the floor. The wood was freezing. His body shivered violently, and he brought his legs back up onto the bed.

I just need to lie down for a few seconds, he told himself.

Fifteen minutes later he woke again. With a groan, he pulled himself out of bed and dressed quickly in the dark. Downstairs the house was dark, the only sound the ticking of the ancient cuckoo clock somewhere above him. He felt his way through the living room to the back door, brushing past the wobbly coffee table and narrowly missing the arm of the old sofa. He almost turned back to try to find some coffee in the kitchen.

Instead, wearing just a sweatshirt and jeans, he rushed outside into the harsh March air to wait for his brother and father to start the milking. His tennis shoes were soaked with dew after ten steps as he rushed across the lawn. But before he pulled open the door to the cow barn, he could hear the loud buzz of the milkers and the grunts of the cows in the darkness. William and Dad had beaten him to the barn.

"Morning!" his father yelled over the pumping machine. Ten cows were lined up in the stanchions, four silver cylinders attached to their udders, pushing milk into hoses that ran into the big tanks next to the eastern wall. John could smell the sweetish sour odor of the cows, as well as the warm smell of new milk. William pulled another cow into place, leading it with a hand on the back of its neck. He glanced for a split second at John, but didn't say a word.

"Here," John said, making his way delicately around the piles of cow droppings and hay that covered the barn floor in mounds. "Let me help."

"I got it," William muttered, securing the cow into the stanchion.

At John's approach the cow snapped its head back, stamping the floor like a bull.

John watched his brother tighten the harness around the cow's neck, and then, without pausing, bend down to fit each teat with a silver pump, his big fingers moving fast and surely. The cow, hooked up like a car at a gas station but in reverse, gazed at John as if in disapproval.

"I'll get the next one," he said, talking as he moved, remembering the procedures even though it had been almost a decade since he'd helped with the milking. It was a simple enough process, but it seemed as if some of the technology had changed since he used to do it. The milking machine and the separator were new, and the separator had a control panel that looked more complex than most computers John had seen. He wondered how much money his father had sunk into the new equipment.

The black and white Holsteins waited outside in a clump of hooves and snouts and tails, bag-heavy and ready to be milked. John grabbed the closest cow by the scruff of its neck. To his surprise, the cow came willingly. He'd never been good with the animals; it was as if they could sense his dislike and contempt, and they rebelled against his touch. Triumphantly, he led the cow into an empty stall and let William strap on the milking contraptions.

After ten minutes of shuffling cows in and out, John felt himself relax. The warmth of the barn, filled with the big animals and his father and brother, mixed with the almost hypnotic hum of the machines that became a kind of rhythm. William wouldn't let John touch any of the equipment, which suited John fine. He liked the simple task of moving cows in and out like a traffic cop.

Leaning against one of the stanchions holding a cow that had just begun milking, John felt his mind begin wander as his eyelids grew heavy. He thought back to the last warm day before it grew cold again. That had been ten days ago back in Chicago with Andrea, trying to sell his bed and couch at the flea market down by Grant Park, close to Buckingham

Fountain. That day seemed like months ago now. After the expense of renting a U-Haul, he barely broke even when two college kids toted his furniture away in their little Toyota truck. The couch stuck out above the college kids' truck bed like a strange checkered growth, propping the mattresses up vertically.

Andrea, at a near-boil ever since Mark and Christine had told her about their plans to get engaged and move to the suburbs, had sat silently on the couch next to John all morning. Her anger spilled over onto him after the couch was gone.

"You didn't have to get rid of all that, you know," she said. "We could live together, share costs, nothing serious, just roommates, you know. I don't know why you let Mark break your lease."

"Whatever doesn't fit in my car has to go," John had said, walking back to the rented truck. It was that easy. When he put it all together, like some problem from high school math, it was obvious that without any money coming in, without a roommate to offset his growing pile of debts and bills, without any money left in his savings, he couldn't stay in the city. But Andrea had wanted to know how she fit into that equation, and John hadn't had the correct answer for her.

Back in the barn, someone was whistling at him. John looked up in time to see his brother yelling his name, the words almost drowned out in the sound of milking pumps.

"John! Wake up, God damn it!" William yelled over the sound of the machinery. He pointed at the door where the cows waited.

John waved him off, annoyed both at himself for losing focus and at William for catching him. Trudging across the manure-covered floor, John lifted his leg over the hoses running to the milker and slipped. He went down on top of one of the hoses, ripping the milking pumps off a cow. The cow began kicking in pain and surprise.

With a strength and speed that surprised John, William was behind him, pulling him to his feet. He pushed John away and walked next to the cow to calm it, swearing the entire time. One of the hoses was dripping thick milk onto the dirty floor.

Once he had the hose reattached, William turned on John. "What the hell were you *doing*, you clumsy shit?"

Dad stepped between the two of them before John could say anything back to William. After giving William a warning look, their father led John outside in much the same fashion that John himself had led cows in and out earlier, his callused hand gripping John at the back of his neck. In the gray light of early morning, surrounded by the cows in the chill air, John could still hear William swearing over the sound of the machinery.

"It was an accident," he began, hating the whiny sound that crept into his voice. "I didn't see it there, and I didn't know..."

His father nodded. "I know. But you got to be careful, John. You know that. Equipment's expensive."

John looked at the combination of cow manure, hay, and mud on his pants. Welcome home, he thought to himself.

"Listen," Dad said, "there's no sense in overdoing it your first day. If you want to go back inside, get cleaned up, get some more sleep, that's fine with me."

John looked away from his father, at the cows and the pasture beyond them. He was tempted. Then he stomped his feet, loosening sticky strands of hay from his jeans.

"No," he said. "I'm here to help, Dad."

His father gazed at him, rubbing his beard, then smiled. "Okay. Let's leave milking for later. You can help me with it tonight if you want, while William's in town at the shop. For now, though, how 'bout you work on cleaning out the machine shed for me."

John wanted to complain about being given such grunt work, but he clamped his mouth shut. Cleaning up after William and Dad hadn't been why he'd returned from Chicago. But if it made him more useful, he had to do it. Call it the beginning of "Projects to Do to Make John More Useful."

Dad gave him a look as if he was expecting a struggle, then he turned back to the barn. "Look, I'd better get back in there. Try not to throw away anything that might be valuable in the machine shed. Just organize everything. It's sort of a mess." He walked back to the cow barn door, then stopped.

His father glanced into the barn, where William was still swearing. With a smile, Dad shook his head. "It's good to have you back, son."

John nodded at his father and walked toward the machine shed, still trying to loosen the clumps of manure on his jeans. He knew the secret was to keep moving, keep trying.

But I just keep fucking up again, he thought, rubbing his arms under his sweatshirt. The sun had turned the eastern sky a soft pink, lighting his way to the battered metal door of the shed. The cold cut right through his soiled sweatshirt and jeans. If only Andrea could see me now, he thought.

"John," she'd said, standing at the parking lot entrance outside the flea market. "Would you just stop for one second and talk to me?"

John had to force himself to stop and look at her. "Andrea," he said, walking back and hugging her. She tightened up on him at first, then she relaxed. Her thin arms circled him.

"You just don't think about the future, do you?" she mumbled into his shoulder. She pulled away from him and put both fists on his chest, pressing on him. A tear slipped down her face, then another. "Come stay with me."

John looked at Andrea without answering her. At some point during the past two weeks since his layoff and Jamie's hospitalization, he had decided to leave the city. A weight was lifted off his shoulders when he'd made the decision, and he was starting to see how leaving was his only true option. And so the ties connecting him to Chicago were carefully being severed: first the handful of people he considered friends from work, then his apartment, then Mark and Christine. He'd miss the restaurants and the night life too, but even before he lost his job he had begun to feel bored of the weekly feasts, and the long nights of drinking followed by waking up at three in the afternoon scared him. He could live without all that. He had to. But that still left Andrea, asking him to move in with her.

"Why?" he asked at last, surprising himself.

"Why what?" Andrea snapped. "I don't know what you're talking about."

"Why should we move in together? We've only known each other a year. We'd probably end up hating each other and breaking up."

"Is that what you're so scared of?" Andrea pulled away from him, wiping a tear from her eye. John felt himself slipping away from her even though they were only inches apart. "So what do you call what's happening to us now? You're going to be six hours away, living on the fucking farm. If that's not breaking up, I don't know what it is."

"Andrea," John began, searching for the right words. When he couldn't find them, he simply plunged ahead with whatever came to mind first. "I need to do something with my life, something bigger than what I was doing."

John stopped himself. He'd never thought about what he was doing in that way before. Was that really what he meant to say, meant to do?

Andrea watched him, her face hardening. Either she would understand him and they would still be friends, he decided, or she wouldn't get it and hate him.

"I'm trying to think about the future," he said. "It's a start, isn't it?"

"Don't throw my words back in my face," Andrea said in a low voice. "You're taking a big step backwards, here, you know that, don't you?"

John shrugged. "Maybe. But it's still a step. It's still *moving*, you know?"

Her face had gone cold at his words, and they had driven home in silence. Two days later he had packed everything he owned into his car at five in the morning, slipping out the day after his lease expired. Nobody had been there to see him off, his car so full of his belongings from his apartment that he could see only slivers of light from the side and rear windows.

In the machine shed, John stopped gathering up empty cans of Pabst and discarded Swisher Sweet wrappers. He stood up straight and stretched, feeling something sharp poking him in his leg. Sticking his hand in the pocket of his jeans, he pulled out his father's rock. His late walk last night felt as if it had happened months ago, instead of only short hours earlier. The lack of sleep was making his head feel light and achy.

"Must have left it in my pocket," he muttered, interrupting himself with a huge, jaw-cracking yawn.

He examined the rock in the harsh light of the single fluorescent bulb above him. It *has* to be an arrowhead, he thought. Its shape was too well-formed to be anything else. Dad wouldn't miss it if I held onto it for a while, just until I'm back on my feet. He rubbed the rock with his thumb and flipped it end over end into the air.

I hope it holds good luck, he thought, catching it and slipping it back into his pocket. I could use some of that these days.

Chapter Three

On the first day in April it did not rain, five days into the
month, William reached above his head for the knotted
string that lowered the attic stairs. He unfolded the steps and
pushed his way up into the partially-finished attic, the joints
of the stairs popping with each step. He was sweating already
by the time he sat down in front of his father's battered trunk.
As usual, his timing was terrible, taking him inside on the
warmest day of the year so far, the sky finally free of rain
clouds.

He knew it was a long shot, but he was hoping to find the
manual for their old John Deere tractor somewhere in his
father's collection of books. Yesterday the tractor had been
smoking and stalling more than it usually did while he and
his father hauled an old tree out of the western pasture.

Kneeling in front of a dusty metal trunk, William lifted the
lid halfway and stopped, thinking about the big oaks and
maples that had gone down in the thunderstorm two days
ago, weakened to their roots by the long weeks of rain that
spring. The sudden winds sweeping across the Iowa prairie
had knocked them over like saplings. He hated seeing the big
trees on their sides, starting to rot. It felt like it was his fault
somehow, that he had allowed them lose their balance and
fall.

But that's the way things worked, he thought, opening the
lid of the trunk all the way. In Iowa, there was no controlling
the weather; it controlled you. And now he had a tractor that
needed fixing before his father started processing yet another
loan, this time for a new tractor. He could imagine the rain-

soaked land of the farm groaning with the weight of debt already hanging over it.

Despite his father's occasional financial screw-up, William still admired the man's determination to keep the farm running, even if it meant working from before light in the morning until long after dark every day. Of course, William knew that his father expected him to work just as hard. William did his best, though there was only so much pleasure to be taken from slopping pigs, milking cows, and driving a tractor. He had more fun at Marty and Russell's automotive shop, tearing apart cars and trucks to find out what was wrong with them, with Russell's heavy-metal music blaring constantly in the background. But he knew he could never tell his father that.

William's let out a low whistle when he looked inside the trunk. Stacked spine-up inside the cedar interior were over twenty thick books, many of them hardcover. Every piece of equipment, from the combine to the milking machines to the power takeoff, had a corresponding book detailing its workings. Grinning like a kid at Christmas, he touched the old books, wondering if many of them were even made anymore. Loose blueprints and papers were stuffed into each available crevice between the books, along with a surprising collection of maps. He wondered who had put the maps there, and who had once used them. Even in the off-seasons of late fall and early winter, William couldn't remember his parents ever traveling. They had been too tied down to the daily grind of the milkings and the feedings and the constant work in the fields.

He leaned back against an old chair covered with bags of clothes and carefully pulled a map from between two hardcover manuals. Unlike the other, newer maps, this map was made of rough yellow paper, drawn on a grid with what looked like fields and rivers bisected by ruler-straight roads, some of the roads only dotted lines. After turning the map from one angle to another, he realized it was an ancient plot map of their farm, plus most of the Jacques' farm to the north up to where it met the highway, and large rectangles of what was now the property of three of their neighbors.

If he remembered his boundaries correctly—and having driven a tractor over and over each acre more than three times a year since he was fifteen, he thought he did—their farm had shrunk more than he'd ever known. He tried adding up the acres laid out on the map, took a guess, and figured that the Koopman land had once been close to three hundred and eighty acres, an unheard-of size from the time the map must have been made.

"When did we sell all that?" he whispered, folding the map back into a small rectangle. He hadn't been able to find a date anywhere on the ancient map.

The attic felt warmer, and the air felt thicker, when he imagined all the history on the map and around him. William suddenly felt very small. As if his problems weren't as significant as he'd thought they were.

He leaned against the chair behind him to stretch and try to clear the almost claustrophobic feeling in his chest. How much more would the farm shrink during my lifetime, he thought. Every year his father talked about how they were almost at the edge of foreclosure, but they had always made it through somehow. William wondered if having John back to help with the work would keep them out of bankruptcy, and the thought made him laugh quietly in the silent attic.

When he shifted his body to get more comfortable, some of the bags of old clothes slid down from the chair onto the floor next to him. William gently placed the old map on the books in the trunk and picked up the bags. He was about to throw them back on the chair when he saw the square box covered in red and green paper between two bags on the chair.

Oh no, he thought, his mouth drying up. The sight of the dancing Santas on the box filled him with dread, but he ignored his own warnings and fished the surprisingly heavy box out from under the other bags that sat waiting for a trip to the Salvation Army that was never made. Two more wrapped boxes were under the bigger box. Wiping sweat from his forehead, he set all three in front of him in a line. None of the gifts were labeled.

I need to forget I ever saw this, he thought. I need to find that manual and get the hell out of here, go out and get drunk with Russell and Marty. Glancing at the rectangular hole in the attic floor leading to the stairs, William took a quick breath and jumped at the high-pitched noise that escaped his lips when he exhaled.

"I don't want to do this," he said, and then he ripped the paper off the first, heaviest box.

A set of metric wrenches, long and lethal-looking in their casings. Hanging from the middlemost wrench was a simple white note, folded in half. She never labeled her gifts on the outside. That way she could keep everyone in suspense, wondering who got what, which present was for whom. Marcy loved that kind of game.

"To my hard-working man. Marcy." The sight of her neat printing made William blink quickly, and he thought of her hiding the note in the box and wrapping it, wondering what she had been thinking at that time. He felt like he could read an entire book's worth of meaning into the missing word "Love" that should have been printed in front of his absent wife's name.

"Nice wrenches, though," he whispered. "Too bad they're not in inches, like I'd asked her." He tried to laugh again in the hot emptiness of the attic. With a dull clanking, William dropped the box on the plywood floor and pressed both hands over his eyes to keep from crying, but it was too late.

Once he started, William scared himself when he realized he might not be able to stop crying. He had tightened a part of his heart and placed all his emotions about that day in December into that hardened part, a corner of his heart he figured he'd never use again. But seeing the neat handwriting on the card had managed to loosen that part of him, maybe for good.

Sitting on the floor of the attic, he heard but didn't quite register the sounds of the stairs creaking and the tentative footsteps approaching him. When a cool hand touched the back of his exposed neck, he jumped, giving himself the hiccups through his tears. His grandmother stood over him, looking down at him with concern and intense curiosity.

"Good God, Grandma," he muttered. "You could've given me a heart attack, sneaking up on me like that."

"But I didn't," she said softly, letting go of his neck and settling next to him on the floor with a groan. She looked away from him while he rubbed his face and dried his eyes on the sleeves of his flannel shirt; he *had* been able to stop, after all.

Grandma made a soft hissing noise of joy when she saw the old map in the trunk. Unfolding it delicately, she scanned the contents and made appraising clucking noises with her tongue.

"1897," she said, glancing at the back. "Where did you *find* this?"

William swallowed hard and tried not to hiccup. "In there, between some manuals. I was looking for a book on the tractor, and look what I found."

"Nice wrenches," she said. "So you going to open those other two?"

"I should just throw them in the garbage, forget I ever saw them."

Grandma raised her eyebrows and touched her hair. She had just gotten it styled again that morning by William's mother. He could tell his grandmother wasn't happy with the results. He could also tell she was dying to know what was in the boxes.

"Oh, what the hell," he said, and opened the lightest package. Inside were five pairs of heavy-duty shoestrings for his workboots with an attached "Don't forget to keep those boots on, ha ha. Marcy" note, a joke between the two of them about how he was always ruining his laces. Grandma gave him a questioning look, but he just shrugged.

"Inside joke," he said with a hiccup.

The third box was narrow and slim. It was covered in shiny green wrapping paper that looked expensive, no dancing

Santas anywhere. Grandma nudged him, and he pulled the wrapping off the box to find a simple gold chain. William never wore jewelry, not even his wedding band after hearing about his father's friend who had lost his ring finger when he hooked his ring on a rung of a conveyor when he wasn't paying attention. No note was tucked away in the gift box.

"Do you like it?" Grandma whispered.

William didn't answer. He held up the chain by one end like a snake. What the hell was Marcy thinking? This was real gold. Even if she had actually given it to him, he would've made her take it back to the store, just as he had returned the gifts he had bought her. In exchange for her wool-lined leather gloves and her silver hair clip, he had been able to buy his friend Russell three sets of the best drum sticks he could find, and two sets of guitar strings and picks for Marty, splitting the money from her gifts exactly in half. In addition to being mechanics, the two of them fancied themselves musicians, and they had been in the process of starting a band when Marcy left. William admired his friends' ambition, but there was no way he'd ever get up in front of anyone and sing.

"I'm glad I kept the gift I got her," Grandma said with a sniff. "Leaving right before Christmas like that. It was the best tasting box of chocolates I ever ate, that's for sure."

"Did she ever talk to you about being unhappy here, Grandma?" William kept his gaze on his hands as he ran his fingers up and down the smooth surface of the chain.

"She never had the time to tell me anything. I may as well have been invisible to that girl, unless she needed to borrow a recipe for one of those crazy concoctions she was always cooking up. I just don't think people were meant to eat pork soufflés with marmalade on them."

He smiled, remembering Marcy, stone-faced, eating all of her portion, then going back for more, while everyone else pushed the food around on their plates. That was back when he ate every meal with the rest of the family, when nobody ever talked about John. His smile was starting to make his face muscles hurt. "She tried though, didn't she?"

"She tried." Grandma turned to him and folded her arms in front of her chest, as if it were cold in the attic instead of stuffy and hot. "But not in the right areas, where it mattered the most."At first, William found himself wanting to come to his wife's defense, knowing his grandmother held grudges like no other, but he kept quiet. Against his will, another memory of Marcy from years ago came tumbling into his mind. He remembered the look on her face when he'd told her, after their plan to rent an apartment in town fell through, that they'd have to live on the farm for a while after the wedding. That had been almost five years ago.

At first she'd thought he was joking. They'd laughed a lot more back in those days. Yet all the time they were discussing it, a part of William had wanted her to refuse the move, to force them to find another place to live. But in the end she had given in peacefully, and they'd never looked for another place to rent or buy.

"I'd better get back to work on that tractor." He stood up and rummaged through the trunk until he found the manual for the tractor under some maps of England.

The phone began ringing in the living room, the sound barely carrying up to the attic. The thoughts leaped back to the forefront of his mind, the timing too good to be true, before William stifled them. Two floors below them, somebody picked up the phone in the middle of its third ring.

"Ready to go back downstairs, Grannie?" William looked down at his grandmother, who hadn't moved. A sudden pang of fear passed through him, and then she groaned.

"I don't think I can get up," she whispered, her voice tight. "My legs are stuck in this position. Just bring me my supper up here, and I'll be fine. That way I don't have to deal with any shit between you and your brother. It's for the best."

"Here," William said, setting down the manual. He reached down and gently pulled her to her feet. Her cold hands clamped onto his wrists. "God, your fingers are like ice, Grandma."

When he let go of her hands, his grandmother suddenly reached around him, pulling him to her. William almost laughed with surprise at her sudden, uncharacteristic burst of affection, but then hugged her back.

"You're such a good boy, William," she mumbled into his shoulder. "Don't you ever forget that. She wasn't good enough for you."

Grandma never called Marcy by her name, William thought to himself, and he felt grateful for it now. He closed his eyes and willed himself not to cry. He didn't think he'd have anything left in him if he started again. "Okay, okay. You're cutting off my circulation, Grannie."

Grandma let go, pinching him on the arm along the way. "What's this 'Grannie' shit? I can still knock you on your butt. Now help me down these stairs, young man. You know, I almost shut the door on you before I heard you up here."

"Well thanks for saving me," William said, surprised by how much he meant it. "Let's go downstairs."

He went down ahead of her, watching her place each foot onto the steps, descending it like a ladder, making sure her knees didn't give out on her. The air felt fifteen degrees cooler in the hallway.

"Don't forget to get those wrenches before you close this place up again," she said, nudging him with her elbow on her way down the hall. She carried the old map in her hands like a priceless heirloom.

William climbed back into the attic. Wrapping paper was strewn across the floor, along with the bags of clothes around the chair. He kicked the paper under the skirting of the chair, tossed the clothes into a corner, and picked up the manual once again. He dropped the bootlaces in his shirt pocket and scooped up the box of wrenches, but he didn't know what to do with the third gift. Staring hard at the gold chain, William considered flinging it into the mounded pink insulation on the unfinished half of the attic, but instead he placed the chain between two thick books in the trunk, the chain folding in on itself until it disappeared.

He closed the trunk and latched it. His throat felt tight. Balancing the box of wrenches on top of the old manual, he set his foot down on the first step and then stopped, breathing out a long breath he'd been holding in for the past minute.

"Merry Christmas, Marcy," he whispered, gazing around at the clutter of the attic, stopping for one last look at the closed trunk and the pile of clothes. There was no way of telling what she had been thinking or feeling when she'd hid those gifts up here. Did she know that she was leaving at that point? Had she been miserable for all four years of their married life here? And was she ever coming back?

With an abrupt turn, William descended the creaking stairs with the box of wrenches heavy and jangling against his chest as if they had a life all their own.

Chapter Four

John hung up the phone with a shaking hand, numbed by the thought that somehow they had found his phone number. The unfamiliar voice on the other end hadn't said much, hadn't needed to, and John felt all his plans turn as muddy as the fields outside. He should've known better than to think he could control his life. "We're waiting for you to come through, John," the man had said, calling him by name as if they were old friends. As if the man on the other end of the line was looking forward to seeing him soon. John hadn't been fooled.

He glanced around the living room, at his grandmother's genealogy book sitting on the couch, unattended, and the TV playing the ag market reports. He had no idea where his grandmother was, and he assumed William was outside somewhere, working with their father. His mother had been in the bedroom since she had come home from school, sleeping off a migraine. John turned his gaze back to the darkening sky outside. If he were still in Chicago, he would be with Andrea right now, having the first drink of the night with just her or even Mark and Christine as well. But he wasn't there, and that was the whole point.

He picked up the phone again and began punching buttons. He surprised himself by remembering the numbers, after all this time away. Two local calls later, he was in his new Mustang with the Illinois license plates, heading into town to meet up with Andy and Tim, guys he hadn't seen in over a year. Hopefully, they would help him forget the voice on the other end of the long distance line.

The first thing his old buddies wanted to do was get beer and go roading. They met at the church parking lot, where every young person in the area with a driver's license showed up at one point in the course of a slow-moving, small-town Iowa evening. Even though John hadn't invited him, Tim's younger brother Tony had come along. John didn't know him well, but he shook Tony's hand after exchanging crushing handshakes with Andy and Tim. Andy motioned for the keys as the brothers went into the gas station to pick up beer for the cooler they'd brought along. In five minutes they were speeding through town, heading for the open roads of the countryside.

"It's nowhere near paid off, and you guys want to wreck it," John yelled from the passenger seat over the insistent guitars of Metallica coming from Tim's boom box. It was all he could do to keep Andy from racing the car full speed down the gravel roads outside town. "Watch this corner, Andy."

"It's like a friggin' rocket," Tony shouted. His knees poked John through his seat in time to his brother's music. Tim had insisted on bringing the radio when John told him he didn't have a tape deck, only a CD player.

"Not bad," Andy said, barely braking as the car followed a curve in the road. Loose gravel spit against the wheel wells and the rear bumper like popcorn.

"Jesus, slow down," John said, but it was no use. Andy never listened to a thing anyone else said. "Ah hell, give me a beer."

"Yeah," Tim shouted. "Drinks are on me tonight, guys, in honor of John's return to the great big nowhere of Holy Cross."

"Gotta drink to that, I guess," John said. John took a sip and barely grimaced. He turned the can up and took another drink, emptying half the can. After almost two weeks of being back, he was getting used to the taste of cheap beer again.

"Nice of you to keep in touch while you were gone," Andy said while Tim was changing tapes. Driving mostly with his knees, he opened his can and took a long swig. He glanced at John, then turned back to the gravel road.

John balled his hands into fists and tried to think of a diplomatic way to answer Andy without making things worse. The wind whistled in through the half-open passenger window. He had no idea where they were; everything looked the same. They were surrounded by the growing darkness and the occasional light from a distant farm

The music started up again, this time Whitesnake. "Turn that down a second, ya damn headbanger," John shouted. Tony kneed John again in the back and mumbled an apology. Both brothers were listening in, waiting for John to answer Andy.

"Look, guys," John said, "I know I didn't see you every time I came home to visit. And I was going to invite you up to my place in Chicago, but..."

"But what?" Andy said. He had both hands on the wheel, gripping it tightly. While Tim had remained thin and still looked like a teenager, Andy had filled out from years of working construction, developing a bit of a belly and huge arms that bulged under his t-shirt. John saw some gray mixed in with the black hair underneath his old friend's baseball cap.

"Ah, shit. You guys wouldn't have liked it up there. There's too many people, for one thing, and a lot of them are different from you. From us."

"So they're better than us, huh?" Tim said slowly, rattling his fingers on the buttons of his portable stereo. "What the hell do you mean?"

"No," John said. "That's not it. Chicago's a huge city. Holy Cross isn't even a damn town. It's different."

Outside, brown, empty fields blurred past, the occasional cow or fencepost dotting the countryside like a shadow in the fading light. Maybe they were right, John thought. Maybe I am somehow ashamed of them, guys I've known since grade school. Guys who had never left this area, and it had never seemed to bother them.

"Whatever," Andy said. He had always been the one to determine the mood of their outings. There was a quiet confidence in him, but also something that made John think he was secretly pissed off at just about everybody, which did wonders for keeping people on their toes around him. Out of the corner of his eye, John saw the brothers exchange a wordless look in the back seat.

A few seconds later, Andy shifted in his seat and eased up off the accelerator. They were still going about sixty on the ruler-straight country road. "So are there any good looking chicks in the city? Models, actress-types, all that?"

"Oh yeah." Relieved, John started in with a full, somewhat exaggerated accounting of some of the women in their power suits he'd known through his job, and made his way to the mini-skirted nightclub crowd, grinning along with his friends, but all the while thinking how pissed Andrea would be with him for saying such things. A part of him hated the way he was talking, but a part of him—the always-seventeen-year-old part—enjoyed seeing his buddies' jealous reactions. And anyway, it's just me and the guys, he thought, finishing another beer. That was the advantage of old friends. You could do whatever you wanted around them and it wouldn't come back to haunt you.

"God, it would be so nice to see some new women instead of the same old dogs that hang out at the taverns around here," Tim said in an almost mournful tone of voice.

"What are you talking about?" Andy shot back. "You're married, dumb ass. You are totally and completely out of the running."

"Doesn't mean I can't look," Tim muttered over his younger brother's braying laughter. John wondered what Tim's wife and little boy were doing without him tonight, while Tim was out roading on a Monday night.

"So how are the wife and kid," John asked, opening another beer. He wanted to keep control of the conversation; he didn't need questions about his own love life. That would lead to a discussion about breakups, if that was what really had happened between him and Andrea.

"Great, man. Here's some photos. That's Alex on his first birthday, and there's Jill and him." Tim was holding his wallet in John's face and breathing his stale beer breath on him when John glanced up at the road. Something dark and massive stood on the shoulder, barely lit by the headlights. It was a cow.

"Andy —" John began.

"Shit!" Andy yelled, slamming on the brakes. The car fishtailed in the gravel, but he managed to keep it on the road by jerking the wheel hard to the right. John slammed his elbow into the dash, Tim's boom box hit the back window, and Tony jammed both knees into John's back. Andy kept yelling "Shit" over and over. The car stalled and stopped dead in the road, perfectly sideways, as the cow, untouched, took its time walking across the gravel in front of them. The engine of the Mustang ticked like a bomb about to go off.

"God damn cow." Andy said, finding his vocabulary again. He pulled off his cap with a shaking hand and ran his fingers through his hair, then replaced his cap. "Anybody hurt?"

John's elbow stung like crazy, but he was okay otherwise. Just angry as hell at the near-wreck, shaking with adrenaline. In the back seat, Tim rubbed the back of his head as he stuffed stray D batteries back into his boom box, and Tony chugged the last of a beer that had been frothing over.

Andy jumped out of the car, turning toward the cow. "Come on, you guys. Let's round up this old bag. The Deutmeyers must have a fence down again."

When John stood up on the gravel, his leg muscles wanted to give out. He felt dizzy from the combination of the three beers he'd sucked down, followed by the abrupt end to their drive. He felt stupid for letting Andy drive his car—Andy had been drinking as much as John had been, if not more. But drinking was what they did when they got together. Otherwise, John thought, we'd probably just sit in silence and feel all uncomfortable.

"Andy," Tony called, kicking up gravel as he jogged over to the runaway cow. "Guess what I'm thinking right now." The black and white cow watched Tony with big, dumb eyes, but it remained rooted to the road.

"Ah, no, don't pull that crap, man," Andy shouted back. Tony slapped the cow on the ass with a dull thud, and it jogged off the road into the ditch toward Andy.

Tim stood next to John, a beer in his hand. He looked at his brother chasing the cow and laughed. "What an idiot. I knew we shouldn't have brought him along."

"Let's just leave the stupid cow," John said. "Someone'll find it tomorrow, and they can worry about the fence."

"Shit, John," Andy's voice came back to them from the darkness next to the field. "You don't just leave someone's cow out running loose. They'll find it tomorrow, I'm sure, but it'll either be lame or run over." His voice softened a tiny bit. "Not everyone is as good a driver as I am, you know."

"Let's tip it, man," Tim said. "That'll keep it in one damn spot."

Tony ran back to the car and dug out more beer from his cooler. He tossed one to John, who opened it and drank, toasting his old friends as he swallowed foam. At least they hadn't changed much. First drunk driving, now cowtipping.

"Give us a hand, John," Andy said, leading the cow down the fence line, looking for the break. "I don't see any other cows loose. Let's get Bertha here back into her field."

"Here it is," Tim called out. He had walked about fifty yards up one side of the fence, and he stood waving his arm. "Send her this way. The hole's down here."

With about fifty prods and pokes, the four men managed to steer the cow down through the ditch and over the downed fence. They followed her into the field, barely lit by the headlights from John's car up the road. If we could just hurry up and do this, John thought, I could get my car out of the middle of the damn road and we could get the hell out of here.

"Assume the position, men," Tony said after chugging the last of his beers. They lined up alongside the cow, Andy with his hands on his knees, Tim in a three-point football stance, John on the cow's ass end with his hands on his hips. Tony stood a few steps back, supervising with a beer can in each hand.

"Welcome home, buddy," Andy said, smiling his first real smile of the night.

"On three," Tony began. "One."

Tim pulled John down lower next to him and Andy. "Can't do this in Chicago, can you?" he said with a braying laugh.

"Two."

"Chicago?" John said, tensing his body and leaning forward. "Where's that?"

"Three!" Tim screamed, and the three men hit the side of the cow at the same time. It simultaneously moaned from deep in its throat and broke wind just in front of John's face. After the impact, the cow went airborne for a fraction of a second, then landed heavily on its side, spattering them all with mud and manure. The cow hit the ground hard, kicking its legs as it fought to right itself. John coughed, almost gagging from the smell, thinking about how he was never going to be able to get away from the stink of cow shit. He'd never get used to it, no matter how long he stayed.

As soon as John stumbled into the house later that night, leaving his ruined shoes on the back steps, the phone began ringing. Grandma and William were the only ones still up, though they looked like they were both asleep.

"Hello?" he said into the buzz on the other end of the line.

"I thought you'd still be up," a familiar voice said. He closed his eyes, reminded for the first time all evening of his earlier call. "This is Andrea."

"I know. I haven't forgotten what your voice sounds like." He winced, regretting his words immediately. His head was still spinning, a headache forming behind his eyes. He wished he hadn't gotten so mad at Andy and the brothers on the ride home. But when Tony had dragged cow manure into his back seat, John had completely lost his temper at him. He winced again at the memory. "How have you been doing?"

"Oh just great. The magazine's two days past our deadline, and I'm backlogged with proofs and stories. Oh, and someone was mugged outside my apartment last night. I was at the hospital with Mark and Christine and missed the excitement. After we saw Jamie we went out and had too much to drink and talked about this guy we used to know who lives in Iowa now. They just put in a bid on a three-bedroom house in Elmhurst. They say hi, by the way."

"Great." The line buzzed louder, then quieted as he listened to her breathing.

"So how's the family?" Andrea said.

"Fine." John glanced around the room, at Grandma resting her hands on the pages of her huge binder, either reading or sleeping. William was sleeping on the couch in front of an old rerun on the television. "Full of energy and conversation, as always."

"Right. I'll bet."

"You should come out and visit with them."

"I don't think so," Andrea said, without missing a beat. "I'm not leaving the city. I spent enough time on a farm when I was a kid." After another uncomfortable silence, Andrea sighed. "Well, it's been great, but I've got to go. Have to get to work early, try to avoid rush hour traffic, you know. Remember all that fun city stuff, John? You'll be missing it soon, and I hope you come to your senses one day. I'm sure you have it all figured out, that it's all part of your master plan. But I can only wait so long."

"Yeah. We'll see." John was getting tired of threats on the phone, voices from miles away promising him what could happen one day. Thinking about the drive home tonight with his old friends, after he'd yelled at all three of them, he felt as if there was something in him that made him disappoint people or piss them off, or both. He knew he probably shouldn't have called Tony a stupid motherfucker for getting

MICHAEL JASPER

cow manure on his back seat. He rubbed his shoulder and neck, sore from holding the receiver to his ear in one conversation after another. "Talk to you later, Andrea."

"Bye," she said after a long pause. The phone clicked off. John hung up and paced around the living room. On the couch, William snorted once, then rolled onto his side. John glared down at the coffee table, littered with three days' worth of newspapers, old hunting magazines, and two empty beer cans. A pile of clothes sat in the chair next to where Grandma sat with her head bent towards her binder.

"Just push that stuff on the floor and sit down, honey," she said without raising her head. John jumped, thinking she had been asleep. He did as he was told and sank into the musty blue armchair. The events of the past month had stayed in the back of his mind for so long that bringing them back out again tonight had reminded him of topics that, like an old injury or scar, probably were better left alone. Or taken care of much sooner.

"Want to hear about your great-great uncle Joseph?" his grandmother asked. "Here's a copy of one of the first photos of him, just before he died an early death from T.B."

John took the photograph out of his grandmother's shaky hands. The man in the picture was balding and heavyset, with light brown hair combed straight back. His pale eyes had a hint of mischief to them, and the carefully-manicured curls of his mustache made him look slightly vain. John envied him for a moment, living in an earlier time when things must have been much simpler than they were now, when people didn't try to kill themselves with drugs or didn't leave old friends behind when they needed them the most.

"I'm sorry, Grandma," he said, pulling himself to his feet. "I'm too beat to hear about him right now. Maybe later, okay?"

Grandma sniffed and lifted her chin, plucking the photo from John's hand on his way past her. She carefully placed the picture into the black plastic mounting on the page in her binder, making a wordless noise of frustration to herself.

Grandma could keep the past, John thought. He was better off living only in the present, not the past or even Andrea's versions of the future. Any other timeframe would drive a person crazy. He could worry himself to death about things he had done—most likely done wrong—or get bogged down in planning each movement toward a goal that kept drifting further and further out of reach. Being easily distracted, John had to choose the present, because anything else forced him to lose his momentum and end up nowhere. The stairs creaked under his feet on his way up to his old bedroom. The upstairs was cooler than the downstairs, as usual, and John hoped he'd be able to get to sleep in the chilly air. He forced himself to clear his mind and forget the drive back to Holy Cross tonight, all four men in the car silent except for the sipping of beer out of cans. John had crossed some line with Andy and Tim and Tony, but he didn't fully understand how abruptly it had happened.

John pulled off his socks and fell back on the bed. He knew if he thought any more about his present situation, he'd end up telling himself that he'd made a terribly foolish mistake coming back home. And he'd never get to sleep. In the two weeks since he'd been back home, he'd slept at the most three or four hours a night. In his mind flashed the image of a cow caught in the high beams of headlights just before the world spun away from him and his old buddies. He rolled over. The world was still spinning. Lying face-first on top of the covers, still in his clothes, still drunk, he was asleep after half a dozen deep breaths.

Chapter Five

William lay flat on his back on the concrete floor of the machine shed, trying without much luck to loosen a bolt on the underside of his father's worn tractor. Flakes of rust trickled down onto his face with each turn of his new metric wrench. Keeping the old heap running had become almost a weekly task, but William took pride in his ability to stretch more life out of the big John Deere. His father stood above him, talking about the farm, not even watching as William worked. From the corner of his father's mouth dangled a cigar, its sweet, tangy odor mixing with the smells of metal, oil, and manure.

"You never can tell one year to the next," Dad was saying, sucking on his cigar. "Last year at this time the new hogs were fat as six month olds. This year they're sickly, runty little things, chasing after their momma's teats, not putting on any weight. Maybe it's the rain affecting them. And it's supposed to rain all week, two inches or more a day, according to the news."

The bolt finally came off, and William scrambled to get out of the way of the falling oil. He sat up, looking at his father's back. Neither of them had said anything more about John helping them with the morning or the evening milkings, and William was glad for it. His brother had become the barn cleaner instead, clearing away the years of accumulated garbage and refuse in the eight farm buildings, moving on to another building after a few days. John was in the cow barn today, and that suited William perfectly. Behind William, oil dripped into the pan, sputtering like the weak rain outside.

He tried to imagine how Dad could tell a sickly pig from a healthy pig—they all looked the same to him. He shook his head and leaned back under the tractor.

"How's it coming down there?" his father asked.

All his life, William had hated the stink of the pigs, even though they were often the most reliable source of income for the farm. Stupid animals that lived in mud and their own filth, their odor carried onto his clothes and sometimes onto his skin, if that was possible. Too soon, the flow of oil from the tractor stopped dripping into the pan on the concrete floor. He looked up and realized his father was waiting for an answer.

"It'll be all right. Just needs a little attention now and then." He wiped his face with the bottom of his untucked flannel shirt, pulling it away damp and covered in flecks of rust. After twisting the bolt back on, he dumped oil into the top of the engine without the funnel he usually used. John had done such a good job cleaning out the machine shed a week ago that William couldn't find anything.

He glanced at his father. "The rain'll let up soon, don't you think?"

"We can only hope. Good thing your mother has her income from teaching." Dad puffed thoughtfully on his cigar. William cringed inside, knowing what was coming next. "Too much rain could be another nail in this farm's coffin, is all. It's ruining the grass where the cows graze. It's making the pigs sick. The crops will go in late for sure this season because of it. Hell, it's not good for us, either. I think your grandmother is so tired of being cooped up in the house with the rest of us, she's about ready to shoot someone."

"She doesn't need rain to be in a foul mood." William wiped his hands on a rag and nudged the pan of oil out from under the tractor with his boot, spilling a few black drops on the already-stained floor. Nodding at the tractor, he said, "I think all it needs is some heavier oil to keep it from smoking so much and dying on you. Something that doesn't burn up so fast."

"I still say we throw this thing out on the junk heap and get a new Deere from Tony's dealership," his father said, avoiding William's gaze. "I saw a really nice one there the other day. It was almost in our price range."

"And how we going to pay for that?"

"We'll talk to our old friends at the bank, of course."

William started the tractor, and let it run, the engine roaring. It sputtered, filling the barn with greasy smoke, then evened out into a dull rumbling. He listened to the engine and smiled. Dad would throw out a dirty spoon before washing it off, he thought, turning off the tractor.

Dad nodded, then turned back to the grimy window. Rain fell silently outside, hitting the glass of the window and streaking the pane. The tools on the workbench had been lined up in a row on the bench next to the window, and all of the beer cans, newspapers, and cigar wrappers had been thrown away. From above him on the tractor seat, William noticed how broad his father's shoulders were, broader than both his sons, he thought, though his belly had started to pull the fabric of his work shirts tight above his belt. William had never realized his father had put on weight until John had teased Dad about it his first week back. Luckily John hadn't noticed how loosely William's own clothes fit him, or how little he ate on the few occasions all five of them ate together. William wasn't about to give his little brother a chance to size him up and assess the damage since the last time he'd been home.

Dad tapped on the dirty glass of the window and looked up at William. "He's been in there all morning, cleaning out that barn." He laughed, stubbing out his cigar on the narrow windowsill. "That's the last thing I expected to see all year— John shoveling manure in the cow barn."

William looked away at the sparrows making a nest in the rafters above where his father stood. He doubted if John was still down there in the barn. The little shit was probably back in bed.

"Let's go see how our rookie is doing in that craphole," his father said. Without waiting for William to join him, he slid the heavy barn door to the right, exposing the gray, rain-spattered sky, and walked outside.

William dropped down to the floor from the tattered seat of the tractor and tried not to feel jealous from the unabashed enthusiasm he heard in his father's voice.

The cow barn stood at the bottom of the sloping yard, where patches of grass fought to break through the saturated ground. The massive wooden structure was over thirty feet high, its roof almost square so as to hold as much hay as possible in its double-hipped loft. Behind the cow barn was the low, tin-roofed hog building, secured behind its own wooden fence. All last week, his father had kept John busy swamping out the years of buildup on the hog barn floor, a job William refused to do, claiming he never had time. On a good day, the breeze would carry the stiff odor of the pigs from the barns farther north, onto the Jacques' family spread and on into town. Today was not a good day.

William followed his father through the outer gate and closed it behind them with a clang. The barn doors were wide open. John stood inside, leaning on one of the six-foot-high milking stanchions. His University of Iowa sweatshirt was soaked through with sweat and covered with flecks of manure and hay. He held a shovel loosely in one hand and took a long drink from a bottle of beer in his other.

"Well I'll be damned," Dad yelled, his voice echoing slightly off the rows of milkers. John looked at him with a weak smile across the newly cleaned floor. The thirty-by-fifty-foot building was close to being spotless. William couldn't remember the last time he'd seen it so clean. He could actually see the original concrete floor, laid close to a century ago by his great-grandfather and his sons.

"You got this cleaned in what, four hours? I don't believe this, do you, William?"

William shrugged and muttered, "Looks pretty good," feeling generous for saying anything at all.

John grinned wider and walked around the barn, admiring his own handiwork and taking another sip of beer.

"So," their father said, resting his arm on John's shoulder, "where did you put all the manure?"

John looked at him blankly. William felt a smile creep across his face as he realized where this was going. Maybe Dad wasn't such a pushover after all.

"I just threw it all out the back door, into the field. Why?" William could hear a whiny tone enter his brother's voice, a tone he had been all too familiar with growing up.

"He just pushed it out the door! Can you believe that, William?"

Just tell him, William thought, tired of his father's antics. John bent over to retrieve his dropped shovel.

"It's got to go on the manure spreader, not out the door!" Dad laughed once more, then slapped John on the back. William turned away before John could see his grin.

"But you guys were working on the tractor, and I couldn't get —" John stopped himself suddenly, as if hearing his own voice rise. He banged the shovel on the concrete floor lightly and sighed. "All right. Bring the manure spreader down here and I'll load it as soon as I finish my beer."

"I'll do it," William said, but his father's voice drowned him out.

"Now, don't get all mad, John," he said. "I'm just giving you a hard time. I'm glad you're back is all. William's always so busy I never get a chance to pick on him. And you did good work here."

Groaning inwardly, William headed for the door. Rain fell lightly on his face when he stepped outside, and he tried to ignore the stench of pigs permeating the air like a fog. Let the two old buddies have their fun, he thought, heading back to the machine shed. Somebody had to keep this place running. Just before he was out of earshot, he heard his father say something to John about raising chickens in the empty shed next to the cow barn, but William told himself he was only hearing things. Working with his father had that effect on him.

A nother thing his father had said came back to William as he was showering that evening before going into town. His friends Marty Thier and Russell Goedken were playing in their band tonight in Holy Cross, at the Crossroads Lounge, and he'd promised Marty yesterday at the shop that he'd be there. Scrubbing at the grease on his hands with a brush, William remembered Dad's defensive tone of voice when he'd asked him why John had really come back.

"He said he'd had enough of the city, that's all. His job wasn't going well, he'd had some problems with money, you know. He wanted to come back here a while, recharge his batteries, you know?"

"So why is he coming back now, when before he couldn't get away fast enough? What kind of mess did he get into in Chicago?" William had felt the old, familiar anger he'd always had for John rise up, and he forced it down when he saw his father's unsmiling face.

"You know, you could ask him yourself. Everyone has problems they have to deal with, okay? John had some money troubles up there, so he's back home. Those are his problems. You've had your set of problems, too, you know."

William caught himself making a face in the shower, mirroring the face he'd made at his father earlier. He had never talked with his father about Marcy and what happened last Christmas. He knew it was killing the old man to know more. She'd said she had to leave, had to get the hell out of here. He still didn't understand what she'd meant, and he couldn't handle the hours of discussion he knew his father would want to have with him. Just thinking about Marcy made William's stomach tighten up, made him lose his appetite, even though he hadn't eaten since late morning. The only person he'd said anything to was his grandmother, late one night in January, and he remembered her eyes going wide behind her big glasses, as if she were memorizing each word to add to her huge genealogy book, which she probably was. The missing wife chapter.

William toweled off, wishing he could wipe away the bad memories as easily as he wiped water off his skin. But the past clung to him like the grease under his fingernails and in the creases of his hands. He pulled on his newest pair of jeans, some boots, and a white button-down shirt. After running a comb through his short brown hair, he clumped down the steps, ready to make a clean getaway from his family for the night.

In the living room, Grandma sat on the couch with a shoebox full of photographs on her lap. William thought about her hug in the attic, her cold fingers, and he felt a tug in his heart for the old woman. John lay slumped down on the opposite end of the couch, almost lifeless after his long day of barn cleaning, and William's feeling of good will evaporated.

"I'm going to the bar, Grandma," he said. He kissed her on the cheek, then felt immediately awkward when he noticed John watching him. "Tell them," he said, nodding to his parents in the kitchen, huddled over a stack of bills and paperwork, "I'll be home late."

Grandma nodded and returned to her photos. John hadn't said anything, but William could almost hear him asking, "Can I go?" as he had all of their lives. William had never felt that he deserved a tag-along, never believed that where he was going was so important that someone would actually want to follow him there. But John didn't say a thing.

"See ya," he said, relishing the hurt look in John's eyes. He was too tired to go anyway, William thought to himself on his way out the door. Shoveling manure was no picnic. He gunned the engine to his pickup and left the farm behind.

The Crossroads Lounge was a converted barn, redone all in black on the inside, so that even on a sunny day it looked like night inside. Sound echoed off the walls and got stuck in the high ceiling, making the place sound twice as full, even if there were only twelve people there, as it was when William walked in the door. The Lounge was the meeting spot of choice for him and his friends, and he had taken Marcy here almost every Friday night after eating with his family.

William sat at the bar and looked around at the empty stools and the people sitting at only three of the twenty tables. Most of the people at the tables had just finished eating their suppers, the hard-core partiers who planned to spend as much of their Saturday night at the Lounge as possible. Cigarette smoke hung over the tables, mixing with the smell of fried food and burgers. William knew everyone in the place except for a stocky blonde girl who was sitting next to Ricky Hoerner, the local playboy, if such a thing was possible in a town of four hundred.

He raised a hand at Ricky and ordered a draft beer from the bartender. Listening to an old Johnny Cash song on the jukebox, he tried not to think about his brother and the way John made him think twice before and after doing anything, like kissing his grandmother on the cheek tonight. Any day now, he worried, John was going to start asking questions and trying to act like an old friend. William wasn't ready to stop being angry at his brother. He wasn't going to give in like his parents and forgive John for disappearing from their lives for years, only to reappear when he needed help. William remembered his mother's tears of frustration when John didn't call or visit. Anger was an emotion he understood intimately lately.

Stop it, he told himself quietly. His plastic cup was almost empty already, the cold beer going down fast as if to drown out his negative thoughts. On the bar next to him, a stack of yellow flyers caught his eye, and he flipped through the pile. They announced the return engagement of Marty and Russell's band, Basskick. William never tired of asking Russell whether or not their band was into "fish rock" or if they just had a killer bassist, when he knew full well they actually had no bassist at all. Russell played the drums for

Basskick, and he would always argue for good half an hour after that.

As if in response to his thoughts, a pair of hands slapped William's back, and Russell and Marty sat down on either side of him.

"You cost me ten bucks, you sumbitch." Russell, small and black-haired, dropped into the chair next to the William's right. "Marty was convinced you'd be here, but I had no faith in you. Figured you'd be out working in the rain and all, or you'd be too tired." He lit a cigarette, then jumped to his feet again before putting it into his mouth.

Marty, a stocky redhead, smiled weakly and sat on the other side of William, looking utterly frightened at the prospect of getting up on the stage. William waved for two more beers and a refill of his own.

"What's this about a return engagement?" he said. He pulled a crumpled flyer from Russell's busy hands. "You guys never played here before. You just did graduation parties."

"And one wedding," Russell said, tapping out a rhythm on the scratched wood of the bar, his eyes bright. "Don't forget that wedding in Dubuque last summer. We rocked the reception hall like no other, man."

Marty took a gulp of his beer and closed his eyes in an attempt to calm himself. He blew out a breath and looked at William. "Heard your brother rolled back into town."

Christ, William thought. I can't get away from him. "Yeah. He's going to live at home with us, mooch off the folks a while. I guess he didn't enjoy the Windy City after all."

"Stupid of him to leave in the first place," Russell shouted. Someone had turned the volume up on the jukebox, and in the past fifteen minutes, the number of people in the tavern had easily tripled. "Jesus, look at all those people, Marty."

Marty glanced around the tavern, his eyes widening slightly. Then he turned back to William. "Think he'll stay long?"

William thought about John talking with Dad in the barn, holding a shovel in one hand, a beer in the other. He remembered how John had wanted to argue with Dad, then stopped himself. "I don't really think so. But..."

"It's almost nine, buddy!" Russell yelled, stubbing out the cigarette he'd been too distracted to smoke. "Sorry, William. Talk to you later." He punched William in the upper arm and left the bar.

Marty gulped down the last of his beer. "We'd better get our instruments together, do a sound check." He put a hand on William's shoulder, and William could feel the slight tremble in his friend's big hand. "Have you and him beat each other bloody yet?"

"Not yet," William said, watching Russell make his way up to the stage, slapping hands with people sitting at tables and milling around next to the tiny stage. Tonight, William didn't want to think about his brother and all the feelings he'd stirred up. He pointed his cup of beer at Russell, who was practicing his drumstick twirls behind a rickety drum set. "Our boy Russell's keyed up, isn't he?"

Marty nodded, his face still serious. "You doing all right?"

"Yeah, I'm cool. So get your ass up there and play that guitar, man. Russell's been talking you guys up for weeks now."

"All right. We'll talk more later. Let me know how we sound, all right?"

"Go on," William said, and Marty worked his way through the crowd to the stage. A ripple of applause went through the farmers, the farmers' wives, the mechanics, the girlfriends, the factory workers, and all the people in the Holy Cross area who knew Russell and Marty and the other two men in the band, Charlie and Steve. Most of these people, William realized, had known the members of Basskick all their lives. Just as they had known William. It was a thought he found oddly comforting, but not as comforting as it would have been only months ago.

After a few opening words from Marty at the lead microphone that was mostly lost in a scream of feedback, Russell clicked his drumsticks together over his head four times, and the band launched itself into its first cover song from its catalog of heavy metal standards from the 1980s. After the somewhat murky first verse, the crowd whistled and clapped as soon as they recognized the song: AC/DC's "Back in Black." Marty's guitar, overamped to compensate for their missing bass, strummed out a steady rhythm as more and more people got up from their tables to dance.

Basskick didn't sound half-bad, William thought, though Russell was overdoing the cymbals and the drum solos. Steve Findley, the lead guitarist who farmed his father's one hundred and fifty acres just up the road from the Koopman place, had a pretty impressive range of metal riffs and licks, and when he turned his back on the audience for an extended guitar solo, a la early Eddie Van Halen, the crowd screamed out its appreciation.

"Someone's going to throw their bra on the stage next," a female voice shouted next to him, her shoulder brushing his. William turned to look at Jenifer Vaske, dressed in jeans and a tight blue sweater, her long hair teased up high in front in true '80s style.

"Hey, Jenifer. Good to see you," he said and glanced back at the stage, his skin prickling. Jenifer and Marcy had remained close friends in the years after their graduation, and a suspicious part of his mind felt like he was being set up. "Like the hair," he said.

"What?" The band had finished their second song, and applause and whistles had drowned him out.

He pointed at her hair. "I like your hairdo," he yelled just as the applause died down. In the sudden silence, a few heads turned back to look at them.

She shook her head and smiled. "Russell dared me to wear it like this. I normally don't wear it this way, you know, like some people here. I must've used up half a can of hair spray."

William nodded. Jenifer had filled out since high school, gotten thicker in the hips and rounder in the face. She had been the skinniest girl in their class, and it had always been a toss-up in his mind who was prettier, Jenifer or his future wife. It must have been having the baby that made her put on weight.

More feedback filled the speakers, and William looked up at Jenifer's face. She was watching him with an eyebrow raised. "I'm sorry," he stammered as the band tried to adjust the sound system. "I just haven't seen you for a while, not since..."

"Since I had Cynthia, right? It's all right. Everybody acts like they shouldn't talk about her, but I don't give a shit. She's five months old tomorrow." She held up her cup of Sprite. "I'd be drinking with you right now, but I'm breastfeeding and all. Thank God I found someone to watch her tonight, or the guys would've never forgiven me."

The band started up again, and Jenifer tried to talk to him a couple more times, then she gave up and waited for the deafening music to stop for a few seconds. He gave her his chair at the bar and they both listened to the band and watched the crowd as Basskick plowed through their version of Warrant's "Cherry Pie."

"God, I hate that song," Jenifer said when the music faded.

"Yeah, it's kind of stupid, isn't it?" William had started noticing the way people would glance over at him and Jenifer, then look away quickly. He told himself not to let it bother him, that he had every right to talk to an old friend from school, single mother or not. "So how have things been at the store?"

"Good. Busy. The usual. It's boring, but it pays the bills. I was sort of thinking about going back to school, maybe study accounting or computers, but that won't be happening for a while. Maybe once she's old enough for the day care at the community college."

Up on stage, Marty pulled a towel from a stool behind him and mopped his red face furiously between songs. The rest of the band was getting ready to play another tune, the crowd pushing towards the stage. Jenifer moved closer to him and whispered, "I have to talk to you."

"What?" William said, his chest tightening at the change in tone of Jenifer's voice. He thought of Marcy immediately, something's happened to Marcy, then Russell's drums punched the air and filled his eardrums.

"Call me," she mouthed, touching his arm, then she moved through the writhing crowd. William watched her as he finished his beer, then he crumpled the cup and followed her. She danced with a group of girls to Basskick's version of Van Halen's "Panama," and then she walked out the door. William stared at the door from the edge of the dance floor, afraid to follow her and hear what she needed to tell him, but needing to hear it all the same.

"William-a!" Marty yelled from the stage in mid-song, replacing the "Panama" in the chorus with William's name. "William-a!"

Everyone on the dance floor turned and shouted his name in time to the music. He froze for a second, feeling his face grow hot, then he raised both arms and yelled out the new chorus along with them. It was what everyone expected, what everyone wanted to see him to do, and it felt good to do it and forget his problems for a while. He sang along with the crowd and his friends' band, slapping high fives as if he were the fifth member of Basskick.

The crowd clapped and stomped in time to the two guitars, Russell broke a drumstick, and Marty popped a guitar string as the band continued for ten more minutes on the same song, ad-libbing their way through solo after solo.

When William finally made it outside, the early spring air cool on his sweaty skin, his ears hammering, Jenifer was nowhere to be found.

Chapter Six

Looking out at the mud of the cow pasture at ten minutes to eight in the morning, John Koopman was finally able to figure out why he had always disliked living on his father's farm. It was the work. Dirty, backbreaking, unending labor. Not at all like what he'd been doing in Chicago. Moving stocks, following the market, and keeping careful mental notes on hundreds of clients had taken up all of his energy during the average work day. As did tracking his own investments, most of which seemed determined to lose value.

When the markets closed for the day, he'd spend two to three hours sorting through the mess of newspapers, client files, and computer printouts he'd strewn across his cubicle. Back then, there was no time to stop and reflect. There was only the present and the immediate future, ticking closer each second. And that had suited John just fine.

Now, after four weeks back in Holy Cross, Iowa, John had been assigned what his father had simply called "the chicken project."

Two days ago—either a Monday or a Tuesday, John wasn't keeping track—he'd cut the knee-high grass outside the long, narrow barn that his father planned on filling with baby broiler chickens. He then strung up chicken wire in a wide circle, outlining the fan of short grass. Yesterday his father had taught him how to use the Skillsaw to cut four holes in the south wall of the barn. This morning, as the sun burned away the early morning fog outside, John had installed the narrow windows into the holes by himself. He was amazed by how simple everything had been. You didn't have to check with a supervisor before you cut a hole in a wall. You didn't have to ask permission even if you *were* using power tools. You just did it. That was reassuring, somehow.

John had hoped that his careful work in the barn that rainy day in April would keep his mind occupied. Getting out of the house and away from the phone helped; if people from the city wanted to contact him now, they knew enough to call late at night. He still went to bed two to three hours later than the rest of the family, even though he was now getting up before the crack of dawn to help with the chores. He'd been sleeping a little bit better in his old room, but he still got only five hours of sleep at the most. A few stiff drinks around one or two a.m. usually helped him fall asleep for good for the night.

Yet as he squeezed caulking into the gaps between the window frames and the somewhat uneven holes he'd cut, with the small barn heating from the space heater behind him and the late-winter sun lifting higher in the sky, John's mind kept returning to Chicago.

There was Jamie's apartment, that last night. Jamie lived in a huge four-story house off Halsted that had been divided into twenty studio apartments. Walking up the four flights of stairs to it, calming himself with each step by the thought of a drink after a particularly busy and unsuccessful day. Just about everything he had touched that last day of February had lost money. Though he didn't know it at the time, it had been his last day of work in Chicago.

His goals for that night had been simple: pick up Jamie and their other friends and meet Andrea at the bar. Jamie and Andrea worked together at a small literary magazine, and John had surprised himself by becoming friends with him over the past year. Jamie was the kind of guy John never would've had anything to do with if it hadn't been for Andrea, the kind of guy who dressed in black and smoked constantly and had lived in the city all his life.

"Let's *go*, man," John shouted through the apartment door after his third round of knocking. When Jamie didn't answer, John tried the door.

"Come in already," a voice mumbled from the futon in the middle of the room. "And shut the door behind you."

Even before he was inside, John could smell pot, which wasn't a new smell in Jamie's apartment, but he could also smell a metallic undertone, something putrid. He pushed the door shut and squinted into the darkness toward Jamie's outline on the futon. A wave of hot air hit him as the heater kicked on in the already too-warm apartment.

"Didn't Andrea tell you we were going out tonight?" John said, trying to keep the anger from his voice. He wanted something to drink.

"Sit down," Jamie said, still mumbling. "I called in sick today. Left early, actually, if you want to get all specific." He left out the "s" on his last word, pronouncing it as pacific. "Pacific," Jamie repeated and giggled.

John pushed a pile of manuscripts off a chair and sat down. "Can I at least turn a light on?"

When John clicked on the lamp next to him, he let out a sharp laugh, though what he saw held little humor. Jamie had both hands over his face, protecting his eyes from the light. His shirt was off, and John could see all the bones of his friend's ribcage. He almost reached out for the lamp and darkness again. But he forced himself to look at Jamie until Jamie looked up at him. Finally, in the strained silence of the hot, rank-smelling apartment, Jamie lowered his hands and met John's gaze. The look in his friend's eyes made John feel everything in his world slip out from under him. Two syringes sat on Jamie's coffee table, and one was empty.

Thirty minutes later, John was driving Jamie to the hospital, screaming at his friend's unmoving body in a hazy dream as they crawled through Friday night traffic.

A horn honked five sharp blasts outside the barns, and then his father called out John's name. John glanced away from the pasture and looked down at his feet. He had been gripping the trigger of the caulking gun tightly in his right hand, squeezing a line of clear compound onto the floor next to his shoe. He forced his fingers to unclench.

Standing in the dusty light from his new windows, John felt a tug of annoyance. *Dad should know where I am by now—I've been down here every day for the past week.* He finished sealing the last window by squeezing a large mass of caulking into a gap between wood and window, intentionally taking his time before he left the barn.

Outside, rain clouds hid the sun, and John's old boots sloshed in the leftover mud. It had rained almost every day since his return. He slipped in the mud as he stepped over the chicken wire fence he'd set up, catching himself before falling, and walked up the sloping yard toward the other farm buildings.

Next to the machine shed sat his father's blue pickup, filled with wire mesh cages. Each cage was stuffed with balls of yellowish-brown fluff. As John approached the truck, his brother William walked out of the house, his face pale, rubbing his temples. John had heard William stumble in at two o'clock the night before, and his big brother still looked hung over. Dad popped out of the truck and left the door open in his rush to show his sons his new prize. The three Koopman men converged on the tailgate of the truck, each man at his own pace.

"What did you do?" William said, sounding like a scolding mother. He glanced for a split second at John, then moved closer to the bed of the truck. "You *didn't.*"

"Oh yeah, I did," their father said. "This *is* a farm, isn't it?"

John could hear the peeping sounds rise in volume even though he stood five feet away. *I can't believe he really did it,* he thought.

"Do you have the shed ready, John?" Dad asked, turning away from William.

John nodded. "You actually got them. I kept thinking in the back of my mind that you were just kidding about it."

"No. I'm dead serious. We can sell most of them in July after they've fattened up, and with the rest we can have fried chicken all winter, hell, every day if we want it. But this is your responsibility."

"Jesus. Chickens. What'll the guys in Chicago think of this?" He picked up a cage and followed his father to the narrow chicken shed tucked away between the hog and cow barns, ignoring the look of distaste his brother had given him when he'd mentioned Chicago.

"Need any help?" William called after them. John followed his father's lead and ignored him, remembering his older brother using the same technique on him over the years.

Inside the shed, John let the chicks loose while his father went back for the last two cages, and soon the floor was boiling with round balls of feathery down. Stepping carefully, he dropped the empty cages outside the barn, then stepped back inside, surveying his chicken project as the first phase ended and the second began. Sun shone in through the new windows, but most of the heat emanated from a round, squat space heater in the middle of the floor. An extension cord snaked up from the heater, connecting to an outlet on the dangling light switch. The floor that he had cleaned was quickly becoming speckled with chicken droppings, and the sound of the tiny birds' chirping was almost deafening.

How the hell am I going to keep these tiny things alive, he wondered.

His father returned with the last of the chicks, rolling them out of the wire cage unceremoniously. A musky smell of feathers and dust filled the small barn as the chicks explored their new home.

"These are tough little buggers," Dad said with a laugh. "But you can't let them get too cold. If we have a cold snap, your ass better be out here with this heater going. Even if it's four in the morning."

John nodded, half-listening. Staring at the chickens in the stuffy barn, he'd been back in Jamie's overheated apartment, books and papers spilled across the floor like chicks in front of him. He hadn't done much to help Jamie, either. The inside of his left arm twinged, and he shivered despite the heat.

William walked in the door, shaking his head slowly. "I hope you got a really good deal on these," he said, stepping around baby chicks darting suicidally towards his boots.

"Well, they weren't all that cheap," Dad said. "But they're worth it. We have to keep branching out every now and then, you know?"

"Branching out," William repeated.

Ignoring his brother, John pulled three chicks from a crevice between the wall and floor and dropped them back into the middle of the shed. He could feel himself grinning down at the little wings and black feet, caught between his memories and the present.

"How many of these things did you buy?" William said in a resigned voice.

John looked at his brother—the streak of grease on his forehead, the way his clothes hung off his body, his face unsmiling. William used to be so much bigger, before Marcy left. John barely recognized him.

"One hundred and eighty," Dad said.

"How long do they take to get big?"

"'Bout five or six months."

"Who gets to kill 'em all?" William looked at John as he spoke, and John felt heat rush to his face. He knew what William was thinking: John the deserter would never do it.

"All of us." Dad turned to look at John as well. "Right?"

"Sure," John said. "I'll help. That's what I'm here for." He tried to keep his voice steady as he looked at his brother. "What, do you think I can't handle it? You'd better decide now, don't you think?"

"Just don't start making up names for them, okay?" Dad said. "Because if you do, you'll never be able to eat chicken again." He winked at John and smiled.

"I don't want to be then one burying baby chickens all spring, is all," William continued. "If John decides he doesn't want to do this anymore, it'll fall on me, I'm sure, to make it work out."

"William," their father began, but John raised his voice before he could say anything more.

"I'm right here, William," John said, his voice tight. The sight of William inspecting his windows and his uneven caulking irritated him, and the way his brother kept ignoring him made him furious. "What is it you're so worried about?"

"What am *I* worried about? You're asking *me* that?"

"Last time I checked," John said softly, "this was Dad's farm, not yours."

"John," his father said. "That's enough."

William stepped toward John. "Last time you checked, huh? And when was the last time you checked? A year ago? Do you know—do you have any goddamn clue—what's been happening here while you're off in Chicago, spending other people's money? You have no idea what's going on here."

"Well, I'm here, and that can't be changed," John said. "Don't worry about these chickens."

"*Don't worry*," William repeated, his voice flat. He shook his head and walked to the door, giving their father a long look. "Where have I heard *that* before?"

He left the barn and sloshed noisily away through the wet grass and mud. The space heater shuddered and switched off, leaving them in silence but for the one hundred and eighty tiny voices below them.

John bit back a response. Nothing he could have said would have been appropriate now that William had brought Dad into it.

His father bent down next to the chickens, looking out the windows. "Don't worry about William," he said. "He needs to let some of his anger and frustration out somewhere, I guess."

"So it's okay for him to take it out on me?"

"Well, we've been having some problems on the farm. And when he sees you coming back from Chicago, you're a reminder of the way things used to be, I guess."

John grimaced and shook his head for his father's benefit. Dad always had a good grasp of the obvious. But in John's opinion, the man did little about what he observed. Much too little.

The two men watched the chickens for a few minutes more. John caught himself thinking about the drive to the hospital with Jamie next to him, how lifeless his friend had looked, and how the entire trip had felt like an overlong, distorted dream, that had ended with the bright lights of the emergency room. John had made sure his shirt sleeves had been pulled down, covering his arms and the tiny, fresh scar on the inside of his left elbow. His nearly-overwhelming impulse had been to slip away, to disappear from Jamie's side.

Back in the barn, his father folded his arms on his chest, as if unsure what to do with himself in the silence they shared.

After wiping sweat from his forehead, creating a pasty grime on his already-dirty hand, John swallowed hard and looked at his father standing next to him. Window of opportunity, he thought, picturing his cubicle in Chicago. The words came out before he could stop himself. "I guess this would be a bad time to ask you to float me a loan, then, huh?"

"Hmm," his father said after a long silence. He straightened and walked stiffly across the barn to the door, scratching absently at his beard.

John had wanted to take the question back the instant he'd said it. The loan was something he had planned on bringing up much later, after he'd proven himself on the farm. After he'd done more than just clean out the barns and set up the chicken house. But he was already tired of waiting.

"I'll have to see what I can do," his father said, standing ten feet away from him, still scratching his beard.

"I just thought, you know, that you could pay me for the work I've done, maybe." John needed to stop talking, but he couldn't help himself "So it's not really a loan. I shouldn't have called it that in the first place. But I can pay you back eventually, if you want. I have some debts to repay, and all that..."

"I'll see what I can do," his father repeated, then walked out the door. John rubbed his face with a dirty hand that filled his mouth with bitterness.

"Shit," he whispered, spitting.

Alone in the chicken house once again, John stared at the chickens whose lives were now his responsibility. They ran into each other and huddled together for warmth next to the ticking space heater. He should have felt guilty for hitting up his father for money, but the only emotion he felt now was dull anger. What had really set him off had been his brother's tone of voice, he realized. It had sounded too much like the sound of Andrea's voice across the phone lines, reminding him of where he'd gone wrong, how he'd let down all of their friends, especially Jamie, on that night, drugs polluting Jamie's veins, as well as John's.

John picked up a chick and held it close to his face, its black eyes almost hidden in feathers, its fluttering heartbeat under his fingertips. The tiny bird struggled and kicked, refusing to give in. Chickens were a long way from humans, he thought, but I'm going to do my damnedest to make sure these chickens make it through the season. At least until butchering time arrived.

Chapter Seven

That spring, everything in William Koopman's life conspired against him. For starters, there was the rain, almost every day for the month of April. The rain would let up just long enough for him to raise his hopes for the spring planting and fertilizing, then the sky would darken again and his day would be spent cooped up in the machine shed of the Koopman farm.

Little things set him off, like his mother begging him to eat supper with them, or his grandmother telling him long-winded stories about past relatives when all he wanted to do was sit on the couch and relax. His father kept talking about loans. And then there was John, living at home again after leaving Chicago, borrowing tools or asking William how to do something, as if he was determined to show his big brother how dedicated he was to his new life as a farmer.

William wasn't buying any of his act. It was all part of the price he had to pay for remaining on the family farm long past the time he should have left. But leaving was more work than staying.

On an overcast afternoon at the end of April, rain threatening once again, William found himself working on the tractor once again. He slid open the door to the machine shed to get some fresh air. Keeping things working on their Iowa farm was taking as much energy as the day-to-day routine of milkings, feedings, and plantings.

William turned away from the rainy sky to look at the tractor. The old John Deere was covered in mud and grease and small shavings of metal that had him worried, but if he understood the manual correctly, it wasn't beyond hope. It would just take some parts, some readjusting, and lots of time.

With John taking care of most of the odd jobs on the farm, whether it was grinding the feed for the pigs, feeding the livestock, cleaning out the pasteurizer, or any of the other endless tasks that used to keep him tied up until late at night, William actually had time. His buddies Marty and Russell hadn't even needed any help at the shop in Holy Cross for the past two weeks. It was a strange feeling, not being needed so much. Maybe something good was going to come from having the little shit around.

Dad had insisted on taking the tractor into the fields that day to begin planting corn, even though it had rained only a day earlier. He said he was tired of waiting, ignoring William. After miring the tractor in the muddy ground on the eastern edge of the farm, he'd trudged the mile and a half back to the farmhouse to get William.

Driving up on the three-wheeler, his father behind him, William could see the tractor was stuck fast.

"We're going to have to get someone to pull us out," he said. "Someone with a bigger tractor." He shut off the engine to the three-wheeler. The big tires of the tractor were sunk in to the axles. "Damn."

Dad was shaking his head, his mouth set in a hard line. William knew better. He'd seen his father's eyes dancing under his cap, as if he was somehow enjoying this. "We've got to get the planting started, William. Let me give it one more try."

"Dad..." William began, but his father had already made his way, slipping and swearing, across the field of black mud. Why even bring me out here, William had wanted to shout after him, if you were only going to ignore me again?

William watched him working the clutch too fast, giving it too much gas. The wheels kept losing their traction, the rear tires digging themselves in deeper with each attempt. Mud flew out from the back tires, covering William from head to toe. When he saw the tractor begin to smoke, William had shouted and whistled for his father to stop. But his father simply hunched his shoulders tighter and slammed in the clutch again. When the engine blew with a sudden pop, black smoke filled the air and tiny shards of metal shot past William's, pieces of engine he'd never find again.

When the smoke cleared, Jim told his son not to worry, that he'd take care of everything. Frustrated and angry beyond words, still feeling how close the hot metal had come to his face, William walked back home through the black, empty fields without acknowledging his father. Dad could clean up his own mess for a change, he thought. I don't want to get killed in the process.

In the machine shed, William picked up a wrench, gripping the cold metal tight in his hand. He tapped out a beat to an old rock song on the bent front wheel of the tractor. Something the guys had played at their concert three Fridays ago. William remembered hearing at least four AC/DC songs from their most recent concert, the same concert where he'd run into Jenifer.

He smiled when he thought about Jenifer's hair teased up in front, listening to Basskick at the Crossroads Lounge in Holy Cross with him. Somehow most of the month had passed by and he still hadn't called her. He had to admit that he wasn't exactly dying to hear whatever it was she had to say.

"I have something to tell you," she'd said, then promptly disappeared. Just like Marcy had disappeared from his life. If it was really important, William figured, she would contact him. He had made a science of following the path of least resistance.

Just like the crops, he told himself, loosening a bolt on the underside of the tractor, everything comes back in time. Things worked themselves out naturally, as long as you fixed what you could to help the process along, like mending a broken fence or inoculating a sick cow. Though Marcy had shaken his firm belief in that philosophy, she hadn't dispelled it altogether. She would call him when she was ready to come back, he figured, and they could pick up where they left off. He'd try to do more for her. She'd be happy even if they still lived with his family on the farm, four years after their wedding. It was a patient man's work, keeping up with nature, but William felt up to the task.

Then all his careful work had been blown apart by John's return, just like the ruined engine of the tractor in front of him. He could almost hear his father's overly optimistic voice trying to convince him that everything would be okay.

Looking at the dried mud covering the tractor, William's smile faded. He fought back the urge to start swinging at it with his wrench, damaging it beyond repair. His stomach rumbled, reminding him that he hadn't eaten all day, and his sense of patient diligence faded like a cheap buzz. I'm wasting my time with this piece of junk, he thought, then he muttered "Chickens." He pictured John and their father down there in the new chicken house, laughing at him and the ruined tractor. But instead of wreaking havoc on the worn-out tractor to banish the memory of his wife and the presence of his brother, William put away his wrench and went inside to call Jenifer Vaske. He hoped she was free for lunch.

You still have your nametag on," he said when he first saw Jenifer at the only diner in Holy Cross, Iowa. He'd been there long enough to drink two cups of coffee and develop a strong batch of negativity for the world in general.

In the process of sitting in the seat across from him, Jenifer paused for a second, giving him a long look, then she sat down.

"I mean really," William continued, unable to stop himself. "Do you really think you need to wear that? Doesn't everyone in this town know who you are?"

"Well, hello to you, too," Jenifer said. She looked down at her nametag, shrugged, and left it on. She pulled her long brown hair out of her face and fastened it with a rubber band from her pocket. "What's wrong with you?"

"Sorry. This rainy weather is getting the best of me." He could smell her perfume over the smells of fried food, and with her hair pulled back, he thought she looked quite nice. "How are you? And the baby?"

"Cynthia's great, but she's teething and not too happy lately. Plus I cut her off," she said, nodding her head toward her chest.

William, still immersed in his own thoughts, looked down at her chest, then realized what she meant. He jerked his head up. "I wish you wouldn't talk about it like that, so openly. You keep embarrassing me."

"Hey, it's a natural thing, you know?" She gave him a quick smile. "But I'll try."

Annie Recker took their orders, her gaze flicking nervously back and forth between them. William could almost hear the gossip wheels turning in her head.

"Was that a look or what?" Jenifer whispered when Annie left.

William tried to smile, but failed miserably when he looked around the full diner, catching the glances of the other customers as they looked at him and Jenifer and then quickly looked away. Remembering the same kind of looks from the Crossroads Lounge, he shifted his weight and looked at his ringless left hand. The heaviness in his chest doubled.

"Hello? William?" Jenifer waved a hand in front of his face, and for a split second he hated her for her brashness and her unwillingness to be intimidated by the other people in town. Then he allowed himself a smile, admiring her for exactly the same reasons.

"Sorry. I called you, right? That night at the lounge—what happened to you?"

"So you *do* remember. I got tired of waiting, I guess. Marty's band isn't near as fun, and nowhere near as good, when you aren't drunk. My ears were ringing for days after that."

"Yeah. I don't think Marty's ready to embark on a solo career anytime soon." Whenever he went to work at the shop, William had been forced to listen to Russell's so-called "bootleg" tapes of the Basskick concert, and he had to admit, Jenifer's assessment was accurate. Painfully accurate.

Annie set plates of food in front of them and asked if they needed anything else. William noticed for the first time that Annie looked just as uncomfortable as he had felt moments earlier, and he felt a touch of sympathy for her. But mostly he felt dull anger, and he waved her off.

"So," he said, "what is it you have to tell me?"

"Well, to be honest, this feels like none of my business, so I didn't want to talk about it unless you wanted me to." Jenifer blew out her breath and rattled her fingernails on the tabletop. "Okay. All right. Let me just come right out and tell you, and if you're mad at me, I'm sorry, but I didn't have any choice in the matter, okay? I know where Marcy's been staying since she left."

William dropped his fork onto his plate with a clatter. "What?"

"Oh God. I'm sorry. She's been calling me, says she has to talk to someone, and, like I said, I know where she's been staying."

William stared hard at Jenifer's nametag, thinking over and over again, So that's the way life is. As he stared, a part of him noticed that Jenifer only spelled her name with one "n," not two like any other Jennifer he'd known. He thought the same thought again: that's just the way life is, and I'm destined to fail no matter what I do. It must be that way, if my wife could leave me after four years of marriage, but still keep tabs on me through someone I thought was a friend. A friend, and maybe something more. If I could kick myself in the head, William thought, I would.

"William, pick up your fork." When he didn't move, Jenifer lifted it off his plate and forced it into his hand. He looked up from her nametag at last. "You have got to quit zoning out on me like that. It's not good."

William took a bite of his Salisbury steak and chewed, tasting nothing. He swallowed. "Where is she?"

"It's a ways from here, I can tell you that much. Keep eating. You look like a scarecrow in your clothes."

"Not hungry. Did you ever think that your brute honesty might not always be the best policy?"

"That's just the way I am," she said, reaching over to take a bite of his steak. She made a face as she chewed. "I can see why you're not eating. Listen. The last thing I wanted to do was to get caught up in the middle of this. This past year was hard enough on me as it was. I know how it feels to be left. The only difference is I barely knew my guy, while you were married to your girl. At least you don't have people looking at you like the town slut."

"People don't think that."

"Yeah, right."

"I don't." William looked down at his plate, then up at Jenifer. It was almost a relief to worry about somebody else's life besides his own. Everyone carried old pains around. "I don't, okay?"

"Thanks," Jenifer said with a smile. "Marcy told me not to tell you I was talking to her, but you looked so out of it and distracted that night at the concert that I felt you deserved to know."

"Did I look out of it that night?" William asked. He thought he'd been doing an admirable job of making it look like everything was fine, that it hadn't hurt him to lose his wife. He hadn't been fooling anyone. Just himself.

Jenifer glanced at her watch. "Crap. I've got to get back soon. Here's the deal. Marcy feels like she needs a face-to-face with you, but she can't do it out on your folks' farm. She thinks she needs closure, and I agree. I know I'm getting tired of her wishy-washiness on the phone about whether she should call you or not. I'm just speeding up the process, I guess. When do you want to meet her, and where? I'll set it up. It'll take some time for her to get here, so I need to know as soon as possible."

"Wait," William said. His heart was beating hard and fast, and the word "closure" stuck in his brain like a sliver. "Wait. Slow down. I thought you didn't want to get involved, and here you are, directing traffic. I'm not even sure if I want to see her. Maybe I don't need closure, whatever that's supposed to mean."

Jenifer shrugged. "All right. That's cool. I just thought— never mind." She waved at Annie for the check. "You can let me know if you change your mind."

"I got it," William said, handing Annie a twenty-dollar bill.

"Thanks," Jenifer said. William felt himself returning her smile, while Annie's eyes went wide as she counted out his change. She tossed a few dollars and some coins on the table with a clatter and scurried off.

With a quick smile, Jenifer shook her head at Annie's behavior as she stood up from the booth. "So. I hear your brother's back in town."

William followed Jenifer to the door. "Don't remind me. I'll walk with you to the store, since it's not raining."

"Sure you want to be seen with me? Rumors will be flying."

"Let them fly," he said, holding the door open for her. The sun was attempting to push though the clouds and the thick, humid air that hung over the town. They passed by the pickups and dirty, rain-streaked cars parked outside the diner and headed for the store. The noon whistle blared out a long tone that rose and fell, and neither of them could hear a thing until it wound back down again. Dogs all over town howled in protest.

"Is he back to stay?" Jenifer said.

"Looks like it, at least for a while." William raised a hand at a neighbor driving past. "Get this—Dad's got him raising chickens, in addition to doing most of the crappy chores I used to have to do."

"Chickens, huh?" Jenifer laughed. "Well, I guess you're glad he came back. That way you don't have to mess with a bunch of chickens. Unless you like that kind of thing. Wasn't he working in Chicago?"

"Uh-huh. I think he got in some financial trouble up there. And no, I'm not all that happy he's back. We never really got along. We're too different, I guess."

They walked past Marty and Russell's auto shop, the air filled with the hiss of a pneumatic drill and the unmistakable blare of bootleg Basskick. Outside the bay doors to the garage area, a portable sign with an oversized arrow on top pointed into the shop, its white face listing this week's special on oil changes and tune-ups. Four letters were missing, and a "5" had been used as an "S" in two places. Marty had forgotten to plug in the sign.

"Now *that* is one place that could use some cleaning up and organizing," William said, pointing into the darkened cave of the shop. "Russell and Marty are good mechanics, but they'll never break even the way they do business."

Jenifer touched his arm, briefly, long enough for William to register a tiny, staticky shock. "Why don't you show them?"

"What do you mean?"

"Why don't you show them how to do it right? You know, work with them, help them get their act together?"

"I already work for them when I'm not working on Dad's farm." He looked inside the shop and saw Russell's boots sticking out from underneath an old Pacer, then they were past the shop and the smell of old oil and exhaust. "I'm lucky to get paid anything by them. Good thing we're all buddies."

"Maybe you should do more." They were approaching Peterson's store, a combination grocery and hardware store. "Think big, William. Maybe they should work for you. Marcy always told me you were a great mechanic."

"Marcy told you that, huh?" Her name tasted like gravel in his mouth when he said it out loud to Jenifer, but that didn't stop a surge of pride from filling him.

"Sorry. I didn't need to mention her, right?" She put a hand on his arm and squeezed lightly. "Thanks for lunch. I'd better get back to work. Think about what I said, okay? *Everything* I said."

William wanted to take a step closer to her, to remember the smell of her perfume, but instead he simply nodded. "Thanks," he said. "See ya."

Jenifer turned and entered the store without another word. A flurry of thoughts ran through William's head, not the least of which was how much he liked Jenifer's quick smiles. Then he scolded himself, thinking about her on the phone with Marcy. Jenifer probably knew more about his relationship with his wife than he'd ever know. He walked back down the street toward the diner and his truck, knowing he needed to get back home and fix the tractor and get ready for the evening chores, but instead he turned into the auto shop, looking for Marty.

Dragging the cord behind him, he found an outlet and plugged in the sign from outside. Inside the shop, the Basskick tape had come to end. All William could hear was the whirring noises of the wheel balancer, mixed with Russell's whistling. Coming up on Russell from behind while he pried a wheel from the dusty machine, William thought he recognized the tune he was whistling. Either "Come on Feel the Noise" by Quiet Riot, or "We're Not Gonna Take it" by Twisted Sister. Russell never gave his music a rest.

William crept up to Russell and grabbed him by the shoulder. "Don't move!" he shouted. He felt Russell's entire body convulse, then his friend spun, crowbar in hand as if to crack William's skull.

"Whoa! Sorry, man!" William yelled, then burst into laughter. "Don't kill me. I was just seeing if you were paying attention."

"Holy shit," Russell whispered, his thin frame shuddering. He rubbed his forehead with a greasy hand, leaving a black smear across his eyebrows. "If I had a weak heart, I'd be a dead man right now."

"That's what you get from listening to that headbanger crap all the damn time—deafness."

"Ha ha." Russell grabbed the tire he was working on and rolled it over to the dismembered Pacer. "So I hear you and

Jenifer Vaske are seeing each other now. I thought I saw the two of you together at the Lounge that night we played, jamming to our music. And to think that it all started at our concert at the Crossroads Lounge."

"Don't believe everything you hear, buddy," William said, nodding at Marty, who stood in the doorway to the office. All they'd done that night was dance and have a couple drinks together at the bar. This town was ravenous for gossip, he thought, popping a cassette out of Russell's ancient boom box. He flipped it over and put it back in. "That is, if you can hear anything at all," he said, and pressed Play.

"Hey," Marty said as the music began again, fuzzy and loud. The two men walked into his office, leaving Russell and his music behind. "Don't you have work to do on the farm?"

"Nah," William said. "My new assistant takes care of all my grunt work for me."

Papers were strewn across the metal desk, covering it except for where a giant black binder sat open in front of Marty's folding chair. The room was humid and musty from the rain. William sat on top of Marty's filing cabinet and continued looking around the office, taking mental notes. Jenifer's idea had taken hold of him. He could probably make it happen, even if it meant not working on the farm anymore. William suddenly stopped looking around the office, shocked that he would even think of leaving the farm.

Marty was digging in a lower drawer of his desk, oblivious to William's silence. "Check this out," he said, pulling out a thin folder filled with lined paper from a notebook. He tossed the folder on top of his desk and gave William a nervous smile, his face suddenly red.

"What's this?" William opened the folder and flipped through page after page of Marty's scribbling. It looked like poems, all written in careful block letters, with as many scribbled-out sections as there were words.

"Songs, dumb ass. I've been writing some new stuff, so we have more than just headbanger covers from the eighties. Not that I don't love Whitesnake and Motley Crue as much as everyone else, but I want to write something original. Expanding our horizons, you know, as a band."

William flipped through the songs a second time. "So you think 'Finger Lickin' Good' is a good song title? And I thought 'Cherry Pie' was bad."

Marty jumped up and pulled the offending song out of the folder. "How'd that get in there?" He balled it up and threw it at the door. "That's Russell's song. He was trying to be a smart-ass. Check out 'Tornado in My Soul' or 'Gonna Freeze without Your Love.' I'm proudest of those songs."

"Not bad," William said, reading the chorus to "Gonna Freeze." "You may be onto something here. Maybe you guys could hit it big," he added, only half-joking, "give a show at the State Fair."

Marty's face turned white at the thought. "I hope not. It's hard enough for me to get on stage at the Lounge. I just like trying something new, being creative. When it's slow here, I can bang out a song in a couple hours."

William closed the folder on the lyrics to "Tornado in My Soul" and forced himself to focus on why he had stopped by in the first place. If Marty wasn't going to think big, William would do it for him. "So how's the shop doing?"

Marty rolled his eyes and collected his songs from William. "Oh, just great. Things are going just wonderful. I'm hoping that the Pacer Russell's working on will bring us a couple thousand to keep us floating. Rent's due tomorrow, and we need to get some new equipment if we want to keep up with the times and be competitive. Everything's just great."

"It can't be *that* bad," William said, sizing up the office again. The calendar behind Marty still displayed December of last year, the month Marcy left him and Holy Cross.

"It's just trying to make ends meet that gets old. I'm sorry I haven't been able to have you come in much lately to help. Or pay you for last month."

"You know," William began, closing the door with his foot and pushing down the sense of betrayal he felt about leaving his dad alone on the farm. If the farm was a sinking ship, he asked himself silently, did that make me a rat for abandoning it? Haven't I already done my time on the farm for the past thirty years of my life? Everyone needed to broaden their horizons, not just Marty with his songs in his folder or Marcy with all her belongings stuffed into her car the week before Christmas. It was my turn to start, William decided.

"Marty," he said. "I think maybe I can help you out here. Do you have a second?" William leaned forward toward his old friend and started talking.

Chapter Eight

Driving east with the farm and the sun at his back, John felt like he was, after all these weeks away, finally going home. He touched the envelope in the pocket of his dress pants and stepped on the gas pedal. Above him, the color faded from the sky, night rising around him with an almost visible motion. More than anything else, it felt right to be moving.

Dad had slipped him the check before supper two nights ago. As soon as John had money in his hands, the confidence he'd lost during his last weeks in Chicago had come trickling back. "This is just between you and me," his father had said, as if expecting William to come barging through the door and rip the check out of his hand. "You've been working hard. You deserve it." John took the check and the guilt with both hands.

After forty-eight hours of agonized waiting, trying not to seem too eager in his father's eyes, John had gone into town to cash the check five minutes left before closing time. With the cash in his pocket, fighting the urge to speed, John drove through Holy Cross, taking in every aspect of the three blocks of downtown—the stone Catholic church, the two taverns directly across from it, the boxy Post Office building that doubled as a tiny library, the diner, and the combined hardware and grocery store. William's truck sat in front of the automotive shop, and John held his breath until he was past, glad not to see his brother this evening.

John hadn't seen much of William since their argument in the chicken barn. He still couldn't believe Marcy had up and left like she did. Despite the fact that she married his brother, he'd always liked Marcy. She was a good-looking girl, with a somewhat mean sense of humor that John could appreciate. He remembered one late night, years ago, when he was home for Thanksgiving, when everyone else had gone to bed. She had bought a fancy bottle of wine that nobody else in the family had liked, and she had gotten smashed, determined to drink it all by herself. And she had started talking about her husband.

"He never stays up late anymore," Marcy muttered, pouring more wine into John's glass. She pinched up her face and deepened her voice. "Have to get up early. Got work to do.'"

John had nodded and let her talk. The wine was pretty bad, but her words made it taste sweeter. At that point in their lives, William was beginning to make John's visits home exercises in guilt, and John was losing all admiration for his big brother.

"Sometimes I just want to do something different," Marcy was saying. "Go somewhere where it's not so damn cold. Travel. Meet some new people." She slid closer to John and almost knocked over the almost-empty bottle of wine. "Isn't that why you left?"

"Mostly. Plus I hate farming. I don't think William or Mom understands that. I think Dad might, but you know how he is. Nobody takes him seriously."

Marcy rolled her eyes in agreement, then leaned forward again. Her blonde hair fell in her face, and she brushed it away with her free hand, the one not holding her glass of wine. "How do you like it there, in the city?"

John looked at his sister-in-law in silence. He had lived in Chicago less than a year, and he had barely been scraping by, living off his credit cards and borrowing from his friends. He was about to tell Marcy all of this, but the hungry, almost desperate look on her face made him lie about the wonders of life in the big city. It was the life he wanted to be leading, the life he felt he deserved to be living. Money, friends, late nights. His story was so good, he almost convinced himself.

Before Marcy stumbled off to bed, she gave John a long hug, her face turning to him in a way that let John know she was allowing him the opportunity to kiss her. Looking down at her face, John realized that his brother William knew this look Marcy was giving him as well. He'd kissed her on the cheek and walked her up the stairs, trying to keep her from falling.

Turning off the narrow two-lane from Holy Cross, John accelerated onto the smooth expanse of the new interstate that led into Dubuque. A construction crew building a huge gas station and truck stop had taken advantage of the longer days by working late, and they were just now breaking for the day. Lights blinked on in the distance across the fields, farmers finishing their work as evening approached. Everyone he saw was engaged in hard labor, and John realized he was one of them now: a pig-slopper, a manure-shoveler, a chicken-feeder.

It would have to do for now, though tonight could change all that. He had his father's loan and his mother's advice to thank for his river adventure tonight. Before dinner one night a week ago, his mother had talked with him about how badly she'd wanted to go out to the casino with her girlfriends from work. She went on to tell John about how, up until a few months ago, she would get together with the other elementary school teachers and gamble at the Diamond Jack riverboat. They'd have a few frozen drinks, gamble away maybe fifty bucks, and have a wild time. John could imagine a bunch of half-drunk, middle-aged women balancing their drinks and their gambling chips while talking at full volume about Mikey or Mary in school that day. She hadn't gone recently, she said, whispering so Grandma wouldn't hear, because the money had been so tight. Grandma didn't approve.

Thanks to the interstate, Dubuque had shot up and spread west toward Holy Cross. The cornfields had given way to hotels, gas stations, and video stores. The traffic coming out of the city was heavy, but it was no Chicago at six on a weekday, when the lanes would slow to a crawl and everyone tuned in to the traffic reports like gospel. As John drove down into the city toward the Mississippi, he thought about the argument he'd walked into the night before in the kitchen.

"Ann-Marie," John's mother had said, the name hanging in the air. John closed the back door behind him and tiptoed to the kitchen. He hadn't seen his mother and grandmother alone together in the same room since he was a teenager. Right about the time Mom had started taking classes at night and talking about getting a job of her own, off the farm. Grandma sat at the table with her back to her daughter-in-law, a game of solitaire spread out in front of her. She casually thumbed through her deck of cards, moving a card here, sliding a group of cards there, before flipping the deck over and starting through it again.

"Ann-Marie," Mom repeated, flipping through the phone book. "Who was that lady who made Dad's birthday cake last year? I want to get William one as a surprise for his birthday next week."

Grandma snapped a card down and smacked her lips over her cards as if deep in concentration. She waited another second before giving an almost imperceptible shrug.

"Was it that Freking girl who married Kenny's nephew? That pretty girl who just had the baby?"

Grandma grunted and gave another tiny shrug. John was getting ready to walk into the kitchen when he saw his mother, phone book still in hand, pull out a chair and sit next to his grandmother. She set the phone book on top of Grandma's cards. John froze, watching.

"Don't you want William to have a good birthday? He's had a rough year. We all could use a little party, don't you think?"

Grandma reached up to move the phone book off her cards.

"Why do you have to be so difficult?" his mother said, standing up. She picked up the phone book and sent cards sliding across the table.

94

"Look what you've done now," Grandma muttered under her breath. She slid all the cards into a pile with a heavy sigh.

"So you *can* speak," Mom said.

John had waited for Grandma to blow up, and when she didn't he hurried upstairs, only slightly ashamed for wanting to see a big fight.

By the time he pulled up to the Diamond Jack on the river, the sky was dark. But the riverboat more than made up for the lack of light. Built like an old-style paddlewheel passenger ship, all three levels of the riverboat casino were glittering with white lights. Neon beer signs hung in the oversized windows, and country music blared from within, making the Diamond Jack resemble a very well-lit, floating tavern.

A thin man with slicked-down hair waved him down at the parking lot entrance. There weren't more than thirty cars in the wide stretch of asphalt next to the river. The man hurried up to John's car with an important stiffness. "She ain't going nowhere tonight," he said through the window. "River's too high."

John opened his mouth to let loose an angry response, then stopped himself. Drumming his fingers in agitation on the envelope in his pocket, he asked, "Can we still gamble?"

"Everyone asks that," the man said with a fake laugh. "Of course. You just can't ride. River's up ten feet over normal, after all this rain..."

John drove off into the parking lot before the man finished. Being close to the action, even if it was taking place on this grounded riverboat, forced him to focus on the here and now, and nothing else would distract him. I could easily make ten grand tonight, he figured, with the money from Dad and a lot of good breaks. The people in Chicago would like to see some of those winnings, with interest.

He parked and walked up the ramp onto the slightly swaying reception area. The cool air hit him in the face and chest like a hand pushing him back, as if in warning. Men with freshly scrubbed faces and stiff denim jeans stood at the five buffet tables outside the main ballroom, filling their plates high while their wives in their best dresses picked at the veggie platters. This was not what John thought of when it came to gambling. Give me a smoky room and four or five guys and a deck of cards over this, he thought as he entered the ringing, blinking, and shimmering ballroom of the Diamond Jack. But, in a pinch, the Jack would have to do.

At a small booth just inside the main entrance to the ballroom, he cashed in all but four of his twenties for chips, saving the rest for tips and coffee. He had vowed that caffeine was the strongest thing he would drink tonight. Alcohol would only slow him down. Pocketing the combination of red, green, and black chips, John turned to survey his options.

Eight rows of slot machines faced him. It would be so easy, his mind whispered, to just pop in a five-dollar token and win a couple hundred just like that. But the slots were for saps, he thought. The glassy-eyed men and women clutching their cups of quarters and dollar tokens in front of the spinning displays, not even pulling down the arm anymore in their need to spend and gamble faster, only confirmed his theory. The prize values of the slots increased as he walked down the aisle toward the real gambling area, finishing with the hundred-dollar slots promising five-thousand-dollar prizes at a minimum, up to fifty thousand in exchange for one black token and a lucky press of the button.

John stopped to watch a blue-haired lady drop a black token into the slot at the end of the line of machines. Chewing at her bottom lip in concentration, she lost a hundred dollars in the time it took to blink twice. It must feel good, he thought to himself, to just drop all that cash and then do it again. He could relate. He turned away before she could feed another token into the machine, her lips twisted in disgust and some strange kind of joy.

Slots were for suckers, but blackjack was for real gamblers here on the Mississippi. John scanned the high tables with their bar stools—mostly empty—and decided on a table with a plain-looking female dealer. She didn't have a full table like the tanned blonde girl next to her, but she had a cute face and a nice figure. John smoothed his button-down shirt and pulled up a chair. The dealer had a friendly smile for him as she dealt him his first hand.

He started small, betting twenty-five dollars only on his best hands, trying not to draw attention to himself. Two of the other brokers at his old firm had done a lot of gambling in their younger days, and they had taught him everything they knew about blackjack. When to stand, when to go for it, how to count the cards without seeming to, how to read the dealers. A waiter brought him a complimentary Coke and a coupon for a free buffet after he won two hundred dollars in ten hands.

He sat out a round after losing five dollars on an ace, a five, and a three. Gathering up his chips and his drink, he grinned at the dealer. "Be back in a little bit." She flipped cards out of the boot that held five decks of cards, barely nodding at him in her concentration. He left a twenty dollar bill on the table for her.

A sudden rash of nerves had taken hold of him. All this money reminded him of the night he'd borrowed from the loan sharks the first time, after he'd started spending too much on the promise of his new salary. Got to take it slow, he thought to himself. He shuddered at the memory of the cold little apartment where he'd gotten his high-interest loan, all in cash, bulging in his pocket like the chips in his pocket now. The only plan he'd had for tonight was coming in with the thousand dollars his father had given him and making enough to keep the loan sharks in Chicago from calling him and harassing Andrea on the phone. He needed to stick to his plan and remain patient.

Sipping his drink, he could almost feel the boat shift with the current of the swollen river. He didn't want to sit still. As his gaze passed over the blackjack tables, the dark-haired dealer somehow looked up at the same time and caught his eye. She nodded her head at the breast pocket of her shirt, where just the edge of his twenty-dollar bill poked out, and she gave him a quick half smile.

John ordered another Coke for the caffeine and sugar. After two sips, he asked the bartender to top it off with some bourbon, and slid the bartender a ten. Drink in hand, he made his way back to the blackjack table with over $1400 in chips and cash in his pocket. The plan, he'd decided, was to make money. Plain and simple.

"Deal me in, Terri," he said, glancing at her nametag. She wasn't as plain as he'd thought earlier. Betting a green twenty-five-dollar token on a ten and a six, he asked for another card. Terri dealt him a five. "Keep it up, Terri," he said and winked at the red-faced man next to him wearing a Kent feed cap. "Keep it up."

The cards spun toward him and were scooped up by Terri's efficient hands in a rhythm that had John almost dancing in his seat. After an hour and four drinks, John had informed Terri of his name, his qualifications as a stockbroker, and how close his old apartment used to be to both Lake Shore Drive and Wrigley Field. Thirty-five hundred dollars in chips sat in front of him. He was brimming with the old confidence he'd feared he'd lost forever.

"Want to know why I'm here tonight?" he said to the man next to him. He felt a twinge of surprise when he realized the red-faced man in the feed cap had left, to be replaced by a white-haired man with shaking hands. He pushed fifty dollars in mixed chips into the middle of the table and tapped on seven and five for a hit. "I'm here to save the family farm. I'm doing it for my dad and my brother."

Terry flipped over a king, and John shrugged and shot a smile at the man next to him. Terri pulled the cards and chips toward her. The old man, probably a retired farmer himself, pretended to ignore John, but John could tell he was listening. Terri dealt out fresh cards.

"Farming's a noble profession, I tell you. Man against nature, making life from nothing, from winter into summer, and back again. I'll stand, Terri." He flipped over a queen to go with the ace Terri had dealt him. The old man knocked a gnarled fist on the table, next to his ten, two, and four. John picked up two black hundred-dollar chips and set them in front of the older man. "For you, Grandpa. Don't spend it all in one place."

Terri clucked her tongue at that, but she couldn't hide her smile. Things could get quite interesting, John thought, watching Terri's hands as she dealt him a five and an eight. The old man gathered his chips and left. John won the next four deals.

At ten, a bespectacled woman in her fifties replaced Terri. John gathered up his chips and followed Terri to the ballroom doors. She was digging in her pants pockets, and when he came up behind her, his own pockets heavy and rattling with chips, she fished out a rumpled pack of Marlboro Lights.

"Got a light, farmboy from the city?" she said without turning. John caught his reflection in the mirrored double doors, and he saw a reflected Terri holding a cigarette in her hand, bouncing a smile at him off the silver door.

"Who you calling a farmboy?" he said, pushing the door open for her and digging around in his full pockets for the matches he'd taken from the bar earlier that night. Things were getting interesting, he thought.

A s kids, John and William had been best friends. With their nearest neighbor their age two miles away, they'd had no choice but to get along. William had been the one to organize the construction of the tree house that had lasted half a summer, and John had assisted him in building a dam across the ten-foot-wide creek that formed the eastern border of their father's land. Sitting on one of the three decks of the Diamond Jack next to his blackjack dealer, his pockets stuffed full of plastic chips, John realized that his brother could never stop working, even as a kid. These days, William seemed like an old man to his younger brother.

"How long you been gambling?" Terri said, lighting up another cigarette, using her own lighter this time. The

Mississippi surged past them thirty feet down, the occasional tree limb bumping against the docked boat, and the floor vibrated with strains of Billy Ray Cyrus.

"Shit. I'm no gambler." John turned to look at Terri. Her cigarette glowed in the subdued lights of the employee's-only section of the deck. Why am I thinking about my dumb-ass brother? he wondered to himself.

Terri flicked ashes into the brown water. "Yeah right. You were counting the cards, even though I had five, six decks of cards in the boot. C'mon, Kenny Rogers. 'Fess up."

"Isn't your break about over, Terri?" John muttered, falling back into his habit of using a person's name to get under their skin. His head was losing some of the fuzzy warmth from his bourbon and Cokes, and thinking about how he used to idolize his brother—and how William had turned on him years later—had soured his mood.

Terri moved next to him and whistled the chorus to "The Gambler," just loud enough for him to hear over the pulsing sounds of the casino inside and the river below. She was a skinny little thing, John noticed, all sharp angles compared to Andrea's curves.

"So why'd you follow me out here?" she said when her whistling failed to get a response from John.

"I needed some air. Too much aftershave in there."

She leaned closer to him. "*You're* wearing aftershave."

"Yeah. But I didn't bathe in it." John was suddenly aware, with Terri standing so close to him, of how much money he was carrying. "I think some of these farmers are under the impression you can cover up the smell of manure with an extra application of Brut."

"That's cold. Those farmers are keeping this boat in business. Them and the guys from the John Deere plant." She reached into her pocket as if to grab another cigarette, then paused. "Tell you what, John the Gambler."

"What?" The cool air was sobering him up faster than he wanted to be sobered.

"Well, we've got a couple private tables here, places where you can make the big bets. And not just blackjack. Poker, all sorts, all combinations." She stepped toward the railing, her white hands standing out against the dark of the river behind her. "You could make tons of money there. Save the family farm and all that."

"Oh really?" John squeezed his eyes shut for a second. He never should have had that first drink. He talked way too much when he was drunk. "And are you the dealer there, too?"

Terri turned back to him, giving him a look that was half excitement, half guilt. "Nope. This dealer's a bit more experienced than me. What do you say?"

"Maybe. Too bad you have to go back to work. You could come along."

Terri pulled at her tie and unbuttoned the top button of her starched white shirt. "My shift just ended," she said, pulling off her nametag and slipping it into her pocket.

The drive from Dubuque to Holy Cross usually took less than fifteen miles, but at one in the morning it seemed to last forever. John took the back streets, trying to find something familiar in the changed river city and its surroundings. The downtown was deserted, no comparison to Chicago's might four hours to the east, and he rolled through stop signs and blinking red lights at intersections without any cross traffic. The land rose up as he drove away from the river, but John's spirits remained as grounded as the muddy riverboat.

At the last stoplight of downtown Dubuque, John passed a darkened police cruiser. He lifted his index finger off the wheel in a down-home wave, and the shadow inside the cruiser moved slightly but didn't return the motion. Probably wondering who I am and how much I've been drinking, John thought. The cop would have plenty of reasons to pull him over, even though he'd stopped drinking an hour ago, right before everything fell apart. Terri had disappeared in those last minutes as well, slipping away like his buzz, leaving him with just a headache and empty pockets to show for all his efforts.

Instead of taking the interstate back home, John turned onto a two-lane road that wandered through the countryside before arriving in Holy Cross. He powered down all four windows and pressed on the accelerator, letting the cold air batter his body and roar past his ears. As much as he hated to admit it, he'd felt a thrill when he started losing that he couldn't compare to anything else. It felt like a weight had been removed from him that he didn't even know he'd been carrying, and he could suddenly see everything with amazing clarity. We don't need money to enjoy life, this feeling seemed to say. So he bet on weak hands, bluffing like mad, double or nothing, anything to win when his inner voice was telling him to lose and lose big. Losing was more intense than winning. At midnight he'd been up close to twenty-five thousand. By 12:45, he was down to his last two chips and the twenty-dollar bill he'd hid in a pocket of his wallet.

John eased his foot off the gas when he saw he was going almost ninety on a straightaway. Braking before a narrow bridge lit by a pair of streetlights, he felt his stomach lurch, and he knew he had to stop.

With the engine still running, John ran to the bridge and lost his complimentary buffet supper over the edge. He wiped his mouth and let vertigo wash over him as he walked to the middle of the bridge. The river was dangerously high, just like the Mississippi. There was less than ten feet of clearance between him and the surging river. Everywhere he went, there was so much water, in front of him and behind him.

"God damn it all," he shouted, the words flying from his mouth with a force he hadn't thought possible. Everything had fallen apart on him again. "God damn it," he whispered. At least I was by myself this time, he thought, staring at the river as it tried to hypnotize him. The water rushed by below him.

John pushed back from the bridge railing and was turning to walk back to his car when an explosion of splashing erupted from the river. His entire body tightened in fear, his empty stomach cramping. When he looked down in the water below, he saw a shape, some animal, caught in the current, so close he could almost touch it. It was a deer, tangled in what looked like heavy telephone wire. The splashing stopped for a second, then began again, even more panicked than before. The deer fought the push of the water, kicking over and over again with its lean legs. But the more the deer struggled, the tighter the wire wound itself around the deer's body.

John watched, fascinated and sickened by the way the deer silently battled the pull of the current. When the splashing stopped for a second time and didn't resume, John felt a chill run up his back. Then the deer was lost in the darkness. Not believing his eyes, hating himself for witnessing it, John stumbled back to his car. He drove home slowly with the windows closed.

At five minutes past two, John pulled up to the house. The window shade in his parents' bedroom moved, and he swore under his breath. He didn't want to deal with anyone else tonight, especially not Dad. He couldn't get the sound of that crazed splashing out of his ears.

His father sat waiting at the kitchen table in his robe. Two glasses sat in front of him. His hair was bent out of shape from sleep, but his eyes were wide open. "I was going to fix you a drink," he said, "but I don't know what you drink these days."

"Dad..." John began.

Dad pushed back his chair and walked to the liquor cabinet. "I think I'll have a whiskey sweet."

John sank into a chair. "Get me a shot glass, will you?"

His father gave him a look, then placed a blue shot glass with a map of the United States stenciled on it in front of him. Dad dropped some ice into his glass and poured in whiskey and Seven-up. Sitting back in his chair with his highball in front of him, he said, "Now, what would you like to talk to me about?"

"You don't want to hear what I have to say." John filled a shot glass full of whiskey.

His father sat watching him in silence. He took a sip of his drink, grimaced, and sighed. "Go on," he said.

John downed the shot and almost coughed it back up. It burned all the way down his throat, into his empty stomach. "Jesus. That's harsh."

"Quit stalling."

"Okay," John said. "Let's just say it's been a rough year, and tonight certainly didn't make it much better."

"I don't want to hear about tonight. You can talk about anything else but that."

"Did Grandma tell on me?" John picked up the bottle of whiskey and poured himself another drink, then got his father a shot glass and filled it as well. He watched his father for a reaction.

"Your mother."

Damn it, John thought. He picked up the full shot glass and motioned to his father. Dad picked up the glass with a wary look on his face. They both drank. His father's eyes looked slightly watery as he blew out his breath. John poured them both another.

"Tell me about Chicago."

"Chicago," John said. "Not a bad place to live, if you like spending money and crime and running into people every time you turn around. I liked it there, though. I liked taking the train across town at night, watching the buildings fly past, trying to make eye contact with the pretty women coming home from work or going out to a club. Doing stuff with my friends."

Dad listened with a smile, the same smile John felt on his own face. His parents had visited him twice in his three years in the city, but only for a day, returning home as soon as it grew dark. As if they had to escape by nightfall. Mom had never approved of John moving there, but he'd always felt he had his father's unspoken blessings.

"I don't know how you could stand it there," his father said. "Too much going on, too much traffic and crime. It made me claustrophobic."

"You get used to it. That's probably what I miss the most— the action. Holy Cross doesn't have much of a night life, you know? Except for that crappy bar where everyone goes to hear John's buddies play heavy metal." John picked up his empty glass and laughed.His father shrugged. "William likes them." He filled both shot glasses. "Let's do another bump."

"A bump, huh? You going to be able to get up in the morning?"

Dad rapped on the table as they drank their shots. "Yeah I will. And you'll be there next to me with the chores, right?"

"Bump," John said, leaning back in his chair. They sat quietly for a few seconds, long enough for John to start thinking about his situation again. He looked down at the table. "I'm not sure if I can go back there."

"Back where?"

"Chicago."

His father answered by pouring two more drinks. John put his hand over his glass, not wanting to drink it until he had explained himself. "It's not just because of my job and my money. I think I may have lost my friends there."

Dad nodded slowly. John recognized the look on his father's face. It was the same look of focused attention that his grandmother wore when she was telling a story from her book. That intensity made John want to stop talking altogether. He thought about his losses from the riverboat, and his desire to talk shrank further.

"Let's just say a buddy of mine got messed up with drugs, the worst kind to get messed up with."

His father sat back and crossed his arms, nodding. "I *knew* it was drugs. I just knew it."

John bit his lip and stared at the full shot glass of whiskey in front of him. He wanted to drink it as fast as he could and loosen his tongue so he'd tell his father everything. But he felt his jaw tighten, locking his mouth shut. When his father looked at him, he forced his words out.

"One night, I found him, all messed up. I had to take him to the hospital, and he almost died. He almost fucking died, Dad. I couldn't handle it, so I just left him at the hospital. I was pissed at him, I was pissed at my friends for not being there with me, and I was pissed at myself for leaving him in the ER. I just left. I quit my job the next day and started packing to come back home. And I don't think I can go back now."

The kitchen was silent. John felt the alcohol in his system, making his words blur together and warming his face to the point that it felt hot to the touch. The bottle of whiskey between them was half empty. He'd told Dad all he wanted to tell him about that night.

"You did the right thing," his father said at last. "You did the right thing, taking him to the hospital. He may have died otherwise."

John shrugged. "I should've stayed with him."

His father didn't answer. They sat in silence until Grandpa Koopman's cuckoo clock in the living room clucked out twice.

"It's late," Dad said. "We'd better get some sleep. I can't say that things will be perfect here, but you are always welcome to stay here, son."

John looked at his father, reminded of something William had said earlier. "Is everything all right here, on the farm?"

It was his father's turn to shrug. "Money's been tight. Last year we didn't break even and had to borrow. And this spring has been one rainy day after another. We don't have a lot of money to spare."

John closed his eyes, wanting to give in to the despair and guilt that came washing over him. His family couldn't afford to lose what he lost tonight. He opened his eyes and picked up his shot glass.

"You're not going to lose this farm, Dad. If we all work together, we can make it."

His father picked up his own shot glass, though he didn't look convinced by John's words. "How are you going to do that?"

John felt it return, the assurance and cockiness he'd learned and needed in Chicago. Back when the money had begun rolling his way, and he could make deals work almost as if by the force of his will alone. "I'll make it work." He held up his glass of whiskey. "To the farm."

His father clinked his shot glass against John's. As they downed their last drink of the night, John felt sure that this was what he had to do at this point in his life. He said good night to his father and began unbuttoning his shirt, his mind calculating what to do next, how to make his latest endeavor see light. The whiskey still burned in his throat as he walked through the darkened house, avoiding furniture and squeaky steps. In the darkness of his bedroom, he could still see the kicking deer, fighting against the pull of the river.

Had the deer had felt fear at that point, he wondered, or did it force itself to fight with all the energy it had left? Dropping onto the bed, John didn't want to know. There was just so much water, pulling everything down with the current.

Chapter Nine

William could hear the music half a mile away. As he drove down the gravel road, the beat of the drum and the tinny whine of guitars thumped in his hears, even over the hammering of his old pickup. He turned onto the driveway, waved at Kenny Findley, and drove to a rickety barn on the far edge of the farm buildings. When he parked his truck, he realized Steve's father had been wearing bright yellow plugs in his ears while he was outside feeding his pigs. William laughed and got out of the truck. He walked into the barn and was hit full blast by the sound of Basskick.

Marty and Charlie raised a hand to him, then returned to their guitars, faces lined with concentration. Russell was too busy trying to beat his cymbals into submission, while Steve attempted to bend the feedback coming from his guitar in an experiment that wasn't working. William couldn't tell if they were finishing a song or just beginning. A few seconds later, Marty stepped up to his portable mike. As soon as he started to sing, there was a sudden pop and a whiff of ozone. The music stopped and the lights went out. Russell continued drumming for another few seconds before realizing he was the only person still playing.

"God damn it," Steve said, slinging off his guitar. "Stupid circuit breaker," he explained to William on his way out of the barn.

"That's the third time so far tonight," Russell said. He walked out from behind his drums and came up to William, wiping sweat from his forehead. "Glad you could make it."

"I am too," William said, opening his mouth to try to relieve the ringing in his ears. "I think." Russell and Marty had both urged him to come to one of their so-called "jam sessions" for weeks, and thanks to his brother's help on the farm, William was finally able to make it.

"We were ready for a break anyway," Marty said, sitting on a stack of baled hay. Charlie continued strumming his guitar, working his chubby fingers through the chords with a squeaking sound, his pick scratching at the strings. Outside, the sky had finally turned reddish orange, the day lengthening by a few more minutes each evening. William noticed with a hint of jealousy that the Findleys had managed to get their crops planted last week. The fields outside the barn were lined in neat, clean rows of furrowed earth, one after the other into infinity.

"When's your next show?" William said, pulling his gaze from the land outside.

"Two weeks," Russell said. "We're doing the end of the year dance at the high school. Nothing like watching a bunch of drunk kids groping each other on the dance floor. But they're paying us."

"You'll probably need to do some different songs, huh?" William said, watching Marty. "Maybe something other than monster rock from the eighties."

"What other kind of music *is* there?" Russell asked. Charlie ambled over, listening, still strumming.

As the lights flickered again, Marty shook his head. "No," he said. "I know what you're thinking, William. Don't make me do it."

"Yeah!" Russell shouted as Steve came jogging back into the barn. "We can do original stuff, along with our repertoire." He ran back to his drum set and began a beat. "Now how did 'Finger Lickin' Good' go again?"

"We should do it, man," Charlie said.

"Do what?" Steve shouted over the sound of the drums.

Marty looked like a trapped animal, caught in a corner. William felt a twinge of sympathy, then he caught himself. "You should do it, man. Your stuff is good."

"The guys don't have any music," Marty said. "All I have are the words."

"We can improvise, dude," Charlie said.

"Yeah," Russell added from behind his drums, "we've been doing that for most of the songs we have music for already."

"Come on," William said. "At least try it. Before the power goes out again."

Marty trudged back to the microphone, but William thought he caught a gleam in his friend's eye. Maybe he'd wanted to do it all along. He just needed a push.

"Let's start out with 'Tornado in My Soul,'" Marty said. "Um, that's just a tentative title, okay? It's sort of mid-tempo, with lots of places for a solo and tempo changes." He began strumming slowly, adjusting the sound and changing chords awkwardly. Charlie listened along, then plugged in his guitar again. Russell provided a driving beat on the bass drum that forced everyone to pick up speed. Steve watched his bandmates quizzically, trying to find a place to jump in with a riff or two, glancing nervously at the overloaded power outlet next to the window.

"Pressure's dropping, ears are popping, wind is picking up speed," Marty sang, his voice hesitant at first. William gave him a tiny nod, and he continued. "You're in my heart, now you're in my head, taking me for a spin."

As Russell and Steve tried to turn the power ballad into an anthem during the chorus—"Tornado! Tornado in my Soul!"—William found himself caught up in Marty's lyrics. He knew it was just a song, but Marty had hit on something, feelings William had been keeping hidden from himself. Since Marcy left, the sense of being thrown around by a twister was something William could understand intimately.

Russell tried again to speed up the tempo, and Marty stopped singing, glaring at him. Charlie continued strumming, while Steve added to the mutiny by launching into an ear-splitting solo.

"Russell!" Marty screamed into his microphone, but Russell continued on, providing a wicked backbeat for Steve's improvisations, cymbals crashing like breaking glass. William could hear cows mooing in pain outside. When Marty shouted into the mike again, the power flickered, giving the music a strange echo effect. One of the speakers sizzled and went silent.

Marty looked to William for help, but William was still caught off-guard, thinking about Marcy and high winds. In my head, taking me for a spin. He could only shrug at his old friend. When Kenny, Steve's father walked in the door, the power went out completely. The drums fell silent, and in the semi-darkness of the early summer evening, the silence hitting him like an open hand, William swore he could hear two tiny pops as Kenny removed his earplugs.

"Thank you," Kenny said. "The cows were too nervous to give milk, all that racket you boys were making." He was shouting, even though the barn was unnaturally silent. "Maybe you guys better practice in town somewhere," he said on his way back out of the barn. He didn't seem to realize that the power had gone out one final time.

Smoke rose from one of the speakers as Basskick broke down their equipment, giving up for the night. William stood back for a moment, aware that he, along with the Findleys' poor wiring, was to blame for the abrupt end of the rehearsal.

Tornado in my soul," Russell said, his voice heavy with sarcasm.

Marty shot William a quick smile and shook his head as if to say, "We tried."

That's all we *can* do, William thought, helping pick up the damaged equipment for his friends' band. No matter what life throws at us, we have to keep trying.

* * * * *

The morning after the rehearsal, William drove fifteen miles to the neighboring town of Cascade, his ears still ringing slightly. He felt a pang as he drove past his family's farm, past the unplanted, saturated ground surrounding the white square of the farmhouse in the distance. The hook to Marty's song had him keeping the beat on his steering wheel, singing "keep it coming round, twisting me up and down, the tornado lifts us away from here." Twenty minutes later he stopped in front of the NAPA store. After weeks of waiting, he'd finally tracked down the last part he needed to fix up their battered John Deere. William paid cash for the gasket at NAPA and hurried home, whistling and thinking about Jenifer Vaske's tight sweaters and quick smiles.

Back home, as William fit the pieces of the old tractor into place like a giant puzzle, he let his thoughts wander. At first he had been consumed by his plans for the shop: he'd been saving his money bit by bit, even though the weekly checks for $300 he received for his work on the farm added up painfully slowly. There was no way he'd ever ask his father for a raise, even though he'd been making the same amount since he graduated from high school. He would still help on the farm, he vowed to himself, though his father would surely see his leaving for a new job as a betrayal.

Now that the idea had been planted, he found the rain didn't bother him as much as it had only a week earlier. At the shop he wouldn't be ruled by the weather.

But he'd also been thinking more about Marcy, which bothered him a lot. Listening to Marty's song had only been the latest incident. Lately he would catch himself holding one-sided conversations with her in his head, sometimes telling her how things would be different, sometimes telling her to go to hell. He could smile at her cooking disasters one second, and feel cold anger at her the next for not even giving him a hint that she wasn't happy. Maybe he just hadn't been paying attention.

And to top it all off, his thoughts move just as quickly from Marcy to Jenifer, which troubled him even more. It wasn't so much the fact that she was a single mother or even that he was still married to Marcy that had him worried. He simply couldn't risk entering into another relationship, not if it could end as abruptly and unpredictably as he and Marcy had ended. Tractors were safer.

"There," he said, wiping grease from the manifold of the engine. It had oil, the parts that had been damaged in the blowout had been replaced, and he'd even scraped the caked mud from the body. He climbed up behind the wheel, pushed in the clutch, and turned the key. The engine growled, then fired into life, blowing smoke out the open double doors of the shed. William let out the clutch and yelled when the tractor rolled forward. He'd squeezed another inch of life out of the old beast.

Testing the engine, listening for the slightest variance in its running, he drove down the sloping yard toward the barns in the spitting rain. He touched the brakes. No response. The tractor rolled down the slope, picking up speed, the engine humming. William shifted into low, turning the wheel hard to the left, but he turned too slowly. He hit the chicken-wire fence and bent it to the ground with the rear wheel of the tractor. He felt a slight bump and looked back see about ten dead chicks in his tracks behind him, crushed under the tractor wheel.

"Shit," William whispered. The tractor rolled partway up the slope, then stopped. He turned off the tractor. Bending the fence back to keep the surviving chicks inside, he caught the half-dozen chicks that had tried to escape. He dumped the chicks inside the fence and was bending down to inspect the murdered chicks when he heard heavy footsteps, then John tackled him.

"Son of a bitch!" John yelled, flailing at him with his fists. "You couldn't let me have this, could you, you bitter son of a bitch?"

William hit the muddy ground hard, missing the hitch at the back of the tractor with his head by a few inches. He tried to draw a breath, but John had knocked the wind out of him.

He tried to block his brother's swings and catch his breath at the same time. John was bigger than he was now, he realized, and John was mad. Neither of them were kids anymore, and William didn't like the odds. Out of desperation, he lifted his knees hard into John's groin. John rolled off him, and they both lay gasping for air next to the corpses of the half-grown chicks, their broken bodies pressed violently into the ground.

"Fucker," John whispered.

"Didn't mean to," William said. "Accident."

"Son of a bitch."

William finally had enough breath to roll to his knees. He used the tractor wheel to help himself up. "What the hell? It's not like I tried to kill your goddamn chickens."

"Shut up," John said. He sat Indian-style on the muddy ground, taking deep breaths and holding his midsection. "The chickens were just the last fucking straw."

"What are you talking about?" William could move his jaw back and forth, but he tasted blood in his mouth. John had popped him a couple good ones before he'd been able to get him off. Somehow he had managed to hit John in the face, and his brother's eye was starting to swell up.

"You know what. You've been nothing but an asshole to me ever since I came back. I see those looks you give me and the way you act like I'm not even here. Hey, I'm sorry I went to college and tried to make something of myself. That's what this is all about, isn't it?"

"Look, I'm sorry about your damn chickens," William said. "But you don't know anything. You think you can just leave for years, never calling Mom, never visiting, until we all just give up on ever seeing you at all, then come back and make it all right with some bullshit story about your job?"

John rose to his feet slowly. "You don't know anything about that. Don't even try to jump in here, William. The water's way too deep for you."

William took a long, slow breath and looked at his younger brother. He hadn't really looked at him directly since his return. John had a couple day's growth of beard on his chin, and his eyes were the same light blue color that William saw in the mirror each morning. He scraped the mud from his boots onto the big rear wheel of the tractor. Somehow he was going to have to find a way to get rid of at least a piece of the bitter anger inside of him, or else he'd become like Grandma's Uncle Hubert or Uncle Albert, and he'd take John down that bitter, divided road with him.

"I think there's a lot going on in both of our lives that neither of us know much about," William said quietly. The chickens stood at the fence, staring at them, a rapt audience.

"What's your point?" John said, his voice uncertain.

"Did you really think I'd run over your chickens on purpose?"

John tensed, looking at the pathetic little bodies in the mud, then relaxed. "I don't know. I guess not." He gave William a warning look. "You're not going to fucking hug me, are you?"

"Nah." William spit blood out of his mouth, trying to get rid of the coppery taste on his tongue. "But I'd like to buy you a beer, if you promise not to beat on me again."

"I'm not ready to forgive and forget, William. Not this or any of the other stuff."

"Neither am I." William resisted the urge to help his brother to his feet. "But I'm willing to at least get started on it."

William was surprised at the number of people in the Crossroads Lounge who remembered his brother and seemed genuinely happy to see him again. He had forgotten that John had been active in almost all of the activities and sports available at their small high school, including football, where he'd learned how to tackle. It was a skill, evidently, that a person never lost. The only extracurricular activity William had been interested in was auto shop and the Future Farmers of America, and he'd never been allowed to go out for sports. Dad had needed his help on the farm.

"Hey John, how's it going?" Ricky Hoerner shouted, slapping John on the back on his way past the two brothers.

"Hey there," John yelled. "Good to see you!" He lowered his voice and looked at William. "Who's *that*, and who is that ugly girl with him?"

"You don't want to know. Drink your beer." So far, nobody had joined them at their table, and the jukebox had remained at a reasonable volume, and William hoped he'd get to talk more to John before the place got too loud. Or before he lost his sense of curiosity and reverted to his old, angry ways. It was awkward, trying to be a friend to his brother; he was used to not being anything to him.

"So how are those chickens doing?" he said, hoping the two beers they'd each had would have been enough for John to forgive him for that afternoon's carnage. He had offered to help bury the chicks, but John hadn't been ready to accept his help at that point.

"You know, it's sort of fun. I used to hate doing anything on the farm, especially anything with animals. Remember when I used to throw firecrackers at old man Jacques' cats? I hated anything on four legs, thought they were too stupid to live." He sipped at his beer and shrugged. "But it's been great watching these chicks grow, get stronger. And it's like, I had a part of that, because of all my work with them."

"Yeah, I know what you mean. I guess that's why I'm still here, why I stayed on the farm. To see the results of all my damn work. You probably think I'm a loser for still living at home, huh?"

"Naah," John said, shifting in his chair.

"Go on, you can admit it."

"Well, I don't think you're a loser." John spoke slowly, as if picking his words. "I just don't know how you can stand living with Mom and Dad like you have for so long."

"Easy. I'm never there. Why do you think I work outside all the time, or down at the shop? Keeps me out of their hair, and vice-versa. I guess we sort of have an understanding."

John nodded. They sat for a while without talking, John waving every now and then at someone who recognized him. They ordered another round of beer and listened to the music from the jukebox, mostly country songs from ten years ago or longer. More and more people came in, the men with their hair still wet from their showers, the women looking made up and bright. William felt the early tingle of a good beer buzz that spread from his empty stomach to his fingertips.

After another beer, his curiosity got the best of him. "So why did you leave Chicago?" he said abruptly.

"I don't know if I'm ready to talk with you about that yet," John said. "Let's talk chickens some more."

"Come on. Tell me what you can tell me."

Some of John's classmates from high school dropped by, asking him how he was doing and promising to buy him a beer later. They looked at William and nodded, but didn't say anything to him.

"God, he's gotten fat," John said, gazing at the group after they moved off to another table. "They all have, even the girls. I guess that happens when you get married. Except for you. What, have you lost like twenty pounds?"

William took a long drink from his glass of beer. "Don't try to change the subject. I just don't have much of an appetite, is all. Tell me about Chicago. At least tell me who's been calling our place and hanging up on me all the time."

"They don't hang up on *me*," John said softly.

"Really?"

"Really. Listen, I owe some people some money. What I told everyone about my job with the stock market was true, to a point. I made some wrong turns, got into some debts, and tried to move some clients' money around. To my, ah, advantage. Do you want all the sordid details?"

"Just what you're ready to tell me."

"You've heard of the saying 'stealing from Peter to give to Paul,' right? Well, I was stealing from Peter, Paul, and Mary and everyone else I could find to give back to Peter." He ran his hand through his hair. "Know what I learned? There are some very cooperative loan sharks in the greater Chicago area who are more than willing to toss some cash my way. But now they want it back, with interest."

"You're pulling my damn leg. This is like, this is like 'Goodfellas' or something. You didn't really go to a loan shark, did you?"

John nodded. "Sure did, bro." William thought he heard a trace of pride in his brother's voice.

"And I thought I had it bad because my wife walked out on me. At least I'm not gonna get whacked." William picked up his beer, then stopped with the glass halfway to his mouth. "You're not gonna get whacked, are you?"

"Hell no," John said. "They'll probably just break my hands or something."

William took a sip of beer, not sure if John was serious or not. He watched the band setting up, a trio of high school kids playing on Basskick's night off. "So how about those chickens, huh?"

"How about those chickens," John repeated. He finished his beer and sat quietly for a few seconds. Then he pulled his chair closer and looked at William with a strange look in his eyes. "Let me ask you a weird question. Can deer swim?"

"What? Are you drunk already?"

"No, I'm serious. I saw the strangest damn thing a few nights ago, outside Dubuque." John told William about the deer in the river, tangled in wire.

"That's wild, man," William said when John finished. He felt the hairs at the back of his neck standing up, and he shifted in his chair, avoiding his brother's intense gaze. "Maybe you were just seeing things."

"No. That's what I saw." John set his beer down. "I think about that deer a lot. I doubt he made it out. No way."

William stared at the inch of beer left in his glass, feeling miles away from his brother sitting next to him. He wanted to ask what he was doing outside Dubuque so late at night, but he knew better. He was making an effort to understand his brother, but John was still a stranger.

John's face was thoughtful, but he looked uncomfortable, as if he'd said or remembered too much. He sat up in his chair. "Hey. I'm going to go say hi to some of those guys over there."

"Sure." When John picked up his beer and moved off, William sighed inwardly with relief, glad they hadn't gotten into a discussion about Marcy. At least now he knew who'd been calling so much. He shook his head. My little brother, getting cash from loan sharks. Sometimes it was better to live a simple life out here in Holy Cross, Iowa.

The band had played two feedback-laden songs, and John still hadn't returned, when William saw Jenifer Vaske. She detached herself from a group of women on the dance floor and waved at William. Carrying a bottle of beer in her hand, she looked a little tipsy. He nodded at her and motioned to his table with a grin on his face.

"Hey there!" he said, surprised at how glad he was to see her. "So what are you celebrating?"

She dropped into the seat next to him. "Freedom."

William looked at her, unsure how to take her comment. He felt a tingling in his body, almost like an electric shock, a sensation he hadn't felt in a long time.

Jenifer laughed. "Freedom from breastfeeding. It was too hard on my, you know whats." Her voice dropped to a whisper. "Plus this is only my second beer."

"Only your second, huh?"

"I haven't had a beer in over two years," she said, then gave a loud "Wa-hoo!" Nobody seemed to notice over the din of the band. "Sorry. Guess I'm a bit too loud." She smiled at him in a way that made him think that part of her drunkenness was for show. "Didn't I see you deep in conversation with your brother earlier?"

"Yes you did. We got into a fist fight this afternoon. But we're cool now. Sort of."

"Good for you, William. Now you're starting to think big."

The band started up again, playing a danceable version of some old ZZ Top song, and William found himself out on the half-full dance floor with Jenifer, moving to the music and laughing, ignoring the looks the two of them were getting. They continued dancing through the rest of the set. He'd never liked dancing before, and he used to only go out on the dance floor with Marcy if she begged him. As he moved to the music, William forgot all about his little brother and Marcy and the farm and focused on Jenifer's eyes. They were a light brown color, and they met his gaze without looking away.

When the music stopped, he bought two more beers. They stood next to the bar, drinking and wiping their sweat away.

"Did you ever want to have kids, William?" Jenifer asked, watching his face closely, as if she could see the answers to her question in the way he held his mouth or crinkled his eyes.

"Never really thought about it. She didn't want them until we had our own place, and I wasn't going to force her into it. Guess it worked out better this way, you know?"

"I never wanted kids. It just happened. I screwed up, didn't use any protection. I was lucky I didn't get anything worse than pregnant. What a jerk."

"You're not a jerk, Jenifer."

"I was talking about the father." She laughed and took a long drink of her beer. "I thought we had something good going, then he dumps me the second he finds out I'm knocked up."

"Shit. I'm sorry."

"Nah, don't be." She finished off her beer and set it on the bar as if something had been decided in her mind. "So, do you want to come to my apartment?"

"Whoa, slow down there. I'm here with my brother, you know."

"Well, I'm going. This racket is hurting my ears, and I want to get some fresh air. See ya."

William hesitated for only a fraction of a second before letting Jenifer give him the slip again. His brother could find his own ride home tonight.

He caught up to her just as she pushed through the door leading outside and grabbed her hand. He'd hoped to see another one of her smiles, and he wasn't disappointed. Holding hands, he walked with Jenifer through town to her apartment five blocks away, even though he knew he was close to making one of the more foolish decisions he could have made at that point in his life. The walk seemed to take less than ten seconds, he thought, his sense of time distorted by all that had happened that day. The lyrics to "Tornado in My Soul" still circled around in his head. They tiptoed up the stairs to Jenifer's upstairs apartment, William remembering her warning about waking her elderly landlords in the house below.

Outside her door, Jenifer went through her pockets searching for her keys, then she bent suddenly in inspiration and pulled the key from under the doormat. "In case of emergencies," she said, grinning crazily. William followed her, still trying to be as quiet as possible.

Jenifer disappeared into her darkened apartment. William made his way carefully around a table and chairs in the kitchen, hating to let her out of his sight. He heard fumbling sounds ahead of him, then Jenifer shouted "Wa-hoo!"

"You okay?" William whispered as she gave another war cry. He found a light switch and clicked it on.

Jenifer appeared in front of him, her face flushed. "I'm fine, I'm great. You should really try this," she added, giving a third whoop. "It clears the lungs."

"What about your landlords downstairs?"

"Deaf as doornails," she shouted, motioning for William to join her in her living room. The kitchen table and the couch were covered in photographs ripped from magazines and square pieces of cardboard and paper. Framed pictures filled almost every square inch of the wall. William walked into the living room, taking in everything, and sat next to Jenifer. She gave out a quieter "Wa-hoo" when he slid closer to her.

"Where did you get all those pictures?"

She shrugged, blushing suddenly. "I put them together. I'm teaching myself how to do it, how to frame pictures with matting so they look nice." She popped up and pointed to a yellow-tinged photograph of an old barn, not unlike the Findley's barn, that was housed in an ornate golden frame with gilt matting. "Next to Cynthia's artwork, this one is my favorite."

"This is awesome. I never knew you did stuff like this." William leaned back and tried to find an empty place on the walls. "I hope your landlords don't mind you put all those holes in the wall."

Jenifer sat by him again on the floor. Next to the couch covered in magazines and pieces of frame, the only other place to sit was an old blue chair with an empty baby bottle sticking out of the cushion.

"You worry too much," she said, and kissed him.

William had to catch his breath before he could return her kiss. Which he did, his hands running through her long hair and down her back, pulling her to him. They were both lying on the floor before he opened his eyes again.

"I'm hoping I can get really good before I frame and mat Cynthia's picture," Jenifer said when they came up for air.

William's head was spinning too fast to follow her train of thought. Then he saw the small red and blue handprints on a sheet of heavy paper hanging over the television, the picture standing out now because it lacked a frame.

"We made that when she was a month old, with some handpaints. I'm not good enough yet at the matting part to do it justice. So I keep practicing with pictures I find." She bent close to him again as if satisfied with her explanation, and kissed him again.

Despite the tingling sensation that Jenifer's touch gave him all over his body, William's eyes kept coming back to the painted handprints on the wall. As good as Jenifer felt, as strong as his need for her had suddenly become, he felt like he'd been doused in cold water. Jenifer had a baby from some other man. He had a wife who wasn't here but who was still married to him.

Jenifer saw his eyes wandering and pulled her head back from him. "You okay?"

William sat up and rubbed his temples, trying to clear his head. The tingling sensation dissolved. "Everything's happening too fast, all at once." He risked a look at Jenifer, afraid of the anger he'd find there.

She sat watching him, her face thoughtful. "I have a confession to make," she said after a few moments. "I wanted to see you tonight. I came to the Lounge hoping you'd be there. I wouldn't have even minded if Russell and Marty's loud-ass band was playing. As long as I got to see you again."

"What?" William blurted out before he could catch himself. "Why did you want to see *me*?"

"Because of lunch that day. Once you got over your obsession with my name tag, I felt like you were actually listening to what I was saying, that you believed in me. You know, all the stuff about taking over the shop, me being the town slut, all that. And Marcy."

William took a deep breath. "I knew she'd come up tonight, somehow. I know you two have been talking, and you must think I'm an asshole after all she's said about me." William looked up at Jenifer, letting out his breath. "That's why I'm surprised you want to have anything to do with me."

"William, let me tell you one other thing, then I'll stop this 'True Confessions' crap. Marcy is a bitch, okay?"

William felt his mouth drop open, but he couldn't come up with any words to defend his absent wife.

"She's a good friend of mine," Jenifer continued, "but she can be a real bitch if she doesn't get her way. I've always taken everything she says with a grain of salt, including all the times she's complained about you." Jenifer reached over and pushed William's chin up, closing his mouth so she could kiss him briefly. "Sorry to be so blunt. But I can't stand someone being miserable like you were that night at the concert. Life is too damn short for that."

William swallowed hard, the lingering dread he'd felt since December melting away. "Jenifer. You don't know how badly I've wanted someone to tell me that. About Marcy. About me."

Jenifer slid down next to him, her hand touching his cheek, not saying a word. Then she was pulling him to his feet, leading him back into her bedroom. She unbuttoned the top button of his shirt, then slid his shirt up over his head. Touching his naked chest, she whispered "Wa-hoo."

William pulled off her shirt and flung it across the bedroom. "Wa-hoo," he answered softly. The sight of Jenifer in her black bra took his breath away. Keep it coming 'round, twisting me up and down, he thought to himself in his speechlessness.

"You can do better than that," Jenifer said, unbuckling his belt. "Gimme a 'wa-hoo.'"

John fumbled with the buttons on her jeans. "Wa-hoo," he tried again.

"Once more with feeling." She pulled off his boots and threw them across the bedroom. Her long brown hair fell onto her bare shoulders, and she threw it out of her face with a quick toss of her head.

"Wa-hoo! Wa-hoo!" William shouted, feeling the air leave his stomach and chest as they both began to laugh, still pulling at each other's clothes. When Jenifer clicked off the light, the last of their clothes falling away from both of them like rain, William thought he'd never get his breath back again.

Chapter Ten

At the end of the night, when the music had stopped and the Lounge was getting ready to close down another Friday, John couldn't find his brother. He'd last seen William around eleven, when Tony and Tim had pointed him out on the dance floor, both of the brothers laughing at the way William moved his skinny body in time to the music of the band. When Tony told him the pretty girl with the long brown hair dancing with his brother was Jenifer Vaske and she had a kid but no husband, he felt a stab of embarrassment and shame for William being seen in public with her. Damn it, he thought to himself a second later. These Holy Cross people are rubbing off on me, making me think the same way they do. He glanced at William one more time, then he forgot about him and concentrated on the game of quarters he was playing with Andy and the brothers.

"Last call, people," the teenaged lead singer shouted into his microphone. The drummer beat on his cymbals to drown out the groans from the audience. "Thanks for coming. Tips are always appreciated." The band began packing up their instruments under the watchful eye of a band member's father, and the crowd surged briefly toward the bar for one more drink.

"Got it," Tony said, hopping out of his seat for one last pitcher of beer. John couldn't remember paying for any of the five empty pitchers that lay scattered around and under their table. He tried to feel his lips, but they were numb. So this was how the people here passed the time, he thought. Lots of drinking and reliving their high school days on a Friday night.

And trying to bounce quarters into cups of beer. Somehow two hours had passed, and he had a good notion William was long gone. John gave up looking for him.

Andy pulled his chair up close to him and nudged him hard with his elbow. "Anybody home, Koopman?"

John shook his head, as if trying to clear the cobwebs that had suddenly appeared there. "Whew. Time sure does fly, doesn't it?" His side smarted from where Andy had elbowed him, but he refused to give him the pleasure of a reaction.

A wide-hipped girl with a towel on her shoulder began piling empty pitchers and glasses onto one table and stacking chairs upside-down on the other tables as she cleared them. She looked like a girl from his high school math class when he was a freshman or sophomore. John wondered what she'd do when that one table was full.

Tony came back, swearing and empty-handed. "God damn rat bastards say it's past last call already." He swayed next to his chair and tried to sit. He missed the chair and sat hard on the floor instead, provoking a long blast of laughter from the three seated men. "Ah, the hell with it," he muttered, and remained sitting on the beer-soaked floor.

"We haven't done that in a while," Andy said, nodding at the table of decimated pitchers and empty glasses. "I forgot how much beer you could put away. Even if you do cheat at quarters."

John couldn't remember ever drinking in a bar with any of his old friends from Holy Cross. At the time, they hadn't been old enough to drink legally, at least not when he used to run around with them. All he ever did with Andy and Tim was drink beer while they were driving around town or at some classmate's house while their parents were away. But he didn't want to spoil Andy's warm memories, incorrect or not. He hadn't drank like that since Chicago, before he ever knew Jamie. "You guys ready to go? They're about to close up shop here."

Tim had been dozing in his chair across from Andy and John, and he woke with a start, his eyes wide for a few seconds before he realized where he was. Both Andy and John laughed at him, and Tim gave a sheepish look before giving his brother, still on the floor, a kick in the ribs to get him up. Tony rolled awkwardly to his feet, lost his balance, and reached out for a table.

"Let's go," John said, pushing Andy and Tim towards the door. He'd seen where Tony was headed. But it was too late. Trying to steady himself, Tony grabbed the table covered in pitchers and glasses and overturned it, sending its contents across the floor in a deafening crash. They were out the door before the bartender could come after them, and they sprinted drunkenly down the block to Andy's souped-up Chevelle, Tony lagging behind, swearing and moaning.

"Oh no you don't," Andy said as Tony came up to his car. "You're not getting in my car with those pants." Tony's jeans were soaked in beer, from his time on the floor as well as from his second fall. "Lose the pants or walk home, man."

"What?" Tony's face was a mask of pain and suffering. John pressed both hands over his mouth to hold in his laughter.

"You're not going to trash my seat, just because you were too drunk to get up off a wet floor." John recognized the edge in Andy's voice, the meanness that bubbled to the surface in his old friend without any warning. He couldn't tell if Andy was faking it or not. "Drop trou, boy."

"My brother, the family embarrassment," Tim said next to John in the back seat, loud enough for Andy and Tony to hear. Andy got in the car and slammed his door behind him, a wicked smile on his face. The muffler boomed in John's ears when the car roared into life. Outside the open car door, Tony stood, alone, his mouth still open and his arms out.

"You coming, numb nuts?" Andy yelled, and Tony jumped into action, unbuckling his belt and pulling down his pants, underwear and all, and hopped onto the passenger seat.

"Damn!" John yelled, dropping his hands from his mouth at the sight of Tony's hairy white rear end. "I can't believe you let him talk you into that." Stretching his Metallica T-shirt over his crotch, Tony turned and gave him a weak smile.

"Keep your pecker to yourself, Tony-boy," Andy said. John and Tim screamed with laughter in the back seat. Tony crossed his legs and acted as if he couldn't hear them. John couldn't remember seeing anything more out of place. Only in Iowa, he thought, wiping tears from his eyes.

Andy drove out of town and onto a gravel road, the car swaying with the changing surface of the road. Tony was asleep in the front seat, his head back on the head rest behind him, bouncing with every bump in the road. He held his T-shirt down with both hands.

Tim turned to him once they'd gained their composure. "So what was your brother doing there tonight?" John thought he heard Andy say something that sounded like "Goody-two-shoes William," but he wasn't sure over the roar of the Chevelle's mufflers.

"We were just having a couple beers together. Catching up on old times, you know." The wind whipped through the car as Andy rolled down his window, the cool air getting everyone's attention except Tony.

"Don't take this the wrong way, but I always thought William was the biggest asshole," Tim said.

Andy laughed from the front seat. "Don't take that the wrong way, John." He touched his brakes at a four way stop and kept going. John wondered if they were going to go cow-tipping again.

"He has his moments," he said. "But I guess it's been hard on him lately. With Marcy leaving and all that."

"Hell, I'd love it if my wife would leave. Then she'd get off my ass for once."

"Don't even try that, man," Andy shouted from the front. "You worship your wife. You'd be crying in your beer every night if she ever left you."

"Yeah, I guess." Tim rubbed his face as if trying to wake up. "But your brother is still an asshole."

"All right. I hear you." John said. "But I won't take that the wrong way."

Andy barked out laughter from the front seat and turned his big car into a tight turn. When he hit the brakes the car started to slide. In the passenger seat, Tony woke up with a loud gasp and grabbed at Andy in a beer-soaked panic, making the car swerve across the gravel. Andy pried Tony's hands off him while somehow steering his car out of its slide, then they were in the middle of the road again, going fifty, then sixty.

"Don't ever pull that shit again, idiot!" Andy screamed. As if part of the movement of turning the steering wheel, Andy swung his right arm in a backhanded arc from the wheel to Tony's nose. John watched from the back seat, numb. His good feeling died the second he heard the crunch of fist meeting face. Tony's nose squirted blood, and he began crying in a high pitched wail.

Looking at the blood, John thought of the broken bodies of the chickens crushed under William's tractor. Then he thought of the needle sticking out of Jamie's arm. In both cases, there hadn't been near the amount of blood that he saw now.

"I think you busted his nose, Andy," Tim said. He reached up over the seat and put his hand on his brother's shoulder, leaning forward for a better look. "God. You dumb ass. You busted his nose. Look at it."

Tony kept his hands plastered over his nose as blood dripped onto his bare, hairy legs and onto the seat of Andy's car. Tim kept his hand on Tony's shoulder, glaring at Andy. John leaned back in his seat, his mouth dry from too many beers. The world was spinning like a car on loose gravel. He wondered if he'd ever make it home again in one piece.

When he walked into a quiet, dark house, John was surprised at how disappointed he felt. He'd expected someone would be up waiting for him when he got home, had almost counted on it. Nothing was turning out the way he'd hoped it would. Instead, everything had taken a surreal turn for the worse. That was the problem with plans—they never worked out exactly how you wanted.

Stumbling over a pile of laundry that had spilled over from the living room chair, he made his way into the kitchen for a glass of water and some aspirin. As he drank, he thought about how he should have been pissed at his brother for deserting him at the Lounge, but he couldn't muster up the energy to be angry, even though he almost got killed on his way home. That would've made William feel good—first some chickens died because of him, then his only brother.

Just as he was reaching to turn out the light, John saw the folded piece of paper on the kitchen table. His name was written on it, in his mother's neat, perfect handwriting. He flipped it over, but before reading it, he reached into the refrigerator for one of his father's beers. Holding the beer against his suddenly-aching forehead, he unfolded the note. "Your friend Andrea called," was all it said.

John took a sip of beer and stared at the words. He could smell smoke on his clothes and skin. Two drops of blood were on the sleeve of his shirt. He wanted to wake his mother and ask her what else Andrea had said. Had she been upset? Why did she call? Did she say anything about me and what happened in Chicago? The possible answers were endless, and none of them looked good for him.

Stuffing the note into his pocket, John carried his beer into the living room and picked up the phone. He dialed Andrea's number and waited as it rang. He could picture her small, cluttered apartment, the tinny ring of her cheap phone. "Wake up, Andrea," he whispered.

On the eighth ring, a man's voice answered. "Hello?" he mumbled.

John opened his mouth, but he couldn't make himself say anything.

"Hello?" the voice repeated. John thought he recognized the voice, but he couldn't believe it. The person on the other end of the line swore, and John was convinced. Jamie was at Andrea's place.

Before Jamie could hang up, John found his voice again. "Hello?" he croaked. "Is this Jamie?"

Now it was Jamie's turn to be silent. Finally, he said, "Hello, John. What are you doing?"

"Hey, buddy. I could ask you the same question. But I won't." John raised his beer to take a drink and saw his hand was shaking. He took a quick breath. "How are you doing?"

"I'm good. Just taking it nice and cool."

"That's good. Listen. I'm sorry to call so late, but I got a message from Andrea." John felt himself talking quickly, trying to control the conversation so Jamie couldn't ask him more questions. "Is she there?"

"She's sleeping. We've had a rough night."

I'll bet, John thought. He hated the protective tone of voice Jamie was using. "Could you wake her up? I need to talk to her."

"Uh, she's not feeling too good right now. I'd rather not."

"Jamie. What the hell's going on?" John tried to keep his voice low. "What kind of trouble have you gotten her into now?"

"Oh, it's not my trouble. I was too busy hanging out in the hospital to get mixed up in any new trouble. This is old trouble. Trouble that someone left here for her."

"Spare me the lecture, man," John said, but without much heat. He was calculating time in his mind, how long it would take for him to get to Chicago, how much gas he had, how much cash. He could be there by six if he left now. "Who was it? Who's messing with her?"

"Your buddies. Who the hell did you get messed up with? They got into her apartment, didn't touch anything but her cat. She came home and found blood everywhere. I just got done cleaning it up."

"Um-hmm." John couldn't stop his hand from tapping on his leg. Each tap was a little bit harder. "I'll be there today, this morning."

"No." Jamie said, his voice hard.

John's mind was moving so fast he thought he'd misunderstood him. "What?"

"No," Jamie repeated. "Don't come here, man. Don't bring your trouble around us. Not unless you've got their money. I don't want Andrea getting hurt. This was bad enough."

"Who the hell are you?" John hissed into the phone, squeezing his eyes shut until he saw white spots flashing in his vision. His hand clenched, and he punched his leg. "Don't fucking tell me what to do. You don't know shit, Jamie. If it wasn't for me, you'd be —"

"I'd be what? Come on, John. Tell me. You've always got the answers. Tell me what you did for me. But don't forget that I'm not the only one that was messed up that night."

"Shut up. Shut the hell up." John felt the sudden urgency in his mind dissolve, replaced by a numb sense of helplessness. Jamie couldn't have remembered any of that. He'd been unconscious.

Jamie took a deep, loud breath. "John. This is a seriously screwed-up situation. If you come back, you'd better bring what they want. Don't come here expecting to make everything better with a smile and some fast talk."

John didn't say anything in response. He looked at his forgotten can of beer on the floor, surprised he hadn't knocked it over.

"I appreciate what you did for me, man," Jamie continued. "But I'm pissed as hell at what you're putting Andrea through. She thinks she's going to get raped or knifed, all because of your money. If you need to get in touch with us, call me at work. Bye."

John hung up the phone and looked around the darkened living room. "Fuck," he said, forgetting to whisper. Through the closed door to her downstairs bedroom, he could hear his grandmother's soft snoring. Everything else was silent.

It was as if the rest of the world had continued on without him, he thought, everyone getting on with their lives and their plans except him. Jamie had gone to the hospital and come back out again. Andrea didn't need him anymore. Even William was getting over his shitty life. But ever since John had left Chicago, it was as if his forward progress had stopped. He was still stuck in the first week of March, but in reality—in the rest of the world—it was already almost June. And his best friend was screwing his girlfriend.

Finishing his beer, John left the empty can next to the phone and grabbed another from the refrigerator. I'm just drunk and getting melodramatic, he tried to tell himself. Jamie and Andrea have always been friends. Neither of them would do anything more. Andrea had always said Jamie was like a little brother to her.

With his beer in his hand, John walked through the kitchen into the mudroom. He started to search the pockets of his father's winter coat, but after a few seconds he realized he had left the arrowhead rock on his dresser upstairs. He didn't have the energy to go all the way upstairs to get it. Tonight, he'd have to try his luck without it. Just like he'd tried his luck at the Diamond Jack without his good luck piece, and he remembered all too well how that had ended up. Closing the door to the kitchen behind him, he walked outside through the back door. Instead of turning toward the lane, however, he headed for his chicken house.

He'd never been down there at night. In the glare from the big outdoor light attached to the top of the cow barn, he followed the ruts in the ground made by William's tractor. They formed furrows in the ground that grew deeper until they came to a sliding halt on top of the chicken wire fence. He caught himself laughing at the anger he'd felt earlier that day when he'd tackled his brother and swung at him. He hadn't tried to punch his brother since he was eleven or twelve. And all over a bunch of stupid chickens, he thought on his way inside the tiny barn.

The room was dusty and eerily silent. John reached for the string to the light bulb dangling from the ceiling, but thought better of it. He didn't want to hear the birds' complaining when he woke them. Slowly, he relaxed the muscles in his jaw that he hadn't even known he was clenching, the whole time worrying about what Jamie may have told Andrea about that night. He realized he'd been more worried about that than about Andrea's safety.

The chickens had grown out of their cuddly stage quickly, John thought. Covered in greasy white feathers, the fat broilers slept huddled together for warmth, even though he felt a bead of sweat breaking out on his forehead already. He envied the chickens and their simple lives. "Even if they are short lives," he said to the sleeping clumps of feathers. "Very short lives."

He drank his beer and sat back against the wall opposite his windows. The adrenaline he'd felt moments earlier, from his talk with Jamie as well as the close call in Andy's car, had left him feeling exhausted. Watching the chickens twitch in their sleep, dust rising into the air from just their breathing, John knew he'd been fooling himself with his desire to exist only in the present. He drank his beer and slumped further down on the floor, thinking about how stupid it was to live only in the present if you haven't taken care of your past.

"I'll have to talk to William," he whispered, his voice slurring his words together. His eyelids felt heavy. "He's gonna want to kick my ass when I ask him, though."

Closing his eyes, he took a deep breath of thick, dusty air. A sudden image of the blood flowing from Tony's nose earlier that night made him flinch. He thought of Tim's hand on Tony's shoulder, and his own fists swinging at William. How far would the ties of blood stretch? he wondered. The bonds he'd made with his family in his two months back home felt tenuous and weak, and he doubted those bonds would extend much further. He'd already tested them with the loan from his father. The last thought John had before falling asleep in the chicken house, a beer in his hand, was whether he would do for his brother what he was planning on asking his brother to do for him.

Chapter Eleven

Waking at three in the morning next to Jenifer, William tried to rationalize what had happened: their night together was just a fluke, a random encounter that they could both write off as a bad choice made during a rough time. Or too much beer on a Friday night. Holding his breath, William slid out of bed and moved slowly toward his clothes piled on the floor. He rubbed his throat, trying to remember why it was so sore. Jenifer woke up when he was slipping on his boots.

"Are you leaving already?" she whispered.

William eased himself back onto the bed, sitting with his back to Jenifer. He remembered their war cries last night and smiled. "Sorry I woke you. I'd better get home so I can get started with the chores." When he put his ankle on his knee to tie his boot, Jenifer put her hand on his leg.

"Does your head hurt as much as mine?" she said, squeezing his leg.

He had to force himself to not get up from her bed. The guilt he'd been feeling ever since waking up threatened to overwhelm him. I'm a married man, he wanted to say. "Yeah. My head's killing me."

The two of them sat for a moment in the darkness, then Jenifer shifted in the bed to turn on the light. Both of them squinted in the sudden light.

"William," she said, pulling the sheets around her bare shoulders. "Did we make a huge mistake last night?"

Looking at his shirt hanging off the bedroom doorknob, Jenifer's jeans in a ball on the floor, and her bra dangling from the lampshade, William laughed softly. He'd never done anything like that in his life, with anyone. Before tonight, Marcy had been the only other girl he'd ever been with. He'd loved every second of last night, in spite of the guilt. Or maybe because of it.

Jenifer followed his gaze and pulled her bra off the lamp next to her. "I don't *want* to know how that got there." Her sheets slid down, revealing the tops of her breasts and one pink nipple. William couldn't look away.

"No." He took her sheets in his hand and slid up closer to her. "I don't think we made a mistake. Do you?"

Jenifer answered by clicking off the light and wrapping her arms around his shoulders, her skin warm and her breath loud in his ears. William allowed her to pull him down next to her again, wanted her to do it. In her warm embrace, covered in her kisses, he was able to forget his wife's iciness before her departure and every numb week since. So much time had passed since he'd truly felt happy, he was afraid he wouldn't be able to get enough now that he'd found it again with Jenifer. Before he left half an hour later, walking back in a daze to his truck parked in front of the Crossroads Lounge, he promised to see her again later that day.

His mother was already awake when William crept into the house at a quarter past four. He had less than an hour before his father woke to start the milking, and he figured he could get in a quick nap before he had to start on the chores. He hadn't spent much of last night sleeping, he thought with a guilty grin. Then he remembered John and the chickens and the loan sharks in Chicago. William had completely forgotten about leaving his brother at the Lounge last night.

"What's wrong?" he said, looking at the pieces of tissue his mother had shredded onto the kitchen table. Her glasses sat on the table in front of her. "Did John get home all right?"

"He got in around two or three, I think. I don't know who gave him a ride home, but whoever it was needs a new muffler."

"Why are you up so early?" He looked down at his mother, her shoulders slightly hunched forward in her light blue robe.

Her face was puffy from sleep, and her eyes looked too small without her glasses. "You should be sleeping in now that school's out for the summer."

"I just couldn't sleep, that's all." She squinted at his untucked shirt and sleep-bent hair and put on her glasses. "Looks like you had a rough night too."

"You could say that." William stretched and inhaled deeply, enjoying the way his body felt both physically tired—he blamed the dancing—and quivering with energy at the same time. He blamed the latter on the way Jenifer had locked her gaze on him after he promised to see her again later that day. He felt like he had passed some kind of test in agreeing to continue what they had started late last night.

His mother shook her head and tried to smile. "When are you going to eat something? You're wasting away. I'm not that bad a cook, am I?"

"Mom, please. I'm just busy, is all." He sat across from her. "Why can't you sleep?"

His mother looked at him and nodded. "I guess you deserve to know this. I don't know why we never got together to discuss all this, you and me and your father. Where does all the time go, anyway?"

"What are you talking about?" William said, inching closer to her. Don't let it be the farm, he begged silently. Not when my life is finally starting to make some sense, in its own screwy way. "What do I deserve to know?"

"We're going to see the lawyer next week. We're going to have to do something about our debts."

"Fuck," William whispered.

His mother gave him a warning look as she tore another piece of tissue loose. "We've been putting this off for too long. Please don't take this the wrong way, but we didn't want to argue with you about it. I know you don't want to have to sell any more land than we have to, but I don't think we have any choice. We need to refinance our mortgage, and with interest rates low right now, your father and Mr. Anderson think this is the right time."

"Dad should've told me before this." William looked out the kitchen window. The sky was turning a weak grayish-blue with the sunrise.

"When could he have told you? You're never around, and the two of you never work together when you *are* here. Not like you used to. And with all the rain this year, and the hogs not doing well, I don't think we can keep the debts from pulling us down altogether. We have to do something."

"So it's easier to just sell out than try to make it work?" William kept his eyes focused on the sky through the window, trying to decide if it looked like rain again today.

Mom grabbed his hand. "I don't want to do this, William. Don't you dare think this is my idea. We're going to visit with Mr. Anderson to see what kind of options we have. I'm going to help out here all summer, get a temporary job if I have to. And we have John to help us out."

William eased his hand out from under hers and stood up. He felt suddenly tired, overwhelmed by all that had happened in the past twenty-four hours. He hated himself for the sense of growing relief that threatened to wash over him. He didn't want to feel glad that his parents didn't need him as much as they used to, that there was the possibility that he could live his own life without the farm holding him down. William heard his father's footsteps in the bedroom, and he wondered how much of the conversation Dad had heard.

"Don't worry," he told his mother. Touching her hand, he pushed the ragged pieces of Kleenex into his own and threw them into the garbage. "We'll work something out. We always do."

Walking upstairs to change into his work clothes, he hoped he wasn't making another promise—his second of the day—that he'd have trouble making come true.

The rain let up in June. William's father had all but written off the corn during the last week of May, but after a string of warm, breezy days, it looked like the plants would take root and grow. William sensed that the cloud of financial ruin that had been hovering over his parents had passed, along with the rain-heavy clouds in the sky above them. But the threat of foreclosure always lingered in every conversation he had with his parents. John's chickens, suddenly fat and tall, stood out in the sun as if shocked that there was no more rain to beat on their heads. The phone had stopped ringing so often, and when it did ring, the person on the other line never hung up when someone besides John answered. And William had fallen for his wife's best friend.

He knew he and Jenifer were involved in the relationship for all the wrong reasons. He knew she knew it too, but that only made their attraction more urgent. He'd meet her at the store, walk with her to her apartment, and they'd make the most of her lunch hour together. Most of the time, even as they were undressing each other with shaking hands and clumsy fingers, they would talk to each other about what had happened to them in the past few years, filling in the holes in one another's memory when they were with someone else or alone. He took her on long drives in his truck, watching the rivers rise after more rain, and she sat close to him on the bucket seat with his arm wrapped around her shoulders. Yet even in their shared caresses and laughter, William sensed it had to end.

On the tenth of June, three things happened that marked the end of William's brief run of intense happiness: John left for Chicago, William met Jenifer's baby for the first time, and the rain began again. William cursed himself for getting so intoxicated and reckless with his newfound joy, after so many months of denying his emotions, but it was such a surprisingly intense feeling for him that he hadn't been able to help himself.

On that day, the skies had begun clouding up by mid-morning. William was in the kitchen, washing up after the milking, when his brother approached him. The two of them had resumed their awkward new friendship, even though

John hadn't let William forget about being abandoned at the tavern so William could go home with Jenifer. He used that fact as leverage against his older brother whenever he could.

"Can I talk to you for a second?" John said. He motioned with his thumb towards the door, casting a meaningful glance at Grandma, sitting at the table with her head cocked toward them.

William dried his hands and followed him outside. He knew that the look on John's face meant bad news, and he wanted to get away from him, as if John carried bad luck in his pocket and was getting ready to share.

"I've got to leave for a while," John said without any hesitating. They stood in the shadow of the machine shed, the air already hot despite the overcast weather. "Don't ask me why, just try and give me a hand before things get really nuts."

"Why?" William asked anyway, trying to force a smile that wouldn't come.

"Damn it, quit screwing around." John shifted his weight from one foot to another as if he had to relieve himself but couldn't. He took a deep breath. "Sorry. I didn't mean to snap at you. It's just that I might be in a whole hell of a lot of trouble."

"You're going back to Chicago, right?"

"Yep."

"So," William said, trying to keep his voice calm. Watching John dance around in the gray morning light was making him agitated. "Do you need money?"

"Yes! Yes. I've been putting this off for too long. I need about five grand. I know you think I'm scum for asking, but you *will* get it back. Just like Dad will get his money back."

"Wait." William grabbed his brother by the arm and turned him around so they were facing each other. "Can you stand still for one damn second? Did you borrow money from Dad? When you knew full well that this farm is going down the tubes? Tell me you didn't do that."

"I did. I went to invest it, and guess what? Nothing. Does that surprise you? Does that make you feel good? Now I have to be in Chicago by tonight, so if you're going to lecture me and not lend me the money, tell me now so I can get it somewhere else."

William looked past John's shoulder, at the rows of corn struggling to push their way out of the earth, the straight lines he had plowed with the old tractor reaching still black, without any signs of green. "I'll get it for you. I've got a couple grand here and there. What do I have to spend it on, right?"

"William. I need it now."

"Follow me in your car and you can leave for Chicago as soon as I get it out of the bank." William's anger faded until all he felt was a strange sort of relief, as if he was glad John was leaving again and he wouldn't have to work so hard at being a good older brother. It reminded him of the feeling he had felt when his mother had told him about visiting the lawyer.

An hour later, John was driving east and William was knocking on Jenifer's upstairs apartment door. He knew it was her day off, but he needed to talk to someone after John's frenzied need for his money. Marty and Russell wouldn't understand the situation, plus they were busy rehearsing for the first of their three scheduled weddings that summer. William was afraid he might not see John again, for one reason or another, and he didn't know how to feel about that. John hadn't even said goodbye after taking the cash out of William's hands. Just a quick "Thanks" and his brother was gone.

Waiting for Jenifer to answer her door, William shuddered. He wasn't used to seeing that kind of desperation in someone else's eyes. People in Iowa were better at hiding their feelings than his brother was. Yet, after all that had happened in the past few weeks, William was afraid of feeling numb all over again.

Jenifer answered the door wearing one of his long-sleeved shirts he had left there, holding a chubby, screaming baby on her hip. Her hair was pulled back into a tight ponytail, and her face looked hard and troubled.

"Well look what the cat dragged in," she said, breaking into a smile. "Come on in." Jenifer held open the door, but William hesitated for a second, almost not recognizing her with her child. He had never seen the baby before that day. She had always been with Jenifer's mother or a sitter. A second later he stepped inside, hating himself for that hesitation and that moment of lost recognition.

"Don't look so shocked. You knew I had a baby." She set Cynthia on a blanket on the floor and rubbed her belly. Gradually the volume of the baby's crying lowered. "William, this is Cynthia. Cynthia, this is your mom's friend William. She's got an upset stomach. She's not always like this. Right, sweetie?"

"Hey there little baby," William said, his voice unsteady. He couldn't imagine ever having a child of his own. He and Marcy had never discussed it. Bending down, he kissed Jenifer's forehead, and then he sat in a chair. A soap opera played on the TV, drowned out by Cynthia's crying. "She's got some lungs. Shouldn't you hold her or something?"

"Be my guest," Jenifer said, gesturing at her baby. "I've been holding her all morning."

"Well, I'll try. I just don't want to hurt her."

"All you have to do is support her head. Sometimes she fights like a madwoman." She handed Cynthia up to him, and he sat with the baby squirming in his arms. She was heavier than she looked, and stronger. "Put her on your shoulder, up high. There you go."

William stood up carefully, afraid he'd drop the baby in the process. After a minute of walking her around the room, William felt the baby relax, and she grew quiet.

"You're a natural," Jenifer said. "So what's going on?"

"My brother," he said, trying to rock his body in an attempt to soothe Cynthia even further. "That's what's going on. He's gone again."

"For good, do you think?"

William shrugged. Rubbing Cynthia's back as he spoke, he told Jenifer about John needing his money, and how he had given him all of what he'd earmarked for the shop, knowing he'd probably never see any of it again. He told Jenifer about John's money problems, holding Cynthia close and feeling her breathe. He knew he could be pulled into a life with Jenifer despite the disapproval of the people in town, in spite of Marcy and her long history with Jenifer and his own unresolved relationship with his absent wife. He knew he could continue a life with Jenifer and not allow himself any regrets. But in the end it would have been a lie and a denial until he dealt with everything that had lead up to this day.

"I think she's asleep," he said finally, his throat scratchy from talking and saying too much.

"Follow me." Jenifer walked into the second bedroom and folded a pink blanket on an old wooden crib. "Put her down softly. Watch her head." Cynthia let out a long sigh after he set her on the blanket. William stared at the peaceful infant below him, so different from the screaming child he'd seen when Jenifer first opened the door.

After a minute of watching the baby, Jenifer took him by the hand and led him to her bedroom. She sat him on the bed and kissed his neck and face, pulling off the shirt she wore that used to be his. William tried to say something, but Jenifer put her fingers in front of his lips and led his hands to her body. Unbuttoning his clothes, she leaned back onto the bed and pulled him to her, and they made love one final, sorrowful time.

William woke an hour later to the sound of rain falling steadily onto the window and the streets. If anything could be depended on this season, William thought, it was the damn rain. He lay on his back and listened to the sound of the drops hitting outside, thinking about what he had to do next. Jenifer stirred a few minutes later, and she nodded knowingly when he told her he needed to see Marcy again.

Chapter Twelve

Jamie's apartment had never looked cleaner or more well-lit. Usually, when John came over to visit him, including his last visit, the place was dark and closed up, with shadowy objects just out of sight on the floor, waiting to be tripped over. John arrived at Jamie's door at about nine at night, his panic at a fever pitch when he couldn't locate Andrea. She hadn't been at her office all day, according to her assistant, and her apartment was being sublet by a lesbian couple who tried to help him locate her even though they never knew her. The compassion on the faces of these strangers was a stark contrast to the hard smile John received when Jamie opened his door to his apartment.

"We've been waiting for you," Jamie said in his new, protective voice, standing back a few inches to let John through. John shook his hand and pushed in past him. "Nice to see you, too," Jamie said to his back.

Andrea sat on Jamie's couch, her knees pulled up to her chest and her arms locked around them. She looked somehow older, even though it had only been a few months since he'd last seen her. After the mad dash from Holy Cross in the rain, going eighty-five to ninety on the wet interstate, he wasn't sure what he'd planned on saying to her.

"Hi there," he said, finally. He sat down on the couch and put his hand on her knees. "You all right?"

"Fine." She gave John a long look, then relaxed her tightened position and gave him a hug. "Where have you been?"

John squeezed her and let go enough to kiss her. She returned his kiss, barely a peck. "What do you mean? I got here as soon as I could."

Jamie settled into the chair next to them, and John had a strange sense of history repeating itself, except the roles had been switched: he was the sick one on the couch and Jamie was the life-saving friend.

"You called over a week ago, John," Jamie said. "We had no idea where you were or when you were coming."

"What is this?" John sat back from Andrea so he could see Jamie. "You know where I've been. On the damn farm, trying to borrow some money from my family before I came out here. It's kind of hard to get a loan from someone who has next to nothing." He turned back to Andrea. "I had to get my brother to basically give me his life savings, and I had to work up the guts to ask him. I'm not sure if he's ever going to forgive me for asking for it, either. But I knew he'd give it to me."

Andrea was silent, and the look in her blue eyes was far from sympathetic. John knew he owed Andrea more than an apology for the way he ran out of the city, discarding all the elements of his old life like worn-out clothes, including her. Especially her. Then he thought about her and Jamie, living here together for who knew how long, and the apologies dried up on his lips.

"John." Jamie was the one to break the silence. Something had changed in Jamie, John noticed, in the way he carried himself and in his appearance. He'd filled out while John was away, and he wasn't so pale and sickly-looking. But his eyes were the same: still burning with intensity and some kind of inner anger that reminded John of his high school buddy Andy, especially when Andy was behind the wheel of his car. In his mind he could still hear the pop of the back of Andy's hand hitting Tony in the face.

"John." Jamie was still looking at him, waiting. "What are you going to do?"

John cleared his throat and sat up straight in the couch. "Well, I have a plan." He glanced at Andrea before turning back to Jamie, and a quick grin crossed her face before she could cover it with her hand. She'd always enjoyed being part of his schemes, no matter how crazy or far-fetched. As long as it seemed like the cutting edge of something new, as she would have said. "But I guess you guys already figured I'd have something planned, huh?"Nodding, Jamie allowed himself his first real smile of the evening. "Let's hear it."

"Well, I've got my brother's cash that we need to plant and make grow. Fast. I'm going to invest some of it with my old buddies down at the office. The ones that'll still speak to me, that is. There's some high-risk stuff out there I've been reading about." John felt everything start to fall into place, as long as he kept his confidence high and didn't stop to think. "While that's being invested, I've got to drop off a chunk to our old friends as a good faith payment. Then I'm open to whatever suggestions there may be from the peanut gallery."

Andrea and Jamie exchanged a look, both of them shaking their heads. Andrea laughed softly. "You always have a plan, don't you?" She nudged him with her foot. "Just don't get in over your head again. And don't you dare run off again when things go bad."

"If," John said, looking from Andrea to Jamie and back again.

"*If* things go bad. But I don't plan on that happening." He stood up, unable to contain himself any longer. He had to get moving.

"Yeah," Jamie said. "That's definitely one thing you never plan for."

Andrea got up and walked to the bathroom. John glanced at the closed bathroom door, trying to ignore Jamie's comment. "Is she all right?"

"She's upset by all this, you know. Jumpy as hell. How would you feel if you knew someone had broken into your place and messed with your stuff? At least your 'old friends' haven't tracked her down here, not yet at least. You're not the only one who's been out of the picture for a while."

John felt the wild burst of energy he'd spent in getting to Chicago start to fade. "Look, Jamie. I know I should've visited you in the hospital. I'm sorry. I just couldn't do it. I haven't been around. You haven't told her about that night, have you?"

"Told her what, man? I don't remember a damn thing. What's there to tell?"

John stared hard at Jamie, the new Jamie with extra flesh and color in his face. This wasn't the same mumbling person who had called in sick back in March, the guy who didn't want to get specific about his condition. John looked for something hidden in Jamie's eyes, but before he could detect any hint that Jamie remembered more than he was saying, Andrea opened the bathroom door, and nothing else was said.

John sat sideways with his feet up on the back seat of Jamie's black Festiva, swaying back and forth every time Jamie hit the brakes. Andrea sat smoking in the front next to Jamie. Every few seconds she would turn to blow smoke out the open passenger window. She'd never smoked before, at least not around John, but now she acted like she'd done it all her life.

"I don't know how you ever heard about those bastards, John," she said, "but I want you to get your loan paid off to them as soon as possible. I told them I'd give them some money for you, but all they wanted was cash, and I wasn't about to give cash to some greasy old guy I'd never seen before." She took a quick drag on her cigarette, and John felt his mouth curl in disgust at the hungry expression on her face as she inhaled. "What I'd like to know is how they ever connected me with you."

"They probably asked for a reference, right?" The car rolled up to a stoplight, and Jamie turned to give John a long look. "So you used Andrea? Jesus, John. The least you could've done was use me, or another guy."

Andrea batted Jamie softly on the shoulder, knocking ash onto his ripped leather jacket. "What, do you think a woman can't take care of herself?"

Jamie smiled and caught John's eye in the rearview mirror. "Hey. At least I don't have a cat."

Andrea's face dropped for a second, as if on the verge of getting upset, then she told Jamie to shut the hell up. John watched their teasing banter with something close to shock. They were acting like an old married couple. He wanted to explain to them how it had come about, how he had panicked when they'd asked for a contact person, and all he could come up with was her phone number, but he kept his mouth shut instead. He knew he never would have gotten away with reminding Andrea about the untimely death of her cat Kerouac the way Jamie just did, but she had let it pass with barely a comment. John decided they were definitely sleeping together.

"This street, right?" Jamie said, pointing to the left.

"Yeah, park anywhere up here and I'll run in." They parked across the street from the drop-off apartment his bookie used. Of the six thousand William had given him—a thousand more than John had asked for—three thousand of it was going away tonight. He hated parting with it when he knew how much more he could make with the entire amount, but the nasty letters Andrea had shown him from her apartment convinced him that a good faith payment was necessary.

"Here we go," Jamie stepped out of the car and moved the seat forward so John could squeeze out. John unfolded himself from the back seat and stood up, facing Jamie so they were inches apart. Jamie broke his gaze first, slapping John on the arm. "Good luck. And make it quick."

John nodded and bent down to see Andrea. She was lighting another cigarette, and she waved distractedly at him. He thought about her smoking in bed with Jamie, and that was enough to get him moving across the street without another word.

There was always someone home at the bookie's apartment, though it was never the bookie himself. John had never met the man, but he knew his voice well from many phone calls. This faceless man's phone number was one of his favorite long distance numbers when dialed from Holy Cross. Unfortunately, the news the voice had given him had rarely been positive. The bookie made payments to the loan shark for him, acting as a middle man to protect everyone involved and to get his percentage of the take as well.

Inside the poorly-lit apartment complex, John jogged up three flights of stairs, feeling more uneasy with each flight. His thoughts had been moving so fast that he hadn't really thought about the bad stretch of neighborhoods they'd passed through to get here. Knocking softly on the door to apartment 340, he didn't have time to worry about Jamie and Andrea in the car. The door popped open after four knocks.

The skinny kid he'd seen here before let him in, nodding calmly toward the leather chair in front of a wide, antique desk. The kid sat back down behind it, his rail-thin body even more gaunt behind the expanse of the desktop. The rest of the apartment was empty except for two computers that sat at either end of the living room area and a table with five phones.

"I'll bet you have something for us, Mr. Koopman," the kid said in a soft voice. John had no idea what his name was, and he didn't want to know. He heard someone talking behind one of the closed bedroom doors, but he couldn't make out what the person was saying.

"Yeah, I've got a payment." He reached into his pocket and slid the envelope across the desk. "Three grand. Tell the brothers that they can lay off my friend now." He'd almost said "girlfriend," but caught himself. He wasn't sure what Andrea was to him anymore.

"Um-hmm," the kid said, running a thin finger through the bills, counting.

"Can I get a receipt for that or something?"

A crooked smile passed over the kid's face above the wide plain of the desk. "A receipt. You never needed a receipt before."

"Come on, man. I trust you guys. But those sharks, I wouldn't trust them as far as I could throw them. As far as *you* could throw them."

The kid reached into a desk drawer and pulled out a pad. He scribbled something on the pad, paused for a split second, and scribbled some more. "You'd be surprised. I've been working out." With a flourish, he slid the paper across the desk upside-down. "I could probably toss both of them further than you."

John picked up the receipt, but didn't look at it. "Thanks." He stood to leave.

"So." The kid remained seated behind the desk, folding his hands in front of him like an executive. "You looking for some excitement, now that you're back in the money?"

"I just gave you all my money," John said, then his curiosity got the best of him. "What do you have in mind?"

"Some people I know get together every Thursday night to play poker. Stakes are high, but the payoffs are sweet. As long as you know your stuff and you don't make a scene if you win or lose, they'll take you in. They're always looking for fresh players."

"Poker, huh?" John thought of the game behind the closed doors of the Diamond Jack and felt himself getting pulled in deeper. Like a deer bound by wire and water. "No thanks."

"No?" The kid looked genuinely disappointed for a second or two. "Here," he said, pulling a card from a different desk drawer and flipping it onto the desktop, where it spun three times. "Edna's Bakery" it read. "In case you change your mind. Go to the back door of the bakery and knock if you want in. Tell them Joey sent you. You can thank me later."

"All right, all right. I'll see." John picked up the card and turned to the door. He fought the urge to read what the kid had written on his receipt. "Thanks," he said, glancing behind him.

The kid was already back behind one of the computers, reaching for a telephone. John walked out of the apartment and closed the door behind him. On his way down the steps, John strained to read the receipt in the unreliable light of the stairwell. Next to the word "PAYOFF" in the kid's neat block letters read "$3000." Below that, "HANDLING" was written next to "$400," leaving the grand total at $2600 at the bottom of the white square of paper. John stopped and almost went back up to the apartment, but he let it go. He wondered how long it had taken his brother to make that $400 that he'd lost just like that. He pushed the receipt into his pocket next to the card for the bakery and returned to his friends waiting for him outside.

A t a quarter to nine the next morning, John got off the train and walked up the crowded street toward the cluster of office towers where he used to work. After making a quick stop at a convenience store, where he slid fifteen hundred-dollar bills across the counter in exchange for three money orders, he felt his steps lighten as he gawked at his surroundings.

He couldn't remember feeling so out of place in the city, not even in his first weeks there fresh out of college. The homeless people on benches he'd been able to mostly ignore, along with the honking cars and the way nobody looked at him. People passed him from behind, as if he was taking way too much time looking around when he should've been focusing on what was immediately in front of him. I just need to get used to it again, he told himself. I've been away too long.

His ears popped in the elevator to the twenty-sixth floor. Too late he realized his mistake: he should've agreed to meet Mark somewhere else for lunch. But he'd been in too much of a hurry to wait until lunch. Standing outside the glass doors leading to Waterford and Johnson, his former employers, he stood with his hand on the door handle for so long the secretary looked up and gave him a quizzical look. Forcing himself to smile as if he'd been caught being absent-minded, he pushed through the door and asked to see Mark. Luckily the turnover rate among the support staff was high, and this young woman hadn't been around to see John carrying his box of personal belongings from his cubicle the morning after he'd left Jamie at the emergency room.

A young stockbroker who had occupied a cubicle two doors down from John earlier that year jogged by, carrying a cell phone and the business section of the Tribune. When he saw John he stopped in mid-stride, his mouth dropping open half an inch, then he continued hurrying down the hall. John nodded at him and tried to look interested in the faded Monet print on the wall.

"Look what the cat dragged in," Mark said from behind him, holding his hand out. Mark shook his hand, squeezing hard once while looking John straight in the eye as if challenging him.

John was getting tired of these reunions. "Hey, Mark. Thanks for seeing me on such short notice."

"No problem," Mark said. He looked around the office, then stepped toward John. "Let's go get some coffee downstairs. There are some folks here who wouldn't be too crazy about seeing you here again."

John followed Mark to the elevator, stepping quickly to keep up with him. Mark stood half a head taller than John, and while Mark had always bragged about how hard he worked staying in shape, John could tell he was getting a bit soft in the middle, trying to hide it with his sports coat. Living in the 'burbs was making his old buddy lose his edge. They bought coffee at a stand downstairs and sat on a concrete bench in the cool morning air that was already moving toward warm mugginess.

"So you want to invest some of your hard-earned cash, huh?" Mark said, unbuttoning his jacket and giving John a long look. "What the hell have you been up to?"

John allowed him the look. He needed Mark's help, though he knew Mark had been pissed as hell at him for leaving the brokerage, and the city, without telling him. Just like John had been pissed at Mark for breaking their lease and moving out of the city. "Jesus, Mark," John said, "you don't want to know all that. I've been working on the farm, and that's about all I've been doing."

"So we talking some long-term investments here, or short, high-risks? I know what my old buddy John would say, but I'm not sure I know him anymore."

John smiled and shook his head. "Look. I've apologized so much in the last day, it doesn't even seem like I'm saying it anymore. But I'm sorry for taking off like I did. I know you helped me get this job, and you probably took a lot of grief when I walked out. But with Jamie getting sick and my own money problems, I just couldn't take it anymore."

Mark nodded slowly. "All right. Christine's still pissed, but she always had a crush on Jamie, I think. She likes the artsy, mysterious guy in black thing. I don't know what she sees in me." He reached into his coat pocket and pulled out a notepad. "But let's get down to business. I hate to rush you, but I've got a ton of stuff to do."

"Okay," John said. That was Mark, all business, all the time, and this was one of the few times John sincerely appreciated his friend's demeanor. He'd been dreading seeing Mark for a long time. "What can you do in a week with fifteen hundred bucks?"

Mark grinned, closing his notepad. "You giving me free range here, partner? No client advice to the broker?" He stood up. "I'll take care of it for you."

"Here," John said, placing the three money orders into Mark's hand. Mark gave him a look of surprise, then slipped the envelope and his notepad into his breast pocket.

"What *have* you been up to?" Mark asked him for the second time.

John only shrugged and shook his hand. He'd never told his straight-laced friend about his under-the-table dealings

154

with his bookie and the loan sharks. That would have only blown a fuse in Mark's orderly mind.

"See you next week, partner," John said. He turned away from Mark and strode down the busy sidewalk, passing other walkers on his way back to the south side. He didn't have any time to waste if he was going to get back up to speed on his poker skills.

Night couldn't come soon enough to John once he'd decided to visit Edna's Bakery. Somewhere in the back of his mind he knew he'd go, and he'd known the second the kid at the apartment had mentioned the opportunity. He remembered Andrea saying something about a dinner with some new advertisers she was trying to win over, and he hoped she'd be gone until late. He wanted to keep her out of his extracurricular activities as much as possible. She knew too much—and was involved too much—already. Only Jamie knew the entire truth about John.

John spent the rest of his morning in a bookstore, flipping through books about poker, until he got so bored he returned to Jamie's and practiced dealing. With the right snap of his wrist, he could spin cards one by one into neat piles in front of three empty chairs, a phantom set of opponents waiting for him to make the first move. When he grew bored of that, he took a nap on Jamie's couch, forcing himself not to tune into the stock market reports on the news networks. He hadn't realized how tired he was until he lay down.

The sky was growing dark through Jamie's windows when John woke up with a start, his back sore from the lumpy couch. For a few seconds, he felt like he was back in Iowa, waking up in the chicken house after falling asleep on the concrete floor, his can of beer next to him. He'd barely been able to move the next morning. When he regained his bearings, he felt a stab of guilt about leaving the chickens in his brother's hands. He knew William had no desire to take care of a bunch of chickens. If I come back and find any of them sick or dead, he thought, I'll take it out on William so bad he'll think the beating I gave him earlier was play-acting.

If I come back, he added silently. The thought surprised him, even though he'd been thinking about it all day long.

Jamie's key scrabbled in the lock, and John rubbed his face and tried to completely wake up. No more thoughts about chickens, John vowed. He had to focus.

"Hello there," Jamie said when he opened the door. "Working hard, I see."

"Fell asleep. How are you?" He felt a new kind of respect for Jamie, for putting up with him and Andrea, even if he was messing around with her. Jamie had made a choice when he gave John his spare key and let him use his place while he was in Chicago, and John appreciated it.

"I'm good. Work was stressful, though. Andrea was a basket case. She won't be home for a while." He sat on the chair across from John and pulled open a drawer on his end table, watching John as if waiting for a reaction. He dropped a plastic baggie and some papers into his lap and began rolling three joints. "So we got any plans for the evening? Or are you flying solo tonight?"

"You know, I was actually thinking about playing some cards. It's been a while, and I know I'm rusty as hell, but I could go for a little gambling. You up for it?"

Jamie lit a joint and sucked in. "Sure," he said, blowing out. He offered the joint to John, but John shook his head. "When we going?"

"Soon as you finish your smoke. You gonna eat anything? I don't want you getting the munchies halfway through a hot card game. I need you to be sharp for me, watch my back."

Jamie took another lungful of smoke and held up his hand like a traffic cop, holding in the smoke. He exhaled. "I'm sharp," he said, and coughed. "Really. As a tack."

"I'll drive," John said. He reached into his overnight bag and fished out the arrowhead-shaped rock he'd found in his dad's coat pocket, its weight a comfort in his hand. He slipped the rock into his pants pocket. If it was an arrowhead, it had to contain some luck to have survived all these years without getting broken apart by tractors and plows. He could definitely use any extra luck he could get. Maybe that's why I done so poorly at the riverboat, he thought. No arrowhead.

John glanced across the room at Jamie. "Leave the joints."

Jamie's hand froze as he was about to grab the last two hand-rolled smokes. "All right, all right," he said.

Back behind the wheel of his car, John threw the parking ticket he'd found under the windshield wiper into the back seat and waited for Jamie. We should've left a note for Andrea, he thought, but didn't say anything about it as Jamie settled himself into the passenger seat.

"So are you glad to be back?" Jamie said once they were moving. John had been surprised at how quickly Jamie had gotten over his initial anger at him. Without Andrea, the tension between the two of them seemed to melt. As long as John didn't think too hard about what he'd missed while he was gone.

"Yeah. I am," John said, as if surprised. "Not a lot to do out on the farm. How about you? You glad to be back?"

"Oh, you know it, man." Jamie's voice was low and lazy as the marijuana took hold of him. "I'd like to kill the fucker who got me started on that shit. Some slouch we worked with. Andrea had him canned and every magazine and journal from here to either coast won't hire him."

John turned onto the expressway and gunned the engine, enjoying the way the car pushed him back into his seat. He didn't want to talk drugs with Jamie.

"Everyone who's ever been on it says the first time is when you get hooked, you know," Jamie continued. "That rush, that numbness everywhere. You know what I'm talking about, right?"

John eased up on the accelerator a fraction. "What?"

Jamie turned toward him. "Man. Don't pull that act with me. Andrea's not here. But I was there that night. I was right there with you. I showed you how to do it."

"I don't want to talk about that shit. You weren't in your right mind, anyway." The lights of oncoming cars spun in John's eyes. He swallowed. "How do you know what happened?"

"I know they found two needles in my apartment, and none of them had any juice in it. But I'd only used once that night."

John stared straight ahead. Their exit was coming up in half a mile. He pushed the gas pedal to the floor and whipped his Mustang onto the exit ramp, braking at the last second. Waiting at the stop light, he turned to Jamie, breathing hard. He couldn't seem to catch his breath. "Why did you do it?"

"Hey, don't put the blame on me. I saw you reaching for it when you thought I was knocked out. At least I showed you how to do it the right way so you didn't shoot it into a muscle and fuck yourself good."

John's head was spinning. He'd wanted to try it, wanted to forget the terrible day he'd had at work, wanted to do something incredibly crazy. And it had felt good, even the cold metal of the needle's tip entering his vein. He'd become a user, a junkie, if only for one night. When the drug hit him, he'd closed his eyes and fallen asleep while Jamie had been convulsing next to him, and for a half hour he'd been too messed up to wake up. Or to care.

A car behind them honked. The light was green, and it turned yellow before John pulled out. With the motion of the car, he felt a weight lifted from him, a weight he'd been carrying since March.

"I hope this doesn't jinx our luck tonight, talking about all this," he said. Jamie only nodded. John turned right and found the darkened bakery. A light was on in an upstairs room, barely visible through the thick shade. John had fifteen hundred dollars in his pocket next to his father's arrowhead.

"You weren't supposed to remember that, man," John said. He shut off the car and looked at Jamie. "*I* barely remember it."

Jamie smiled a cold smile at that. "That's what friends are for. To keep you from forgetting."

They stepped out of the car without a word and made their way to the back door of the building, ready to try their luck. The summer night had grown cold, and John wished he'd brought a coat. He touched the wad of bills from his brother, the money he hadn't earned and didn't deserve. For some reason, John kept thinking about chickens, and all he could do was laugh quietly next to Jamie as they waited for someone to answer the door and let them in.

Chapter Thirteen

W hy don't you ever talk with me anymore?"
His grandmother sat at the kitchen table next to William, her eyes hidden behind her glasses as she waited for him to answer.

William didn't know what to say. His breakfast sat untouched in front of him, the fried eggs cold and hard. Between picking up John's abandoned chores and working more at the shop, William agreed he hadn't been around much lately.

"I've been busy, Grandma," he said, draining the last of his coffee. "Why can't you talk to Mom and Dad, instead of me?"

She shook her head, a dismissive frown on her face. "They don't have time for me, and your mother, I'm still mad at her."

"You're still mad at her? About what?" He watched her try to remember the root cause of her anger toward his mother. She stammered and twisted her lip and didn't say anything for a few seconds.

"You don't even remember!" William laughed, then softened his tone when he saw the hurt look in her eyes. "Was it because she went back to school and became a teacher? Is that it?" William thought of his own anger at John, at how much energy and time he had wasted when he could have been getting to know his brother again. And now he was gone, along with all of William's savings. "You can't hold a grudge like that, Grandma. It doesn't hurt you to do some dusting and wash some dishes while Mom brings home a steady paycheck. God knows we could use the money these days."

"I'm an old woman. I shouldn't have to work so hard. I raised six kids in this house, running and cooking and cleaning all the time, while your grandfather managed the farm. Now with the four of you working on it, it's still not making a profit."

"Well, it's just the three of us now. And watch how loud you say stuff like that. We're doing all we can." William put his hand on her shoulder. "You know what? There's been something bugging me ever since you told me that story about your Uncle Hubert and Uncle Albert."

"Don't patronize me, young man," she snapped.

"Don't get ugly with me," William said in return. "And I'm not patronizing you. I just want to know why Hubert and Albert were so mad at each other. You never told us."

"I'll tell you when John comes back from the city, and I'll tell you both." Grandma sniffed. "I don't like repeating myself."

"Would you tell me before I wring your neck?"

Grandma sat back in her chair and thought for a few seconds. She put on her serious, storytelling face, and began. "This is all second and third hand information, of course. My uncles didn't like to talk much in the first place, and they liked talking about each other a lot less. But their whole disagreement boiled down to an old work horse."

William smiled, feeling the years slip away as he became a kid again, listening to his grandmother's history tales. She kept a wary eye on him as she spoke, as if expecting him to try to sneak off when she wasn't watching him.

"One winter, right around the turn of the century or so, a blizzard hit. The snow was so thick nobody could make it to town for weeks. Most houses had snow up to their windows, so you could walk out a window like it was a door. If the windows hadn't all been frozen shut, that is. The brothers hadn't stockpiled much food, and they ran out after the second week. Hubert wanted to take the workhorse they had and cut a path through the snow into town, risking the cold and his own health. They dared not come to our house begging for food, or my grandfather would've chased them away for being foolish and wasting their food in the first place. Albert wanted to simply shoot the workhorse and eat it while the snow melted. They argued for days, growing hungrier and crazier, until Albert gave Hubert the choice: shoot the horse or he'd shoot him. They ate horsemeat for the rest of the winter, getting terrible stomach ailments, and they never spoke again."

William clapped. "Excellent story. You made it up, didn't you? Right there on the spot. That was very good."

"I did not make anything up. That's the truth." She reached out and pinched his arm lightly in her icy fingers. "Thanks for listening, you ungrateful little boy."

William grinned at her, enjoying the sparkle in her eyes. The sound of footsteps outside reminded him of the day Grandma surprised him up in the attic. He owed her everything for being there for him that day. His parents came in, and the sight of them in their dress clothes made William's smile freeze on his face.

"How'd it go?" he asked. His mother was white with anger, while his father simply looked beaten.

"I don't think we're going to be able to recover after all this rain," Dad said. "The bank is offering to buy out our loan from us, and I think we have to take it."

"That's what he and Tony Anderson think, at least," his mother spat in disgust. William looked at her. He couldn't remember the last time he had seen his mother so upset. "I think the bank sees a good deal on some good land, and it sees us as a couple of suckers."

Mom glared at Dad, who only shrugged his shoulders. The four of them looked at one another, letting the facts sink in. "Well," his mother said finally, "I guess I'd better change clothes and feed the damn chickens before they starve to death." She stormed out of the kitchen and slammed the bedroom door behind her.

"Are you just going to give up, just like that, Dad?" William hated the whipped expression on his father's face, recognizing the look from his own reflection from only a few months ago. Way back before John came back and turned everything upside down. How fitting, he thought, that the little shit isn't here now.

"I don't want to lose it," Dad said, rubbing his face and leaning on the doorframe. "But I can't live with this debt hanging over our whole family, either. And don't look at me like that, Mom. Things have changed one hundred and eighty degrees since your time farming with Dad. The prices we get haven't changed much since then, but that's the only thing that hasn't changed. It's all factory farming now. No family farm's going to make it much longer." He loosened his tie and started to say more, then he just walked out of the kitchen to change clothes, his shoulders slumped as if his dress clothes weighed him down like a man underwater.

William and his father had planned on baling hay in the northern fields that second week of June, but it had rained the day they were going to cut. With nothing better to do and nobody around he could talk to, William drove to the Crossroads Lounge at three in the afternoon and began drinking. Jenifer was at work, and he couldn't bother her with his problems, as much as he wanted to see her. Not after he'd asked her to call Marcy for him. William was tempted to invite his father, but he was afraid Dad would be a miserable drunk, making him feel even lower than he already felt. All his luck was shifting again.

For an hour, William drank by himself, thinking about the changes in his life since last December, back when he was still living with his wife and he barely knew who John or Jenifer were. Back when he and Marcy would get up together to start the milking, then she would check on the pigs or grind feed or go for a walk down the lane. He never asked her to get up with him, knowing she should've slept the extra hour before leaving for work at the insurance office in town. On cold winter days when the icy air hurt his skin, she would stand tight against him as he waited for the cows' udders to empty into the milker, and she'd talk about who was filing a claim or what new law she was learning about from the memos she typed out at work.

William looked at the half empty pitcher of beer in front of him, next to his single glass. Before she left, he wondered, when was the last time Marcy had come out in the mornings with me? It hadn't struck him at the time, but he realized now that she hadn't gotten up much at all during the past winter. He'd blamed it on the cold and her longer hours at work. Picking up his glass, he took a long drink, hoping it would keep the memories away, but all the while wanting the bittersweet pain those memories brought.

William thought about that day in December, and the rock he'd caught in his hand from her tires as she left. How he couldn't feel even the slightest sting of pain, despite the cut it had made on the inside of his palm. The numbness had begun even then, as he stood in the dirty snow in his bare feet. "You'll be back," he said as her car plowed away up the lane and down the long straightaway. He threw the rock, striped with blood from his hand, over the barbed wire fence and into the frozen field. It disappeared into the field, the snow an eerie grayish-blue color from the rising winter sun. Then he went back inside and, for the first time since he was a kid, slept through the morning chores.

William shook his head and poured more beer. "I have to go," she'd said. He had no idea why she felt that way. Was there someone else, waiting for her to finally get up the guts to run to him? Maybe someone who wanted a family of his own, someone who would move away from the house where he'd grown up. He thought he and Marcy had agreed that they would have kids as soon as they found their own place to live. And anyway, William thought, they spent too much time together, either working or with his family, for her to ever slip away for an affair. Though she *had* started working longer hours at her job this past winter.

"Hell no," William said to himself. Her boss was old, his father's age, and the only other person Marcy worked with was some young kid who was already married. When he realized he'd spoken out loud, William glanced around, suddenly aware of how pathetic he looked, a lone man sitting at a table with one pitcher and one glass, mumbling to himself. My wife fucking left me, he wanted to say to the turned backs of the other customers in the nearly empty Lounge.

After he grew tired of beating himself up with the past, he called the shop and told Marty and Russell to join him as soon as possible for some serious drinking. They arrived less than fifteen minutes later. William knew he could count on his old friends to be there for him. Either that or business at the shop was slow again.

Russell carried a too-full pitcher of beer to the table slowly, not spilling a drop, then turned his baseball cap backwards. "To what do we owe this beer-drinking pleasure?"

"To the rain," William said. "The rain and all the farms it's been ruining all summer." He drained his glass and pushed it over to Russell for a refill.

"Yeah, I'm glad my folks got out a couple years ago," Marty said. "It's just not worth the effort you put into it."

"It all turns to shit," William muttered. "To manure. To fertilizer."

Marty refused to give in to William's bad mood. "Come on, William," he said. William could have sworn Marty had been in a good mood ever since introducing his original songs to Basskick. "You know what I was thinking about this morning at work?"

"I'm afraid to ask," William said, rolling his eyes at Russell.

Marty gave him the finger and kept talking. "Your mom and dad's seed party a couple summers ago. When your dad cut that deal with one of the seed salesmen over in Petersburg. I remember chowing down on hamburgers and your mom's kick-ass potato salad while your dad tried to explain the advantages of the different kinds of seed corn on his test rows. Then there was all that free beer the salesman had brought along."

"That was some experiment," William said. "Dad had all those hybrids, and he'd planted too much on his test plot, ended up using over three and a half acres of the test stuff. And only three of the hybrids even did anything."

"Yeah," Marty said, "but I think everyone had a blast that day at the cookout, all the seed reps and the neighbors. I did."

William shook his head. "I know that seed salesman made a bundle off the neighbors. Some of that corn was almost two feet over our heads."

"Your dad's a good farmer," Russell said quietly.

William glanced at him, then Marty. If Russell was humoring him, he was doing a damn good job of hiding it. He'd never given his father half the respect his two old friends were giving him today. All William could see at the time was how much space the test plots were taking up, how big a cut they'd end up taking in their own production to do a favor for some seed salesman.

"That was a good year, too," he said, smiling in spite of himself. "Lots of sun, and just the occasional downpour. Nothing like the dumping we've been getting the past few months."

"Can't control the weather," Marty said.

Russell drained his second glass of beer and poured more into everyone else's glass, then his own. "This rain is costing us gigs, too, man. We had two outdoor parties cancel on us. We gotta get more experience playing places other than this dump."

"I'll drink to that," William said, draining half his glass.

"You two sound like a couple of bitchy old ladies, complaining about everything," Marty said, sipping his beer and looking at William. "Slow down before you get sloppy and start bawling."

"Oh trust me, I'm beyond that," William said, forgetting about his father and remembering everything else from the past year. "I've had more crap fall on me the past few months than anyone deserves in a lifetime. You should write a song about that." He picked up his beer and set it back down again, trying to organize the thoughts that seemed to be slowing in his mind. "And to top it all off, guess who's coming back to good old Holy Cross to visit?"

"No. Is she really?" Marty leaned back in his chair. "How'd you get a hold of her?"

"Who?" Russell asked.

"Jenifer's been talking to her."

"Who?" Russell asked again, then he saw William's face. "Oh. Her."

"We have to get some sort of closure, I guess," William said.

"What the hell is closure? What's that mean?" Russell blurted out, as if to make up for his momentary confusion only seconds earlier.

"I don't know, bud," William said, "but if I can get her out of my system and get my life back on track, it'd be worth it to see her again."

The three friends sat around the table, holding their drinks.

"You're not going to take her back, are you?" Marty asked quietly.

William looked at him in surprise, but didn't answer. In the silence that followed, they all quickly finished their beers and motioned for a waitress to bring them another pitcher.

After three straight days without rain, a minor miracle, William and his father were able to bale hay for the first time all summer. His spirits had begun to rise. Four days before Marcy was to visit, William invited Jenifer and Cynthia to a park overlooking the Mississippi River in Dubuque, and she accepted. He hadn't seen her since the afternoon John left. They stopped at a drive-through on the way to the park and brought the bag of food to a rock that commanded a sweeping view of the wide, brown river below. As they ate their lunch on the rock, Cynthia napped in her car seat next to them.

"I'm glad you brought us up here," Jenifer said. She folded her legs under her and looked up at the sky. "You don't know how good it feels to get out of town sometimes."

"It *is* nice, isn't it?" William's mind had been miles away, thinking about baling hay and fixing the tractor, which had broken down for what looked like the final time. He inhaled deeply, smelling the flowers on the hillside and the freshly-cut grass. "I wanted to see you again, before Thursday."

"The big day, huh?"

"Yeah. I feel like, well, I feel like I've treated you badly."

Jenifer looked at him without saying anything. Cynthia shifted in her seat below them, then fell back to sleep.

"I shouldn't have come over to your place that night, and all those days and nights after that." Trying unsuccessfully not to grin at the memories, William continued. "It was pretty fun while it lasted, though, wasn't it?"

Jenifer bit her lip and nodded grudgingly. "The most fun I've had in a long, long time."

"But it wasn't right for me to see you, not while I'm still legally married, and not while I'm still —" He stopped himself before actually saying it, before admitting he was still in love with Marcy. He didn't know if it was even true. "I took advantage of you, and I'm very sorry, Jenifer."

She ran her hand down the edges of the rock, letting her fingernails scrape the hard surface, then she slid down onto the blanket next to her baby. There was a small smile on her lips. "Don't think you can get away with this. I'm not going to let you take all the guilt for our time together. I wanted this to happen as much as you did. I liked spending time with you, being with you. It would be tempting to let you be the bad guy, but I think I was just as bad, if that's the right word. And I'm supposed to be Marcy's best friend through all this."

William slid down to the blanket next to her and lay on his back. "You know what? I think sometimes everything was better when I was still shell-shocked about her leaving, and I didn't do anything but work."

"No." Jenifer reached across him and held him in a brief, strong hug. "It's better to feel something, in here," she patted his chest, "even if it's for the wrong reason, than to feel nothing at all. I firmly believe that."

"You may be right," William murmured. "I hope you're right."

Jenifer smiled at him and looked away suddenly, as if she were going to say something more and thought better of it. William turned away as well, watching the muddy waters of the Mississippi roll slowly past below them.

They rested in the sun until Cynthia began to stir, then William gathered up the blanket and their lunch bags. They drove past the statue of the huge bald eagle guarding the park entrance, the eagle's black eyes following them on their way out of the park and back into the real world. On the way back to town, William tried more than once to try to talk with Jenifer about something, anything, but Marcy's return hung over every possible conversation topic like a shadow. Jenifer must have felt it as well, and she closed her eyes and slept the fifteen-minute ride home. Cynthia, in her car seat between them, also slept deeply, Jenifer's face reflected in her round features.

As they approached Holy Cross, the steeples of the Catholic church rising into view above the fields outside of town, William felt a wave of sadness wash over him. A piece of his life was ending for him, and for the first time in over half a year, he felt true regret at what had happened and how things had turned out. It wasn't just him now; he'd involved Jenifer and her child. He gripped the steering wheel and clenched his mouth shut against the involuntary moan that tried to escape his lips. Slowing the truck, he passed the co-op and the diner. He glanced at Jenifer, and she was watching him with half-open eyes. Neither of them spoke until he stopped in front of her apartment.

"Let me help you," he said, turning to the baby's car seat, but Jenifer had already unbuckled it and slid it off the seat. William thought she was going to walk away without saying anything to him, her back straight as she walked towards her apartment. Then she turned. "See you later," she whispered.

William moved to open his door and go after her, but he knew he couldn't. Too much was happening, too fast. Too much had already happened, between the two of them.

On his way home, retracing his path through town back to the farm, William stopped in front of the gas station to let an old farmer back his pickup out of a parking place. As he waited, he looked to his left and saw John's friend Andy gassing up his car at the station while Tony and Tim stocked a red cooler. Tony looked up and saw William. When William waved at him, Tony broke into a jerky dance in time to some unheard music. Tony's dancing was made even more comical by his two black eyes and bandaged nose. Tim doubled over in laughter, spilling ice and loose beers from his hands. William stepped on the gas and drove past the brothers and Andy, knowing that if his brother were back, he'd be there with his friends, laughing at him as well. He put on a poker face and shook his head at them to let them know he didn't care what they thought, that they could have their fun while it lasted. They weren't worth getting upset over.

Chapter Fourteen

John woke at ten on a Wednesday morning with a screaming headache. He sat up holding his head and began a mad scramble for his clothes, afraid of William's wrath for being late once again with the morning chores. He knew he'd overslept. By the time he'd pulled on a T-shirt he realized he was sitting on the old couch in Jamie's Chicago apartment, not his single bed in his drafty bedroom back home. He closed his eyes and lay back on the couch with a guilty sense of relief.

The last few days had blurred together. After the all-night card game at Edna's Bakery last Thursday, the details became a bit muddled. He had walked away from the game that night with over twenty thousand dollars in cash after an unbelievable run of luck. Jamie had been at his side the whole time, he knew, and they had been celebrating ever since. Somewhere in the fog of his brain he could remember Andrea yelling at him, reminding them of how worried she had been, but John couldn't tell whether she was aiming her anger at him or Jamie.

After another half hour, John pulled himself up off the couch. He reached his arm out to get his pants and knocked over an empty bottle of gin in the process. He left it spinning on the floor and picked up his wallet and his jeans. There were only a couple of twenties in his wallet, which didn't surprise him. He never carried much cash there. His roll of bills was in the front pocket. Feeling like a two-bit gangster, he sat down in his shorts and T-shirt to count his earnings.

As he flipped through twenties and hundreds, sorting them into separate piles, his headache lessened. He and Jamie had stayed up late last night drinking gin and Kool-Aid, a favorite creation of John's from his college days, and Andrea had stormed off to bed at midnight, asking them without much hope to keep the noise down. "Some of us have to work," she said, glaring from Jamie to John. Listening to Jamie's muffled groans and swearing as he worked his way out of bed, John wondered how much more Andrea would take.

"God damn it," John said, staring at the neat piles of wrinkled money in front of him. They weren't tall enough—he was about five grand short. There was no way he and Jamie could've blown that much cash in the past four or five days. Jamie had quit playing cards with the guys at the bakery once John started winning, so John knew Jamie had barely broken even. All the other players eventually quit as well, except for two: a fat guy named Bill and a quiet kid in a sports coat and tie. John had kept betting more and more, and these two guys tried to call his bluff each time, while the rest of the players sat and watched in stunned silence. John had won twenty-one thousand, five hundred and fifty dollars; the number was etched in his brain. But apparently someone had taken a twenty-five percent cut.

Jamie stumbled out of his bedroom, holding a hand over his eyes. His matted black hair stuck up in the back and hung in his face in the front. "Good mornin'."

"Hi," John said, quietly folding the bills in front of him. He pulled on his jeans and slid the cash into his front pocket. "How's the head?"

"Terrible. Where's the coffee? Didn't you make coffee?"

"Nope." John stood up and followed Jamie into the kitchen.

Jamie stopped with his hand on the refrigerator door. "What?"

"What do you think you're doing?" John asked.

Jamie gave him a baffled look, and John felt everything fall into place: how Jamie had taken Andrea in, how she'd come willingly, how protective Jamie had become of her. How Jamie felt responsible now, as well as expectant. As if someone owed him something for his hard work.

"I don't know what you think you're doing with Andrea, but don't fuck with my money, all right?" He stepped toward Jamie. "I'm short about five grand."

Jamie let go of the refrigerator and crossed his arms in front of him. "I don't know what you're talking about."

"Jamie. Don't mess around here. That money's for my family."

"Hey. I just want my cut. I was there with you, helping you. Come on."

John turned and walked away. He bent down and picked up the arrowhead from the floor. The night of the card game he thought he was going to rub it smooth. It must have fallen out of his pants pocket last night. "What did you spend it on?"

"All right, you tight-ass," Jamie said, stalking from the kitchen into his bedroom. "I'll let you have it, even though you wouldn't have been able to win so much if I hadn't gone with you to back you up." He shouted through the open bedroom door. "And it was only about four grand, not five."

John waited as Jamie threw clothes and books around in his bedroom. It was time, John knew, to return to Holy Cross. He'd give Dad as much as he could afford to give him; he owed his father that much. Beyond that, he wasn't sure what he'd do. All his debts would be repaid at that point, at least the emotional ones. That still left the loan sharks and their steadily accruing interest.

"Here," Jamie said, shoving a loose pile of money into John's hand. John grabbed Jamie's wrist and turned his arm so he could see the inner elbow. Jamie jerked away when he realized what John was doing. "Fuck you, man!"

"Did you already shoot it all up? Is that where my missing thousand went? Right into your arm? That was my family's money, Jamie."

173

"I'm off that shit," Jamie said, heading back into his bedroom. "That's just great. I help you out and that's how you treat me. I didn't have to put you up here and all that, you know. I don't owe you a thing."

"I know," John said, surprised at how calm he felt. "We're even." He started gathering up clothes and shoving them into his bag. He realized he'd been wearing the same shirt for the past two days, but he didn't have anything else that was clean. He stopped packing for a second. His clothes, he knew, smelled like pot and sweat. As much as he hated to admit it, he wasn't all that different from Jamie and his heroin, living like a slob for the past few days. He just hadn't gotten hooked.

Taking one last look around the apartment, at the mixture of Jamie and Andrea's belongings, the blankets and pillows thrown across the couch, he called out, "See ya." There was no answer. Without another word, John opened the door and left Jamie behind.

It was a day of deal-making, visiting old friends and acquaintances, and moving money from one place to another. At half past noon, John collected another parking ticket while he was talking with Mark. He tossed the ticket into the back seat along with the others he'd picked up in his time in Chicago. Mark knew what he was doing, and he'd come close to tripling John's money in a week. Mark's assistant had taken care of most of the business, and Mark showed up only at the end to shake hands briefly, looking comically afraid that someone would see him with John. Before rushing back through the glass doors to his cubicle, Mark said to come see the house he and Christine had bought in the suburbs, then he was gone.

John left the office and went to the bookie's apartment for another partial payment. Ten thousand would have to do for now, even though the interest was killing him. The skinny kid wasn't there, but an older guy who could've been the kid's father was there, and he reminded John of the amount he still owed. He was almost halfway there now. The thought didn't give him much comfort as he drove to his next destination.

After circling the blocks for twenty minutes looking for a spot, John parked in a handicapped space and ran up the four flights of steps to Andrea's office. She was in a meeting, and he almost ran back downstairs and left without seeing her. This would make two departures for him from Chicago in half a year, two good-byes to the woman he used to think he loved. When she came out, she gave him a withering look, then noticed his agitation.

"Are you on your way back home?" she said, waving at a couple of people passing by in the hall. She wore her reading glasses, and she looked focused and slightly agitated.

"Yeah."

"I'd like to come along."

John gave her a look. He hadn't expected that reaction from her. "What? Why?" he blurted out. If she returned with him, everything changed.

"I don't want you running out on my life again. Though I'm not sure why I even care, the way you and Jamie have been carrying on lately." She moved closer to him. "As long as we're back in a few days, I'll go with you. I've got some vacation days I can burn."

John wanted to say something more, but she stepped away, promising to meet him downstairs in five minutes. It was almost three o'clock already, and he wanted to get out of Chicago before rush hour hit. He'd have to come back to Chicago in a few days to bring Andrea back. As much as he hated the way she was trying to control him, he couldn't simply abandon her again. If there was a chance they could work things out, he'd try it. He trudged downstairs, thinking once again about how everything had shifted around, but he was still stuck, moving only in circles, unable to adapt.

They dropped by Jamie's place so Andrea could grab some clothes for the weekend. John stayed in the car, trying to figure out a plan though his mind was wiped clean. He almost put the car in gear and drove off, leaving Andrea to Jamie and the city forever, but before he could summon the courage, she came out the front door carrying an overnight bag.

"Jamie wasn't home," she said. "That's strange. He wasn't at work, either."

John shrugged, not wanting to think about what Jamie was doing in his free time. He had a feeling Jamie was a part of his past now, and as a result, he didn't concern him anymore. They made their way to the expressway, the traffic growing heavier on their way out of the city.

Andrea turned to put her bag in the back seat and placed her hand on John's arm for a brief second. "He was glad to see you again, I think."

"It was nice," John said, and it was more or less true. The truth had become a flexible thing in the past few months. He felt himself relax at her touch, though in his mind he was thinking about how Andrea had slept on a futon next to the kitchen the whole time he'd been at Jamie's. Not once did she invite him over to sleep with her. Feeling like he deserved her poor treatment for leaving her with Jamie and their angry friends, he'd never complained or asked her to reconsider. All in the past, he thought to himself. Water under a burned bridge.

"So. You going to give all that money to your dad?" Andrea said after ten minutes of silence. John drove around a semi trailer and set the cruise at eighty, thinking about her question.

"A good chunk of it, probably. Half of it went to my bookie already. Why do you ask?"

"I don't know. I mean, it is a lot of money."

"Yeah, and they *need* a lot of money. Do you think I should keep it all and let them lose the farm?"

"No, of course not. It's just that, well, Jamie told me how much you'd won, and I know how in debt you are."

"Don't worry about me, Andrea. I can take care of myself." The thought of her worrying about him irritated him, and he had a sudden image of William following after him, checking how he'd done with the caulking on the newly-installed windows of the chicken house. "Maybe you need to worry about Jamie more. He tried to take some of my money. To buy more heroin."

"What? Is he using that shit again? He promised me he'd never do that." She sat up straight. "Are you sure about that? Maybe I should go back."

John almost stepped on the brake to turn off the cruise. "What are you going to do for him? If he wants to kill himself, he's not going to let you stop him. If that's what he really wants to do."

"Why are you acting this way? He's been a good friend, to both of us, through all of this. Don't you care about what happens to him?"

John glanced at her. "I do, Andrea, but up to a point. If he can lie to us about that, what else isn't he telling us?"

Andrea sat back in her seat, a sickened look on her face. She didn't say anything more.A light rain had started to fall, and she traced a line of rain as it slid across her window, biting her lower lip.

"I mean, I find it awfully convenient that he offered up his place for you, the second he thought you were in trouble," John said. I need to shut up, he told himself, but the look of anguished concern for Jamie that he'd seen on Andrea's face set him off even more. "And you just came running."

"I was scared. Someone broke into my place."

"And there was Jamie to comfort you."

"This is going to be a long ride. Okay, John, total honesty time here. I'll be one hundred percent straight with you, if you do the same to me."

"No, no, no. What's in the past is done." John tried to force his body not to squirm under her gaze, but it was to no avail. He could still feel the cold needle tip, the warmth flowing through his body, the blood rushing in his ears.

"I'll start," Andrea said, as if she hadn't even heard him. "We shared his bed that first night, and a couple nights later.

But nothing happened. We just slept, and he stayed next to me, and that was it. I was scared. Nothing happened."

John looked at her, then back at the road. He knew from the set of her jaw that she was going to tell him what he'd suspected, and he wouldn't be able to stop her.

"Not those first nights. But one night, after I'd gotten off the phone with some mean, angry guy on this farm in Iowa, the two of us got to talking. We drank a while, getting good and smashed, then the next thing I knew, we were in bed together."

John hit the wheel with his hand. "God damn it, I fucking knew it."

"Just that one night, John, and I'm sorry it happened, but it must have happened for a reason. That night he told me what you did, why you were so slow in getting him to the hospital."

John turned on the air conditioning to keep the windows from fogging up. The humidity was making him sweat.

"The fact that you left him at the hospital doesn't bother me as much as the fact that you never told me you shot up with him that night. Like you were some kid, experimenting with your first beer or your first joint. You never told me. How can *I* trust *you* after that?"

"Let's not talk about trust right now, okay?" John said softly. Now that they both knew each other's secrets, he felt an emptiness inside him, as if knowing about Andrea's infidelity had taken something physical from him. In an hour they crossed the Mississippi River at the Iowa border, the river high below the span of the bridge. John searched the brown water, trying to find something that wasn't there in its muddy, foaming depths. Further south he could just make out the lights of the Diamond Jack, but that was definitely not what he was looking for. John blew the air in his lungs out of his mouth with a soft hiss. He was no closer to making a decision about what to do with his life than the last time he'd crossed this river. He was just circling and circling.

* * * * *

Y ou must have heard about the accident," his mother said the minute they walked in the door, more of a statement than a question. John hadn't even set his bag down after introducing Andrea to her and Grandma. The last half hour of their trip had been made in complete, utter silence.

"What accident?" he said when his mother didn't elaborate. He tried to work the soreness out of his lower back and legs, while Andrea settled onto the couch next to Grandma.

"Oh, John," his mother said, hugging him hard. "You haven't heard, have you? How could you have, in the city?" She let go of him and glanced at Andrea. "It was Andy and the Johnson boys. They were out late Sunday night, on some gravel roads. I heard they were drinking. They went into a ditch, and Tony was thrown from the car and killed. His brother's in the hospital, and Andy's okay, just has a couple scratches."

"Jesus. Those idiots," John whispered, thinking about cowtipping and drinking on the road.

"John. Don't be that way." His mother rested a hand on his, and John felt himself want to give way to tears with her touch. He fought the sensation. "I'm sorry, honey. The funeral is Friday. I thought that was why you'd come back. I'm sorry to drop this on you like this."

John looked over at Andrea. "I don't suppose you packed anything you could wear to a funeral, did you?" he asked, trying to muster a smile. Her eyes widened in surprise, and John felt even worse. "Just kidding. You can stay here during the funeral. I'm sure Grandma would love to talk to you. Those guys were my friends."

William came in the door, his hair wet from the rain. He looked like he'd lost even more weight, John thought, but that was crazy, not in a week and a half. William nodded at him, shook Andrea's hand when John introduced them, and went upstairs.

"What's wrong with him?" John whispered. He felt like all the progress he and his brother had made had been undone by his sudden departure to Chicago. The money, John thought, wasn't helping close the rift.

"He's caught up in the accident and the farm. A lot of people his age are taking this pretty hard. I guess he saw them the night of the accident, buying beer. He's kicking himself for not doing anything."

"I should talk to him," John said. He stood up, needing to get out of the oppressive closeness of the living room. His mother stopped him and pulled him and Andrea into the kitchen instead.

"They were wild, everyone knew that, but they didn't deserve this," his mother was saying. Andrea sat nodding across the table from Mom, both hands wrapped around her coffee mug. John wondered what Andrea thought of his mother, wearing one of Dad's old shirts, muddy jeans, and ankle-high work boots, still dressed from doing the chores John used to do every night.

"His poor family," Andrea said, wiping at her eyes. "Especially the brother that survived. He must be eaten up with guilt."

While his mother and his girlfriend discussed funerals and accidents, John tried to act interested in what they were saying. Andrea seemed morbidly fascinated by the whole accident and funeral proceedings, which bothered John slightly, but not as much as those two silent tears. He wondered what. He wanted to believe that the real reason for her crying was her night weeks ago with Jamie. He barely knew Tony himself, not enough to feel tears come at his death.

"How do you think Tim is going to handle this?" his mother said, turning toward John.

He felt his mouth open, but no words came to him, too busy thinking about his own problems. The ring of the phone saved him.

"I'll get it," he said, rushing away from the kitchen table, glad to be away from the melodramatic tones from either side. He picked up the phone on the second ring. "Hello?"

"Hey there." The female voice on the other end was unfamiliar, and she didn't give John a chance to identify himself before she plunged ahead. "Just wanted to let you know that tomorrow is going to work. Be at the church sometime tomorrow afternoon. I'm not sure when she'll get in, so I'll call you in the morning when I know for sure. This is going to be good for everyone involved, William, and I'm glad you're doing it. I'm glad I could help. I just want..."

When she paused, John took the opportunity to break in. "What? What do you want?"

"I just want you to be happy is all..." Her voice became tentative. "William? Is that you?"

"Well, sure it is. So where's she been staying?"

"You know I can't tell you that. It's a ways from here, I'll tell you that much."

"John?" His mother's voice piped up from the kitchen. "Who's on the phone?"

"Hey." The voice on the other end of the line went cold. "Is this John? What are you trying to do, you asshole?"

"Wait a minute, don't get all pissed at me. You never gave me a chance to identify myself. Who are you, with all your plans?"

"When your brother gets home, have him call me. Jenifer. He knows my number."

John felt his face flush, but he ignored it. "So where's Marcy, really? You can tell me."

"No, I'm not going to play that game. I've heard enough about you to know better than to trust you with anything. Tell your brother to call me when he gets in."

"Okay, okay. I will. Listen, Jenifer, I'm—"

"Good-bye."

"—Sorry," he finished lamely. The line went dead, and John felt like a fool, apologizing once again for his poor behavior. He hung up the phone and felt himself smirking in spite of himself at the anger in Jenifer's voice. For some perverse reason, he always felt slightly pleased when he'd pissed someone off with just a few words or a small action. Then he returned to the morbid discussion in the kitchen, rubbing his mouth to remove the expression from his face.

It wasn't until late that night after everyone else had gone to bed that John had a chance to talk to William. After Andrea had gone to sleep upstairs, William came downstairs, looking haggard. They sat at the kitchen table with a beer each, though William barely touched his. John hadn't wanted to talk about it, but once he got started, he enjoyed seeing the shocked disbelief on his older brother's face. It beat talking about the accident and the funeral coming up on Friday.

"You don't know how many ways a person can make money, William," he began. "But you need cash to make more cash. I had a buddy of mine throw what you gave me into stocks, bonds, some high-risk stuff, and they all paid off. Then I got to sit in on a big game of poker. We're talking two-hundred-dollar opening bets. It was unbelievable. I lost hard at first, almost had to cash in early, but I hit all the breaks. I got your money for you, plus what I borrowed from Dad." He tapped his fingers on his lower lip. "Don't tell anyone this, but I'm close to being out of debt to those heavy hitters, too."

"You still owe them? Why didn't you use our money to pay them off?"

"No," John said, looking him square in the eye. "I had to pay you guys back first. Plus, all that cash still wouldn't have covered what I owe, bro."

"Jesus."

"Yeah. 'Jesus' is right." John watched his brother's face as he spoke. "So. What's up with you and this Jenifer chick?"

William stiffened, his hands suddenly tapping out a rhythm on the table top. "How do you know about her?"

"Oh, I have my sources," John said. "Actually, she called tonight, while you were in the shower."

"And you're just now getting around to telling me?" William stood up and went to the sink, running water onto the dirty pans stacked up below the faucet. "God damn, John. That was an important phone call."

"Why was it so important?"

"Nothing," William began, then turned off the water. "It's just... never mind. I'd better call her." He started walking toward the living room, then stopped. "Shit. It's almost eleven. She's in bed, for sure, and I don't want to wake the baby." He stood in the middle of the kitchen, his clothes loose on his too-thin body, swearing and rubbing his hands on his jeans.

"William." John pushed his brother's chair back so he'd take the hint and sit in it. William remained standing. "Jenifer said you're supposed to meet Marcy in front of the church tomorrow—"

Before John could finish what he was saying, his brother had taken three long strides across the kitchen and grabbed the front of John's shirt, pushing him back in his chair until he was dangling on two chair legs. He could feel the muscles in William's arms quivering as he held him.

"If you tell anyone about me seeing Marcy tomorrow, I swear to God I'll kill you. Nobody knows about this but me and Jenifer." William's eyes were almost crazy with anger, and John was too surprised to speak. Slowly, William backed up, letting John's chair fall forward onto all four legs again. William let go of him and stepped back. "You really know how to fuck things up when you come back home, John."

John felt his heartbeat begin to slow, and he felt his anger begin to rise. "Are you saying things weren't fucked up before I came back?"

William shook his head and looked down at his hands. "Nobody was supposed to know she was coming back tomorrow. Then you're here a couple hours and you find out, just like that."

"Hey. I'm not going to tell anyone, okay. Just call Jenifer tomorrow and she'll tell you what time you need to be at the church."

William nodded. A small smile crept across his face. "So was Jenifer nice to you on the phone?"

"She called me an asshole. But other than that, she was sweet as can be."

William rubbed his face with both hands and laughed. "God. She's not afraid to say what's on her mind."

"I hope you didn't mess up my shirt, grabbing me like that. At least you didn't drop me on the floor, you skinny bastard. I could feel your arms shaking."

"Just trying to hold your fat ass up took all my strength. Listen, I'm sorry I blew up. I shouldn't have. You should've given me the message sooner"—his voice began to rise, but with a visible effort, he restrained himself—"but that's okay. And anyway, it's good to have you back."

"Good night," John said, then added, "you big asshole."

William grinned and shook his head. "Good night, you little shit."

John watched William left the room. He closed his eyes and listened to the stairs creaking. Despite the joking around he and William could still do after all this time, it didn't feel good to be back. There was too much suffering here, too much death. He smoothed his shirt and tucked it back into his pants. He was more of a stranger now than when he came back in March, and he'd always be that way. But he couldn't tell his brother that. William had enough on his plate for now.

Chapter Fifteen

At ten minutes to midnight on the day before his wife was to return, William walked away from his brother in the kitchen downstairs, feeling the elements of his once-simple life start to swirl around him: Marcy's arrival tomorrow, the money he'd lent John, his offer to Marty and Russell, Tony's funeral on Friday. Every time William closed his eyes, he could see them: Andy gassing up his car, Tim laughing as Tony waved his skinny arms in a mocking dance. And William had only smiled and drove away. In the days since the accident, all the people of town could talk about was the wreck, how many times the car had rolled, and where it had landed in the Deutmeyer's field two miles outside of town.

At the top of the stairs, he made his way through his darkened bedroom without a light. The small desk with her mirror, perfume bottles, and hair dryer sat next to the bed, untouched for over half a year. In the closet, he knew without looking that there were four or five pairs of her shoes, and in the dresser were extra socks and panties she hadn't had time to pack. Marcy had left hints and reminders of herself everywhere he looked. The only thing she probably regretted not grabbing was her recipe box. It sat gathering dust on the night stand next to the bed. She used to flip through constantly, adding new concoctions to it or devising new twists on an old favorite. Maybe she could cook them from memory now.

William sat on the bed, feeling as claustrophobic as the day Grandma had found him in the attic. The wrenches, the shoelaces, the gold chain, Christmas gifts his wife had run off too soon to give. Marcy hadn't had time to retrieve those, either. He put a hand over his eyes and tried to laugh, but the sound that came out of his mouth was far from happy. He heard his brother step slowly up the stairs, walking softly but still making noise on each squeaky step. William couldn't get over how quickly he'd grabbed John by the shirt and held him dangling over the kitchen floor, how angry he'd been. And it was all because of Marcy.

She used to spend every Saturday night with her girlfriends. William hadn't thought about those nights in a long time, when he'd go out with Russell and Marty, and she'd go out with four or five other girls from town, sometimes with Jenifer, sometimes not. In a way, it was like high school all over again, when they'd drive to Dubuque to go to the mall or to a movie, or just cruise around town, honking at everyone, a car full of girls stopping next to a car full of boys. That's what they had been, even into their late twenties: boys and girls.

At some point, Marcy had stopped spending her Saturday nights with the girls, but William still got together with his buddies. Maybe we all should have gone out together for a change, he thought, too late, alone in the bed he used to share with his wife. He rubbed his chest, feeling his ribs through his T-shirt.

"I have to go," he whispered. In the silence he reached across the bed for the recipe box, thinking Marcy would want it tomorrow, but in the dark he misjudged his reach and knocked it to the floor. The carefully organized cards scattered across the hardwood floor like mice. He left them on the floor. The thought of Marcy somewhere else instead of there next to him, sleeping alone just like he was, allowed William a small sense of relief from his worrying. All they shared now was their own solitude, if she was indeed alone.

After another minute of tossing and turning, he convinced himself that she was, and that allowed him the respite from his worries so he could finally fall asleep.

* * * * *

William woke before his alarm and ran through his chores, finishing early and avoiding his brother and father. He couldn't slow down if he wanted. Momentum was something he'd never felt before. Before today, he'd been content to let each day run into the next, maintaining a steady constant, no highs or lows. But this Thursday morning felt like a countdown, as if he had only a certain amount of time allotted before his momentum ran out.

Skipping breakfast, he walked up to John's girlfriend. "Has anybody called this morning?"

Andrea glanced up from the local newspaper, looking like she was surprised to hear him talking to her. "No. I don't think so." She gave him a sheepish smile, a smile that for some reason reminded him of Jenifer. "I just rolled out of bed."

William wanted to give her a hard time for sleeping in until almost nine, but he was able to stifle it. "You're on vacation, right? You might as well sleep in. Though I bet you never thought you'd spend your vacation on a farm in Iowa."

"Not really," she said with a laugh.

William didn't know what else to say to her. Her presence on the farm bothered him, like a tickling in the back of his mind. He thought about asking her when John was planning to take her back to Chicago, and if he was going back with her, but he didn't need to. The past few days, he could see the telltale signs on John's face, though William knew John thought he could hide his feelings from him. The way John kept looking at the time, or how he sat without listening to one of Grandma's stories, or how he stared off into space while running the milkers or herding the cows in and out of the barn.

William realized he was standing next to the phone, waiting, and Andrea was doing her best not to show how uncomfortable he was making her. "Sorry," he said. "I'm just expecting a call. I'm supposed to meet someone—" Before he could finish, the phone rang.It was Jenifer. Without wasting any time, she told him to meet Marcy at two in front of the church. Her voice was cool, unemotional. He pictured her holding the receiver away from her mouth as if trying to keep him at a distance. William thanked her and she hung up before he could say anything more. His face felt hot as he said "Good-bye" into the silent phone.

Instead of hanging up the phone, he hit the disconnect button and dialed up the number to Marty's shop. He left a message for Marty to get his paperwork in order, that he'd see him around four or five. If John was telling the truth about having the money William had lent him last week, William knew he had to act now before either of them could have second thoughts. He hung up, feeling like a rock rolling headlong down a long hill. I'll definitely tell Dad about working at the shop, he thought. Tomorrow.

John's girlfriend was looking over at him from behind the paper, a strange smile on her face. "You look like you've got a plan."

"I guess. I didn't really think of it like that, but you could call it a plan."

She gave the paper a snap and folded it in half. "I can relate to that."

William gave her a questioning look, but she wasn't looking at him anymore. What a strange girl, he thought, and left the house shaking his head. No, he thought, she didn't look anything like Jenifer.

After tinkering with the tractor for an hour, William walked down to the chicken shed. He spent a long time watching John's chickens run inside their enclosure. He sat on the step leading into the warm chicken house, birds pushing past him on their way in and out. Mindless, stupid animals, he thought, as a hapless chicken chased another that had found a grain of food on the ground. The chicken would peck at the chicken eating the food, trying to get the other chicken to drop it. But the only thing that happened, time and again, was that the other chicken would swallow the grain, then punish the clueless chicken with a round of pecks.

The chicken did it over and over to different chickens, reacting to the others but never getting anything in return. William watched until he couldn't stand it anymore, then he walked past the chickens, kicking the hapless chicken in the ass on his way out of the pen.

H e was half an hour late for his meeting with Marcy, having stopped at the diner for three cups of coffee that he stretched over forty-five minutes as he planned his actions for the next few hours. The diner was empty, as if in preparation for the funeral tomorrow, and Annie gave him a sympathetic look when she first filled his cup. William promptly ignored her and handed her back the menu. He didn't have time for accidental deaths and mourning. It gave him a stab of pleasure, as he sipped his coffee in the diner, to think about Marcy worrying and waiting for him while she sat in front of the church.

At two thirty he pulled up next to her in his truck, surprised to see that she was still driving her old, battered Chevelle. The license plate was from Iowa, though it had expired in March. For some strange reason, he thought she would have wanted something nicer than a six-year-old car as she started her new life. Marcy burst out of her car the second he pulled up, seriously overdressed and obviously angry. She wore a dark blue blazer with a matching skirt, and a no-nonsense white blouse under the blazer. In the eighty-five degree heat, she had to be stifling. William remained in his pickup.

"You're late," she said, walking up to his window.

"Nice to see you, too," he shot back, but his confidence had been undermined by her sudden appearance half a foot in front of him, her eyes blazing and her perfume in his nose. She had given him a sudden, shocking reminder of why he'd been miserable without her for the past half year. He forced his voice to remain calm. "You cut your hair."

She backed up a tiny bit, actually looking at him. She touched her short blonde hair, pushing a loose strand back into place. "And you've lost weight. Aren't you going to get out?"

"Let's go for a ride instead. Hop in, it'll be fun."

Marcy bit her lip. "I thought we could, you know, go inside where it's nice and quiet, and talk. I heard about the funeral tomorrow. It's awful."

No way was she getting me into that church, William thought. They had been married in the same church almost five years ago, a day that was a blur in his memory, but a happy blur. That would give her too much of an edge. He started the engine and leaned over to his right and opened the passenger door for her.

"No funny stuff, okay?" she said, and hurried around to the other side of the truck. After slamming the door behind her, she watched William warily as she clicked on her seat belt. Her face had a flushed look, a natural blush he remembered from when she was upset or angry.

"No funny stuff, I promise," William said as he backed up and drove into the street. His confidence returned in a rush at the uncertainty in her voice. The Marcy he used to know would never have used the term "funny stuff" to describe anything.

They drove in silence, except when William would point out the swollen creek that had burst its banks under the two bridges in Holy Cross. Rain and flooding had been William's constant companion all spring. Finally he stopped next to the last bridge at the edge of town and turned off the engine. Marcy looked at him with uncertainty in her eyes.

"I just wanted us to talk, away from town, that's all." He smiled, feeling himself slowly coming to terms with the haphazard array of emotions hitting him as a result of finally having her back. "You look nice. Very professional."

"Thanks. So do you," she added, trailing off. "Have you been sick? You look different."

"Nah. Just lost some baby fat." He turned in the seat so he was facing his wife. For some reason he thought of John, how he had shown up when William had been at his lowest point, and how John had never asked him about Marcy. He wondered if his brother would stay on the farm, but William seriously doubted if either of the Koopman sons would be able to stay at home forever. "Do you have a new job now?"

Marcy gave him a quick look and glanced away. "Yeah. I'm working for an accounting firm as an assistant. But I may be going to school to be a stewardess."

"Really?" William thought about her handing out peanuts and serving coffee. As far as he knew, neither of them had ever been on a plane before.

Marcy nodded. "I thought it would be a good way to see the country. I've always wanted to travel."

Through the windshield just to the left of Marcy, William could see the dark water flowing past the muddy riverbank. He turned away from the water towards his wife. "So Marcy, tell me, why did you leave?"

She lowered her gaze for a second, touching her hair as she tried to come up with a response. He knew in that instant she had just gotten it cut, and she had gotten it cut for him, to get his reaction to the new Marcy. "I just had to go, William. I was losing myself there on the farm, working all the time. We never talked about getting our own place anymore. It was killing me to stay there with you."

"I never did anything to hurt you."

"But you never did anything to help me grow. And we were going to start our own family, but we never did. We kept getting stuck on the farm, in our little bedroom, just one more month, one more year. "

William made a face at that. "You never said anything about wanting to start a family. It was always just you and me."

"That's not the issue. The issue is why we can't stay together."

"We can't stay together?" William said. His words had started out as a joke, but they had come out of his mouth sounding totally serious. No funny stuff, he'd promised. "Why not?"

Marcy looked at him. She started to say something, changed her mind, started a second time, and then changed her mind again. William forced himself to wait her out, to make her talk. After another few seconds, she blurted out, "Do you want me back?"

"That's not the issue, is it?"

"What is it with you? It's like you want to argue. You never wanted to argue before."

"But that was when I wasn't doing anything to *help* you." The world flickered past outside like the sunlight bouncing off the river, reflecting onto the roof of his old pickup. "Maybe this is helping you. It's sure helping me."

"God damn it. Don't throw my words back at me like that." Marcy folded her arms and sat back in the seat. "Let's go back to town. I see now this was all a big mistake."

William made no movement to start the truck. "So why *did* you come back? Other than the fact that we are married, that we did promise to honor each other, and that neither of us can get on with our lives until we come to some sort of agreement." He reached over and touched the thin gold ring of her wedding band on her left hand. "I see you still wear this."

"I do," she said in a small voice. "I hate how my hand looks when I don't have it on."

William felt himself being pulled toward her, painfully aware that if he'd only reach out to her and put his arms around her, she would come back to stay. All he'd have to do was take her by the shoulders and pull her close. He fought the urge, surprising himself at how easy it was to do.

After a moment, William nodded and started the truck. He backed carefully onto the road from the muddy shoulder. Something had shifted in his mind, like a dull pain in his temples that had finally gone away. "Remember when we were looking for places to live before we got married?"

Marcy was looking at the ring on her finger. "Um-hmm," she said without looking up. She swayed from side to side in time with the motion of the truck on their way back through town.

"Remember how we couldn't find any place, how nothing worked out for us? And I told you we'd have to spend the first few months after the wedding living on the farm?"

"I thought I was going to die."

"But you let me talk you into it, then once we were there, things got so busy, and we never bothered with looking for a place to live. I think about that a lot."

Marcy finally looked over at him. "Why?"

"I think that I wished you would've fought me a little bit harder, resisted me more."

"That's not fair. That was years ago."

"I know. And you wanted us to be happy." He turned into the parking space next to her car, in front of the church, and forced himself not to look at his watch. "But I think this is one of those times where if you want this to work, you're going to have to convince me. Because I can't let you back into my life right now. At least not yet. Maybe never."

His heart was hammering when he bent across her to open the door for her, and he kissed her cheek on his way back to his seat behind the wheel. "It's up to you now."

"What —" she began.

"I'll see you, Marcy. Take care of yourself. It you want to talk, you know the number." He watched her slide off the seat and drop to the pavement below. With a dull thump, her door swung shut, and she was framed in his passenger window, her face expressionless. As he backed his truck out into the street, Marcy raised an unsteady hand to wave goodbye.

William drove away without looking back.

* * * * *

Two blocks later, after the adrenaline had worn off, William got the shakes. Did I really do that? he kept asking himself. Did I really say that? Sitting in the middle of Main Street Holy Cross, William wondered if he'd forever closed the door that he'd been trying for so long to reopen.

But there was no sense in stopping now. He forced himself to keep driving until he reached Russell and Marty's automotive shop. He honked his horn in front of the big garage door so they would let him in, but only silence answered him. Staring at the dented door, his truck reflected three different ways in the three oval windows, he thought about what he'd said to Marcy, possibly the last words he'd ever speak to her.

"You know the number," he repeated, raising the skin of his arms into goosebumps. He killed the engine and let himself in the back door of the shop.

An old Firebird sat at one of the work bays, the hood down. Tools lay scattered around the front bumper next to empty quarts of oil and a set of jumper cables. Russell had been hard at work, it appeared. His radio sat on the roof of the car, blowing out static.

William took a deep breath and felt his knees almost give out. He held onto the Firebird to keep from falling over. Somehow he'd said what he'd most wanted to say to Marcy. She wouldn't have let him drive away if she truly wanted to come back. William had to believe that if he wanted to continue his life.

When the church bells up the street began to ring, not the hourly gong but a melody announcing the start of a service, William realized where Marty and Russell were. He'd heard Grandma talking about the special service tonight before Tony's funeral tomorrow, but it had slipped his mind until that moment. Most of the town was probably there. William forgot the lyrics to the song he was whispering as he thought about how Tony Johnson had been thrown from the back seat of Andy's car, through the back window as the Chevelle rolled, then he'd felt nothing more. William sat in the abandoned shop, listening to the church bells echoing off the walls and the equipment around him, and he made no move to leave.

A t half past eleven at the end of one of the longest days of his life, William lay in bed, trying for the second night in a row to sleep. His stomach ached with hunger, even though he'd heaped seconds and thirds onto his plate that night at supper. He wondered if he'd ever get a good night's sleep again. Giving up, he rolled out of bed, kicking loose recipe cards out of his way as he pulled on jeans and a T-shirt, and went downstairs.

The living room was covered in blue light from the TV. John had fallen asleep on the couch, and Andrea sat on the floor, leaning back on the couch in front of John, watching TV with the sound off. She had her knees pulled up to her chest, and her face was shadowed in the soft light.

Afraid to startle her, William cleared his throat at the bottom of the stairs before entering the room. "Midnight snack," he whispered with an awkward wave of his hand, and she nodded back at him. When he walked through the living room, his shadow raced around the wall in the blue light of the TV and caught up to him at the entrance to the kitchen.

Everything in the refrigerator looked good to him. He felt like he hadn't eaten in ages. He pulled out slabs of roast turkey, slices of ham, a block of cheese, pickles, mustard, lettuce, and mayonnaise, and began constructing a mammoth sandwich. He almost made a side sandwich of braunschweiger and mayo, but he didn't want to overdo it. He was cutting the sandwich into two massive wedges when Andrea walked into the kitchen in her oversized T-shirt and sweat pants, yawning.

William looked at the wreckage of food on the kitchen table and looked at Andrea. "I guess I got a little carried away."

"I see that." She pulled up a chair and sat across from him. Her eyes looked puffy, as if she had been crying. "So did your plan work out?"

"My plan." William stopped with the sandwich halfway to his mouth, trying to figure out what she was talking about. He'd been focused on eating. He took a bite of his sandwich. "Oh, my *plan*," he said, his mouth full. "Sorry."

Andrea gave him another curious smile and waited for him to finish chewing.

"You know," William said, forcing himself to put down his sandwich, "I think it just may be working out. But I can't really tell. It's too soon."

"Hopefully it will. Work out, I mean."

They sat for a few seconds in silence. William took another big bite and chewed slowly. He swallowed. "You guys are both going back to the city after tomorrow, aren't you?"

"I can't say." Andrea looked at her hands as she spoke. Then she laughed and pointed at his sandwich. "You're going to have major indigestion if you eat all that."

"I feel like I could eat a horse. I've had a busy day. A crazy day."

"Really? Tell me about it."

William watched her, almost suspicious, but she seemed genuinely interested. "Well, I told my wife, who's been gone since Christmas, to basically take a flying leap today," he began. "And I'm thinking it was probably the best thing I could've done." As he talked about that afternoon with Marcy, parked next to the swollen river, William felt the tension that had been wound deep inside his chest begin to ease. He talked, and as he talked he went back to that cold day in December and even earlier than that, to the mornings he used to share with Marcy. He talked, and he forgot about Andrea sitting across from him. When he ran out of things to say, he realized he'd been talking for almost twenty minutes straight. Andrea rested her chin on her hands on the table, her eyes wavering as she struggled to stay awake.

"I'm sorry." William let loose with a long yawn, his jaw popping. His plate was empty in front of him. "I was totally boring you, wasn't I?" Andrea started to shake her head, but William waved her off. "I've never talked to anyone about that before. I guess you got the long version."

"Feels good to get it off your chest, doesn't it?" Andrea said, stifling a yawn of her own with her hand. She gave William a guilty smile.

"It does. And thanks for listening. Really. I'd better get to bed. You going tomorrow?" William could tell she had no idea what he was talking about by the blank look on her face. "To the funeral."

Andrea's face flushed quickly. "Oh. I don't think so."

"It's okay. You shouldn't have to go. You didn't know him."

"No. I should go. It's the right thing to do." Andrea pushed her chair back. "I just don't like funerals. I had a bad experience when I was a kid, when my Grandpa died. I sort of freaked out when I saw him in his casket. At the wake. I was only six or seven."

"That's okay. You don't have to explain anything. I wish I didn't have to go. Nobody wants to go to a funeral."

William pushed his plate into the middle of the table, frustrated that Andrea had misunderstood him. They sat in silence for a minute, then two. It wasn't as uncomfortable as he would have thought. Then Andrea stood and walked into the living room without another word.

After a few seconds, William stood and followed her into the living room. She had taken up her seat in front of the couch again. A black and white movie played silently on the TV.

"Hey, Andrea," William whispered. "Thanks. Again." He moved toward the stairs, then turned to look at her sitting next to John, who hadn't moved a muscle on the couch. "Say. Do you like to cook?"

"Why?"

William gave Andrea a crooked grin. "Are you interested in some recipes?"

Chapter Sixteen

As far as John could tell, most of the people in Holy Cross, if not all, had crowded into the church for Tony's funeral. Sitting in the fifth pew from the front, he tried to keep his head low. William sat next to him, looking like a scarecrow in his old suit. Incense mixed with the smell of perfume and sweat in the warm air of the church.

To create the slightest hint of a breeze, the ten-foot-high stained glass windows had been cracked open, saints floating sideways above their heads. John refused to look up the long middle aisle at the dark brown casket sitting on wheels in front of the altar. When the last hymn had been sung, Tim and his wife and son walked past, and John could only nod at Tim's blank stare and try to put an encouraging expression on his face. A devastated Andy and his family followed them. After everyone had filed slowly out into the June sunshine, John knew that today was the day he would once again leave Holy Cross.

After the burial service at the cemetery, the Koopmans drove back to the farm. Mom kept looking back at John, wedged between William and Grandma, as if expecting an outburst at any minute. "His poor family," she said, more to herself than anyone else.

Grandma clucked her tongue at that and elbowed John as she turned to stare out the window. He had overheard Grandma and his mother talking with Andrea about the wreck and the funeral that morning, and he knew Grandma held little pity for his dead friend, killed for no reason but stupidity, in her opinion. Andrea had tried to be polite as

Grandma carried on, then she begged John when they were alone to not be included in the funeral activities. He didn't ask her why. He wished he could have avoided it as well, if only to save himself from the looks of barely hidden disgust and blame on the faces in the church. "Why are you still alive," they seemed to ask. "What have you done that makes you so special?"

John watched the erratic growth in the rain-soaked cornfields around him as they rode up the lane. Dad would be lucky to get much out of this year's crops, he thought, his mood darkening further. Maybe I should just keep my money instead of throwing it away on the farm, he thought suddenly. I'd definitely need it in the city.

"Who wants to help inoculate some pigs?" his father said as everyone got out of the car. His only answer was the opening and slamming of car doors. The rest of the family hurried toward the house, led by William, his coat and tie already off. A desperate feeling rose up in John as everyone moved away from him. He'd missed his chance to tell them, all of them at once, about his leaving.

Andrea greeted him with a long hug and a kiss that set his grandmother to grumbling. "Hello," he whispered when Andrea released him. It had been a long time since he'd felt her arms that tightly around him.

"Are you okay?" she said, watching him closely.

John shrugged and looked at his parents' closed bedroom door. "I didn't get a chance to talk to them."

"John." Andrea spoke in a harsh whisper. "You have to if we're going to leave today. What are you going to do with the money?"

John gave her a look of warning and didn't answer. Tony's death was proof enough that he couldn't stay in Iowa any longer. I never belonged here, he thought, watching his brother in his white dress shirt fill a plate with potato salad and ham in the kitchen.

"At least talk to your brother," Andrea whispered and walked upstairs. John glared after her and entered the kitchen.

"Hungry?" he asked his brother's back.

"Starving," William said. He dropped his plate onto the table and sat down. "Get some of that summer sausage. Old man Jacques made it from the deer he shot last winter. It's unbelievable."

"Nah. I'll pass." John stood behind a chair and gripped the sides. His brother crossed himself, said a silent prayer, and dug into his food. He must have no idea about me leaving, John thought. "When you're done eating, can you come out and look at the chickens with me?"

William nodded, eyebrows raised, chewing.

"I just wanted you to check them out, that's all." John let go of the chair when he heard their father in the living room. He'd tell them one at a time if he had to. He left the kitchen as the back door slammed behind his father.

"Dad. Wait up." John followed his father outside, the screen door slamming shut a second time. Dad had already changed into his work clothes, and he was on his way to the hog barns.

He gave John a questioning look and waited for him to catch up. "Aren't you a little overdressed to feed the hogs?"

John didn't answer as they walked toward the barns. The air was muggy, and the sky hinted at more rain. It hadn't rained at all while John was in Chicago last week.

"I wanted to talk to you about something," he said at last. But when the two men stopped walking and he looked in his father's eyes, John couldn't think of anything to say. He touched his leg and felt something sharp. "Where did you find this?" He reached into his pants pocket and pulled out the arrowhead.

Squinting at the rock, his father took it from John and rolled it in his fingers. "It's just a rock, isn't it?"

"It was in your coat pocket. I found it there a few months ago. I figured you had put it there for safekeeping. It's some kind of arrowhead, isn't it?"

His father stared at the rock, then looked at John, his blue eyes unreadable. "That," he said, "is a rock. If I put it in my coat pocket, I don't remember doing it." He handed it back to John. "But that's not what you really wanted to talk to me about, is it?"

John squeezed the rock in his hand. He watched his father's face—expectant, ready to console—and he thought about the money he'd brought back for his father and the farm. John knew he had to leave before the afternoon was over. The funeral had only been a distraction for him, a speed bump in the road out of Holy Cross. A light drizzle began to fall.

"No," he said. "I just wanted to ask you that."

His father touched his beard. "Okay. If you're sure." He waited another second, then said, "I'd better go feed those hogs before they start eating each other."

John began walking away in a different direction from his father, cursing himself with each step for not telling him anything. After ten steps he pulled back his arm to throw the arrowhead over the top of the barns as hard as he could. But before he let go of the rock, he stopped and pushed it back into his pocket. You make your luck where you can, he thought, telling himself he wasn't ready to just toss it all away.

Surrounded by chickens, John waited for his brother. Still in his dark blue suit, his tie tightened against his throat, unaware of the heat around him, he sat down in the doorway to the shed. The chicks ran across the fenced enclosure, fighting for seed. They had only weeks left to live before the butchering started. He wondered what it must be like to face death, and he thought of how close he had come with his buddies, Andy driving John's Mustang or his own car with abandon down narrow gravel roads. Andy's Chevelle was totalled now, sitting in the fenced lot of the salvage yard like a reminder of their stupidity. As John watched in silence, the chickens circled around and raced each other for food. When William approached, John was shaking his head and laughing.

"What's so funny?" William asked, his voice unsteady. He had changed into a pair of old jeans and a blue T-shirt, and John could see the knowledge of his departure on his brother's unsmiling face.

"Chickens," he said. He felt his voice come from someplace outside of himself, a self-assured volume he used all the time at his old job. "Now that's funny. Raising chickens is a freakin' hilarious job. You feed them, you keep them warm, then you chop off their heads and pluck them and eat them. Hilarious."

"You got a better line of work in mind?" William stepped over the chicken wire fence, his feet hitting the ruts in the ground made by the runaway tractor all those weeks ago.

"You know what? I do. Know what else? It doesn't involve sitting here in the middle of nowhere." John stood and lightly kicked a chicken out of his way. The closer William got, the more agitated John felt. "I did my time here. I put in my work, did what I could do to help."

"You don't have to do this," William said softly.

"I've got your money, and Dad's." John felt himself talking faster, his mind speeding up as he formed his plan. "I'll leave it on the vanity in your bedroom on my way out this afternoon."

"Don't think you have to prove anything to me. You should stay."

To William, his choice was as simple as that. Stay or leave. But leaving was the only choice that made sense anymore to John. There was nothing for him here. "Take care of the chickens for me."

"So that's it?" William said. "You're just going to leave again?"

"My brother," John said, listening to the cockiness in his voice and enjoying it, "I am already gone."

He jumped over the chicken wire and walked away from William as fast as he could without running. On his way up to the house from the chicken barn, John noticed how weather-beaten the old farmhouse was, the thin siding covered in gray streaks where the rain had stained it. The barns also needed painting, and William's tired tractor sat rusting inside the open door of the machine shed. The odor of animals filled the air. John balled his hands into fists to keep from rushing into the house, collecting Andrea, and speeding off in his car without leaving anything for anybody. That's what she wanted him to do, he knew, and the money was part of the reason she came back to Iowa with him. But after the turmoil of the past few months, John could live with those facts now. Slipping through the back door, he hurried upstairs to count out his cash.

Andrea sat waiting for him next to their packed bags. "How'd it go?" she asked.

"All right. He took it well, I guess."

"Your dad?" She stood and picked up a bag. "Or your brother?"

"William. He'll tell Dad for me. Let's drop off the money I owe them and get the hell out of here. I can't stay here any more." John pulled the wad of bills from the side pocket of his overnight bag. Andrea had packed everything for him, he noticed, counting out the six thousand dollars for William and the one thousand for his dad. The sight of his once-again empty bedroom made him lose count, and he had to start again.

Andrea stood looking out the window as he scribbled out a quick note to his father. He could almost hear her holding her breath. He counted out fifteen hundreds and slipped them into his pocket, then the rest of the cash went on top of his father's thousand, money for the farm. The roll of bills in his pocket felt dangerously thin, and his eyes strayed to the green pile with his father's note resting on top of it.

"That's all you're keeping?" Andrea had turned and was also gazing at the two piles of money on his old bed.

John felt a final pang of uncertainty, then he thought of his father in the barn his second week back, slapping him on the back and saying how glad he was that John was home. I owe him more than just money, he wanted to tell her, but the words stuck in his throat. Walking out of the bedroom, he set William's money on the old vanity Marcy used to use, then stuffed his father's wad of bills in his back pocket.

On his way out the front with his bags in his hands, John saw his grandmother in the kitchen. She was standing at the window, her back to John, and he could smell something cooking in the big Crock-Pot next to her. He had to say something before he left. He didn't know when he'd be back.

Clearing his throat, he walked up next to Grandma and tried to see what she was looking at. "Doing a little bird-watching?"

She heaved a loud sigh and shook her head. "They never stop working. All three of them." She pushed up her glasses by crinkling up her nose as if she'd smelled something bad. "Back when your Grandpa was running the place, we'd take the whole day off if someone had just died. It's not Christian, all this working."

"You can say that again," John said. When his grandmother gave him a curious look, he motioned for her to sit at the table next to him. He could hear Andrea's light steps on the stairs, going back for more of his belongings. "Tell me something from your book."

"Oh, you never wanted to hear anything from there before," she said, her voice hard at first, then she softened. She patted his hand. "I know—I haven't told you the rest of my story about my uncles. William was asking about that just the other day."

"Okay," John said. He racked his brain to remember the story she'd told months ago. "Tell me that one."

"I didn't tell you why they were so mad at each other. Why they split up their house."

"Well?" John said after ten seconds of waiting. He could hear Andrea stepping softly down the stairs, and he looked at Grandma. She didn't seem to have noticed.

"It went back to when they were in Germany. Something about who was going to get to come to America first. Like it was a contest that could be won. Times were bad in Germany at the time, and passage tickets weren't cheap. And it wasn't a piece of cake to get to the ships, either, if you could afford a ticket. A lot of money was needed. If only they would've helped each other instead of trying to see who could leave first. But Hubert worked non-stop, even dropped out of school, and he was able to leave before Albert."

Fighting the urge to look at the clock, John nodded along with his grandmother. When she paused, he scrambled to put together what she had been saying. Something about boats and money and leaving home.

"The funny thing was, Albert came to America barely a month later. He was mad as can be. Maybe they would have been better off if they would have stayed right there. Maybe then they still would have been friends and not bitter brothers who never spoke."

John sat with his hands folded on the table, waiting for his grandmother to finish, a prickly sensation creeping up his spine when he realized what she was saying. As she finished, he began to stand, angry at the guilt she was trying to push onto him, but she grabbed his wrist with a cool, tight grip.

"Visit us more than you used to, will you?" she said.

John began to deny it, but she tightened her grip and pulled her to him for the briefest of hugs. "I'll try," he whispered, and left her at the kitchen table. His eyes suddenly felt sore, and he couldn't stop blinking.

Andrea came down the steps with a bag, mouthing the words, "Let's go," to John. Pulling himself together, he put a finger in front of his mouth and opened Grandma's genealogy book. Making sure his grandmother couldn't see him from the kitchen, he wedged his father's money for the farm into the book, leaving a tiny edge of paper sticking out. He almost called out a goodbye to his grandmother, but thought better of it and walked out of the silent house without another word.

His car was again packed full of all his belongings, plus Andrea. He started the engine and turned around in the driveway. Idling in front of the house, he looked at the fields, the house, the machine shed, the barns, and the trees beyond. His dark suit was already flecked with dust, he noticed. He glanced at Andrea. She was staring out at the farm as well, and from his perspective she looked like a stranger. They sat there with the car idling for close to a minute. When John saw his brother walk up from the chicken house, he put the car in gear and drove away.

Chapter Seventeen

Up at the top of the barn, the daylight was starting to fade. A bale of rain-heavy hay fell twenty feet from the top of the conveyor and landed inches away from where William stood bent over, coughing and spitting to clear hay dust from his lungs. He hated stacking hay. He knew he'd be congested for the next two to three days, but he also knew that he couldn't let his father down, even if it was almost nine at night. They'd been waiting all week to bale this final field of hay, and William had come over as soon as he had been able to get away from the shop.

He left the falling bales for a few seconds more so he could climb down from the stacks and turn on the light, but the hundred-watt bulb added little illumination and more shadows to the rafters of the barn. The bales were dropping at a faster pace as Dad sped up in a mad dash to finish before total darkness. William stacked and coughed and spat, finding his rhythm despite his aching arms. Even though his clothes weren't as loose as they had been earlier that summer, he didn't think he was so out of shape that he couldn't keep up with his dad.

July had arrived before he'd even had a chance to enjoy the rest of June, and in a few days it would be August. The corn crops would most likely give a fairly decent yield in six weeks or so, he and his father agreed, but nothing like other years. Dad was preparing to sell most of the pigs that fall, and William did not look forward to butchering close to two hundred chickens in a week. It had been a long and unproductive growing season, the rain taking a toll on everyone and everything.

Between bales, William looked at the darkening sky outside. His back was beginning to ache, and his hands felt raw inside his gloves. Now that he was working full-time in the shop, he was growing unaccustomed to this kind of work. Marty had been more than happy to turn the paperwork over to him, and William discovered he had a knack for balancing the books, even if he had to sit behind a desk for a few hours. Marty worked on the cars more when he wasn't perfecting his songwriting ability, which freed up Russell's time so he could practice his drumming.

Dad had better slow down before he kills me, he thought, dodging the bales that kept coming at breakneck speed. He was behind again. Close to twenty had fallen in a rough pile, and a couple of bales had broken free from their twine, lying in a mounded pile of loose hay. Maybe this was Dad's way of punishing me. At first, his father had taken William's career change personally, but William had assured him he wouldn't leave him hanging. Not the way John had. Despite himself, William sometimes missed having John around, and he felt like he owed his brother something for helping him get out of his rut. But he wasn't about to take a trip to Chicago to say thanks.

William threw a bale onto a stack and felt something in his back give. He was just about to yell down at his father to stop when the elevator shut off. "That's it," Dad yelled up, his voice muted by the stacked hay. He sounded out of breath, which made William feel better as he coughed up more dust. He felt like he'd been kicked in the back with a steel-toed boot.

His father came up the ladder and stood with his hands on his knees, sweat streaming down his face. He nodded at the bales strewn across the floor. "What's the matter, can't you keep pace with an old man?"

"Shit," William said, balancing precariously on the stacked hay to reach the last bales that had fallen. If he took little steps his back didn't hurt as much. "You must've had help down there. Grandma was tossing hay off the wagon for you, wasn't she?" He handed the bales down to his father.

Dad slid his big hands around the twine for all six bales, three in each hand. "I don't like baling at night, is all. Too dangerous working in the dark." His blue work shirt was stained a darker blue with sweat except for a dry patch under his belly. He threw the bales against the wall and hurried back to William for more. "Can't do it by myself, you know."

"This is the only time I could help, Dad," William said. "You've got to understand that."

Dad looked up at him. In the shadows made by the bulb high above them, his face looked drawn and tired. After a long moment, he reached his hand up to help William down from the stacks. "I'm glad you came by."

"No problem. You'd better have some cold beer in that fridge of yours."

"There might be," Dad said, turning off the light on his way down the ladder. "It's the least I could do for such good work. Even if you are a big-time businessman now."

At the bottom of the ladder, William squinted to see if his father was serious, but he couldn't make out his expression. Then his father clapped him on the back and laughed, actions that spoke more to William than any words of thanks his father could ever say. They walked together through the still-warm darkness of late summer towards the house, sneezing and dripping in sweat.

So when are *you* leaving?" Grandma asked as soon as he sat down at the table with a beer and a box of tissues.

"Don't listen to her, William," his mother said. He caught the scolding look his mother shot Grandma, and he covered his smile by loudly blowing his nose.

"Who said anything about me leaving, old lady?"

"Don't start showing me a lack of respect, young man," Grandma began. "I know what's going on around here."

William twisted of the cap to his beer, slid it in front of her and got up to get another. "Do you want me to leave?" He directed his question at his grandmother, but he watched his mother for an answer. Dad was already in the shower in the downstairs bathroom. William waited for an answer.

Grandma took a sip of beer and grimaced. "Do what you want to. That's what you boys seem to do best."

William smiled and shook his head. Now that John was gone, she was determined to be mad at *me*, he thought. He was about to say something to her to defuse the situation, but his mother beat him to it.

"I've about had it with you, Ann Marie. I won't have you talking that way to my sons. Even if one of them isn't here to defend himself." William looked at his mother, noticing the tight look of her suntanned face, admiring the determined set of her shoulders. He thought about her staying up late so many nights this summer, working on the books, doing some innovative accounting with the money John had left them. They would most likely have to sell a sizable chunk of land to cover the lost crops, but because of those long nights, they would be able to keep the farm.

William leaned back in the chair, trying to lessen the pain in his lower back. His mother hadn't so much as mentioned John since he left last month, and he felt the room grow warmer even though she hadn't said his name. He could imagine how hurt she had been when John left without saying goodbye to her.

"I'd like to stay living here, Mom," he said softly. His grandmother sat turning her bottle of beer in silence, and Mom leaned against the counter, rubbing her temples as if she had a migraine. The shower stopped, and a sudden silence filled the house. "I don't want to leave."

His mother smiled at that, and Grandma took a sip of beer. William pulled another beer from the refrigerator, the last one in the drawer, and passed it to his mother. The three of them clinked their bottles together and drank a toast to their endurance and patience, and above all, to the farm.

* * * * *

By the first of August, the shop had picked up more business, enough to keep all three bays full most days. William had begun running ads in the Dubuque newspaper, and there had been talk of a possible television ad featuring Basskick. With the radio thumping next to the office door, Russell was hard at work under someone's pickup, while Marty changed the oil on an old Pinto. In mid-July they'd had to clear out space for the third bay, where William was pinstriping an old Camaro, something he had taught himself how to do between crunching numbers at the shop and milking cows at home. The precise work, after three straight hours, was making his eyes want to cross. He had plenty to do, but he wasn't so busy he couldn't slip away on his lunch break, and he left the job for later that day. Enough time had passed, he thought, and he wanted to see her again.

He washed his hands as best he could and stepped outside the shop. Passing the flashing arrow sign listing this week's specials, he began walking. A warm breeze blew a fresh scent over the town, with the salty hint of muddy fields underneath it like a reminder.

A thin mutt padded past him on the way up the sidewalk, but when William reached down to pet it, the dog passed him by without a look. Three kids rode past on the other side of the street, balancing fishing rods and tackle boxes on their handlebars. He waved at old man Jacques passing in his pickup and crossed the street, stepping over the clots of mud thrown from the tires of pickups and cars. Holy Cross was a town suspended in time, just the way William liked it. Not even as the church bell gonging once for the one o'clock hour could break the peaceful spell of the town.

He opened the door to the grocery/hardware store softly, trying not to make too much noise. He saw her immediately, stocking shelves with her back to him. He thought about how her skin felt under his hands, and how he could make her smile in a way she never did for anyone else. Then he thought about the look in her eyes before he took her to her bedroom, on the day they ended their headlong affair. He had almost walked out the In door twice when Jenifer finally turned and smiled up at him.

"Hey there," she said. "How's the shop?"

"Busy. How are you?"

She shrugged. "I'm here. Cynthia's healthy. We're both just fine. I heard your brother moved back to Chicago."

"Yep. The Koopman brothers have abandoned the family farm, you could say. I'm sure the whole town is talking."

Jenifer gave him a smile. "You have to hate that, don't you?"

"Let them talk." They stood there in the store, facing each other, trying to avoid each other's eyes. William wanted to leave, but he couldn't. He had to at least try. "So anyway. There's this band playing tonight at the Crossroads. They play some good old-fashioned rock, plus some original stuff. I was wondering, if you weren't too busy, if you'd like to go see them. With me. The band's called Basskick, and I hear they're pretty good. If you like that kind of thing."

"Really?" she said, her lips pressed together. "I think I could go for that. I'm always willing to try something new."

"You won't be disappointed. I promise." He wanted to say more to her, apologize for everything, but the look on her face told him she understood. He hoped he was right about that. "I'll pick you up around eight tonight."

"Eight o'clock," Jenifer said, the familiar smile returning to her face, the smile he caught himself thinking about as he worked. "I'll be there."

William waved at her and walked out the door, turning toward his shop. He walked slowly through Holy Cross, enjoying the summer weather, amazed that his life had turned out this way. High above, the sun had burned away the clouds in the sky, and, as far as William could see, there was not a hint of rain anywhere.

About the Author

Michael Jasper loves to explore the places where the normal meets the strange. In pursuit of this fascination, he has written and published over a dozen novels, three story collections, sixty short stories, and a digital comic with artist Niki Smith.

In the past he attempted bartending, teaching junior high, painting houses, being a secret shopper, working construction, and many more jobs; he prefers fiction writing. For his day job, he works as a technical writer.

He lives with his family in North Carolina, and his website is **michaeljasper.net**.

www.ingramcontent.com/pod-product-compliance
Lightning Source LLC
Chambersburg PA
CBHW022142240626
47153CB00007B/2474